Sage

Enchanted Series Book 1

Trish Moran

Publisher's Note:

This is a work of fiction. All names, characters, places, and events are the work of the author's imagination.

Any resemblance to real persons, places, or events is coincidental.

Solstice Publishing - http://www.solsticeempire.com/

Chapter One

'Bye, love. Have a good day,' Jim Warland called out to his granddaughter as she set off for school that morning. He smiled as his wife placed a fresh pot of tea on the table and sat down opposite him at the breakfast table.

'I think we made a good move, Ellen,' he said.

'Yes. I was quite worried about how things would turn out.'

His wife sighed. She thought back to the event that had changed their lives seven years previously. That stupid drunk driver who had killed their son Philip and his wife, Daphne, leaving them to care for their nine-year-old daughter, Sage. Plans for her and Jim to retire to The Valley had been put on hold as they felt that it would be too much to uproot Sage from her friends and familiar surroundings at that time. When she was about to start in the sixth form at school, her close friend, Kate, and her family moved to America and Sage was pleased with the suggestion to make a new start in The Valley, especially as the house they had planned on buying all those years ago, had come back on the market. Over the past seven months, Sage had settled in well at Briar Lane School and made new friends.

'I still can't quite believe that we are finally in our dream house. What a coincidence that it came back on the market again when we were finally ready to move. It's like it was meant to be,' Ellen said to her husband. 'And now we've finished renovating the house—well, all the big jobs anyway—it's time to think about the garden.' Ellen opened the newspaper. 'The Orchard Nursery has a spring sale on at the moment. We could drive out there and take a look at their roses. And maybe pick up some bulbs. March is a good time to make a start on the garden.'

'We could grow a few vegetables, too. I wonder if they have greenhouses?' Jim added.

***

'Oh, you'll get some lovely flowers on those!' their neighbour, Mary Goodall, exclaimed later that day as Jim gingerly unhooked a prickly stem from the boot of the car and placed a small rosebush beside several others by the car.

'Hi there, Mary.' Ellen smiled as she picked up one of the pots and placed it near the front door. 'We're going to plant these two in the front garden and the rest along the fence in the back garden. They'll add a nice splash of colour when they bloom.'

'Here, let me help you.' Mary picked up one of the pots and followed her around the back of the house.

'Thank you. If you just leave that over by the fence until we sort out where to plant them,' Jim said as he joined them.

Mary peered around the garden. 'You're getting it into shape, aren't you? The last owners weren't too keen on gardening.'

'We had noticed! It's taken Jim the best part of a month to level out that plot in front of the shed. It was full of rubbish.'

Mary walked towards an overgrown area beside the back door. 'Is the herb bed still here?' She knelt down and pulled up a handful of long grass. 'Look, there's still some mint and borage—it takes a lot to kill those off. And here's some betony and sage. It wouldn't take too much work to replant this area.'

Jim scratched his head. 'I don't know which of those are weeds and which are herbs.'

'Oh, I can help you there,' Mary offered.

'Hi, Nan, Grandad. Hi, Mary.' Sage and another girl stepped into the garden and dropped their school bags onto the garden bench. Sage was tall and slim with long, ash blonde hair and pale green eyes, while her companion, Sophie, was shorter. Her dark brown, curly hair was pulled back into a ponytail with several strands escaping to make a halo around her face.

'Hi, Mary,' Sophie said, kneeling beside her aunt. 'Isn't that wolfbane? And that could be hyssop.'

'Well spotted, Sophie.' Her aunt gave her a proud look. 'You've been brushing up on your—'

'Herbs.' Sophie supplied quickly.

Mary blinked and stood up. 'Yes, herbs. Good. Well, I'd better get going. Let me know if you need any help, Jim, won't you? Oh, and before I forget, Ellen, three copies of Dolores Silver's latest romance arrived at the library this morning. I put one aside for you.'

'Oh, thank you, Mary. I've just finished "Wherever Her Heart Leads." I'll pick it up tomorrow.' Ellen smiled. As the gate closed, she turned to the two girls. 'I've a lasagne and salad in the fridge, if you're hungry?'

'Thanks, Nan! I could eat a horse after basketball practice!'

Soon the two girls were seated at the kitchen table, working their way through generous portions of lasagne.

'How come you know so much about herbs, Sophie?' Ellen asked her.

'Oh, I help my aunt in her garden. And I learnt about them from my Gran.'

'It is nice to have fresh herbs for cooking, isn't it?' the older woman continued.

Sophie looked puzzled for a moment. 'Oh, yes. And for lots of things.'

'Such as?' prompted Sage.

'Erm, remedies for headaches and to help you sleep…stuff like that, you know.'

'And love potions and spells?' Ellen laughed. 'Here, have a drink of water,' she added as Sophie began to cough.

***

Her mother was on the phone as Sophie arrived home later that evening.

'Mary, you can't force these things. If it's meant to be, it will happen without your interference. If not, it won't.'

'But Denise. There are too many coincidences! They wanted to move back into The Valley seven years ago but circumstances prevented them; then when they were able to move, the house suddenly became available again.'

'The Applebys moved north to be near her mother after she fell and broke her hip. It was lucky timing.'

'And their name. Come on now—Warland.'

'There is no Gifted sign in any of them...'

'Sage is still sixteen. Sophie hasn't shown any signs yet and she's a month older than her.'

'Yes, but we know she will. It's in the family.'

'I *knew* the Warlands were of our kind as soon as I saw them. Mark my words, Denise.'

'But as they present as NGs we are not allowed to allude to it at all. You know that, Mary.'

'Don't worry, I won't do anything silly. I know the rules.' But once she had put down the phone, she added, 'But I might give a few helpful nudges...'

Denise shook her head as the call ended. She knew what her sister was like. Just then there was a rattle of the letterbox.

'But we've already had mail today,' she muttered as she made her way to the hall.

She was almost knocked over as Sophie appeared and picked up a thick cream coloured envelope with trembling hands.

'Sophie, did you just...?'

'Yes, Mum. I did! And this must be my invitation to Alora's!' Sophie waved it excitedly.

Her brother jumped back out of the way a moment later in the lounge.

'Oh, no,' he groaned. 'Another one to watch out for!'

'Sophie.' Her mother had followed her into the lounge. 'Take it easy. Start with baby steps or...'

There was a crash as something hit the floor.

'Oops! Sorry, Mum!'

Chapter Two

'I can do this,' Sophie muttered as she made her way into the school building with Sage the next morning.

Her friend frowned. 'Are you okay?'

'Fine. Why not?' came a strangled reply. 'I'm just going to get something from my locker.'

As Sage and the other students walked into the classroom, Sophie leaned her forehead against the cool, metal locker door and closed her eyes. At the sound of a bell, she grabbed her books. She didn't want a late mark. Desmond, the class dreamer, was just in front of her heading for the seat beside Sage. The only other available place was directly in front of Mrs Duke's desk, right under her watchful eye, a seat to be avoided at all costs. Sophie closed her eyes and concentrated.

'Hey, watch where you're sitting!' she shouted as Desmond sat on her knee a moment later.

Both Sage and Desmond looked up, surprised to find Sophie on the seat beside Sage.

Desmond blushed a deep red. 'Oh, I'm sorry...I didn't see you there...'

'Oh, yeah, like I'm invisible,' she retorted, pulling out her books. 'Did you do that past paper homework, Sage? I only got as far as number four, and I'm pretty sure most of it is wrong anyway.'

Sage frowned as Desmond shuffled off to the empty front seat. 'Erm, the questions were quite hard.' She gave an embarrassed laugh. 'You know, Sophie, I didn't see you come and sit down, either. You seemed to move very quickly.'

'That's me, a quick mover!' She laughed.

'I'm so glad it's lunchtime.' Sophie rubbed her growling stomach three hours later. 'It's quite warm today, shall we eat outside?'

'Yes, the canteen is looking pretty crowded,' her friend replied. 'My lunch box is in my locker. I'll go and get it.'

'I'll grab a bench before they're all taken.'

Sage looked around a few minutes later as she stepped outside. Her mouth fell open.

'Sage! Over here!' Sophie was shouting from a bench on the other side of the field.

'How on earth did she get over there so quickly?' Shaking her head, she made her way across the field. She was so engrossed in her thoughts that she failed to hear a shout.

'Get out of the way!' A boy was running towards her, waving his arms wildly. Several other students were watching her with alarm on their faces.

There was a resounding smack as something hit the side of her head. She felt a searing pain; then everything went black.

***

'Thank goodness, she's opening her eyes! Sage, are you okay?' Sophie was leaning over her. Sage could see blue and white wisps rising from her.

She noticed other coloured strands swirling in a cloud above her head. A mixture of dark red mixed with blue strands rose from Mr. Bell, the sports teacher, and a tall boy standing next to him. They drifted across and formed a cloud above her.

'What was she doing walking across the field in the middle of a game of cricket?' the teacher said.

'I tried to warn her,' the boy stammered.

A woman hurried over and placed a cold compress on Sage's head. 'The office has rung for an ambulance. It'll be here in a few minutes. They said not to move her. How are you feeling, love?'

Sage blinked as blue and orange wisps rose from the woman and mingled with the thickening, swirling mist above her own head. 'It's very colourful.'

The two adults and the boy exchanged bemused glances. Sophie knelt down and took Sage's hand. 'You'll be fine. Just take it easy.'

Sage felt herself drift away again.

***

The next time she opened her eyes she was on a narrow bed in a small, curtained cubicle. A nurse came in and smiled at her. Wisps of orange and brown rose from her and settled in circles over the top of the bed. 'You've had quite a nasty blow to your head. How are you feeling?'

'Sore,' Sage grimaced. 'What are all those colours?'

The nurse frowned. 'What colours?'

Sage waved vaguely at the ceiling. 'All those wisps, making a sort of cloud…'

The young woman filled in a chart at the foot of the bed. 'We'd better get Dr Collins to check you out. It's probably the knock you've had.'

Sage's heart leapt as she heard the familiar sound of her grandparents' voices. She smiled and attempted to sit up as they came into the cubicle, but winced and lay back down again.

Blue and white strands rose from her grandmother as she grabbed Sage's hand, 'Oh love, are you okay?'

Her grandad's brow furrowed as he looked at the nurse. 'How is she?'

'She's had a nasty blow to the head and it might have affected her vision, hopefully, temporarily. I expect we'll need to keep her in overnight to check for concussion. The doctor will be along shortly.' With a bright smile, she disappeared.

'What have you been up to, love?' Her grandmother squeezed her hand. Despite her calm demeanour, her own hand trembled slightly. Sage looked at the swirling pattern of colours overhead and waited to see if they would comment on it. She looked up. 'The décor is kind of …unusual…isn't it?'

Ellen frowned. 'Are you okay? What happened? The woman in the school office told me you were hit pretty hard by a cricket ball.'

She gave a wan smile. 'Oh, it's nothing serious. I just wasn't looking where I was going. I've a terrible headache, but I'll be fine.'

Her heart raced. No-one could see the colours except for her. She prayed that she hadn't damaged her sight permanently.

The curtain opened and a young man appeared. 'Hello there. I'm Dr Collins. I've come to take a look at you, young lady. The nurse said that you were having trouble with your sight. What exactly is the matter?'

'Well, everything seems to be a bit colourful, that's all.' She waved towards the growing cloud above her.

Dr Collins didn't seem to notice anything unusual. He pulled a small torch out of his pocket and looked at each of her eyes. 'I can't see anything out of the ordinary, but I'll book you in for an MRI this afternoon.' He turned to her grandparents. 'As you probably have already been told, we'll keep your granddaughter in for the night in case of any concussion. All being well, she'll be able to go home tomorrow.'

Two hours later, Sage was wheeled out of the scanning department.

'Well, everything looks clear. We're happy that no permanent damage has been done,' Dr Collins told her and her grandparents. 'We'll most likely be able to discharge you tomorrow morning, young lady.'

'That's a relief.' The blue wisps surrounding him were changing to a pale yellow as her grandfather smiled at her.

'The porter is here to take you to ward eight. You'll be ready to sleep now, I'm sure.' Dr Collins smiled. He walked away, leaving a trail of orange and brown wisps.

Fifteen minutes later she was lying in a corner bed in a small ward.

'We'll have to say goodbye until tomorrow, Sage,' her grandmother said as she smoothed down the blanket. 'How are you feeling now?'

'Much better. Just a bit tired but I'm sure I'll be ready to go home tomorrow.'

'Yes. The doctor said a good night's sleep should sort you out. We'll see you tomorrow,' her grandad said.

'Are you okay, Ellen?' he asked his wife as they left the hospital.

'I've a touch of a headache myself,' she replied, rubbing her brow. 'Probably a bit of stress from today's events. I'll be fine.'

Sage looked around her. There were five other beds with children ranging from ten years old to around sixteen, her own age. She smiled at the girl in the neighbouring bed who gave her a weak wave in return before closing her eyes. Sage felt alarmed as dark blue and white strands left the girl and made their way upwards, some drifting above her own bed. The cloud was a thickening mass as more strands and wisps rose from the people around her. No-one else seemed to be aware of this strange cloud. The nursing staff carried on their duties with wisps of blue, yellow, orange, and brown rising from them, drifting across to settle above Sage's bed. All acted as if nothing was out of the ordinary. Sage bit her lip. Was she going mad? She decided it must be her secret.

Shortly afterwards, the night staff came on to the ward. Most of the patients were in bed apart from two young girls who were playing a computer game in the corner.

'Come on, you two,' a nurse told them. 'Make this the last game now. You need a good night's sleep.'

'It's too early to sleep, Evie,' one complained. Sage noticed her orange strands flicker and change to a vivid blue.

'You can read your book for a while if you're not tired yet.' Sister Evie hugged her. 'Tell you what, once I've done the meds round, I'll pop over and we can have a little chat about your op tomorrow, okay? There's nothing scary, everything will be fine.'

The girl nodded and made her way to her bed. The nurse looked around at Sage and her eyes flickered wide for a moment. 'Sage, isn't it? I hear you're probably just here for the night after a nasty bump on the head.'

'Yes, I'm feeling much better already. I'm sure I'll be fine again tomorrow.'

'I'm Sister Evie,' she said coming closer to her and tidying up the few items on her bedside table. 'Are you new to this?' She glanced at the cloud of colours above Sage, then with a movement of her hand the cloud disappeared. She briefly opened her palm to show a pile of small, shiny discs of different colours. They reminded Sage of the slivers of crystal she had seen in a craft shop.

'What are they? What did you do?'

'You're *very* new to this, aren't you, love?' The nurse slipped the discs into her pocket. 'Sometimes a blow to the head can trigger it. Is it in the family?'

'I don't know what you're talking about...'

'You're going to need some guidance,' Evie whispered as she straightened the blanket.

'No! I'm fine apart from a headache.'

'Evie. Can you take the meds trolley around now, please? Mandy will help you.' A man stood in the doorway.

'Coming.' She gave Sage a quick smile and disappeared.

Sage watched as different coloured strands unravelled above people's heads, some floating across to hover over her bed. Most of the strands from the patients were different shades of blue though two, including the pale girl in the bed next to her, gave off wisps of a white mist that she found quite depressing. Many of the staff had a range of orange colours and some also had different shades of brown. She sighed as she watched the cloud above her growing larger. She opened her hand and glared at a long blue strand as it curled above her. To her surprise it began to shrink and a moment later a blue crystal disc appeared in her palm. She narrowed her eyes again and fixed her gaze on a dark red wisp. Nothing happened except that she felt a sharp pain in her head.

'Condensing takes practise,' Sister Evie said as she placed a container on her bedside table. 'Here are your painkillers.' She glanced up and Sage watched as the strands disappeared to be replaced by a handful of crystal discs which Evie placed beside the pill container.

'Here's some fresh water, love.' A young nurse put a jug down beside the discs, seeming unaware that she was knocking some of them to the floor. Sage moved to catch them.

'Have you dropped something?' The nurse looked down on the floor.

Sage shook her head. 'No, I...'

The nurse smiled and continued to the next bed.

'It's okay. She can't see them,' Evie whispered as she bent to pick up the discs. 'I'll disperse these on my way home. Which school do you go to, Barrows?'

'No, Briar Lane,' Sage replied, taken aback by the change in subject.

The nurse winked. 'I'll get someone to speak to you, very discreetly, don't worry.'

Chapter Three

'I've been at home for three days now, Nan. I really feel ready to go back to school. I can hardly feel the lump at all now.'

'Are you sure, love?' Her grandmother frowned. 'You still have a bit of a dazed look in your eyes now and then.'

Sage looked down and bit her lip. She was finding it hard to hide how distracting the strands of colour were. With a bright smile, she fixed her eyes on her nan's face, forcing herself to ignore the wisps swirling above them.

'I'm just thinking of all the schoolwork I have to catch up with. The sooner I get back, the better.'

Her grandfather put his newspaper down. 'I think she'll be fine, Ellen. The doctor said one or two days' rest should do it. Sage's right, she can't neglect her school work, she's important exams coming up in a couple of months' time.'

Sage took a deep breath as she set off for school the next morning. For a moment she felt overwhelmed by the number of wisps and strands that detached from the people passing by and accumulated over her. Over the past few days, she had only to deal with the colours from her grandparents. She had made several attempts to "condense" the wisps, with about a twenty per cent success rate. She had been relieved to find that at the end of each day, as she grew tired, her connection to the swirling cloud lessened and she was able to open her bedroom window and watch the colours float away into the night.

A crowd of chattering girls were entering the school gate as she reached it.

'Sage, you're back. Are you okay now?' one of them asked.

She nodded. 'I'm fine, thanks.'

She tried to keep her eyes off the colourful wisps as they rose up from the group of girls.

'Hey, Sage!' A shout made her look around. Sophie ran over and gave her a warm hug. 'I'm so pleased you're okay. Your nan said you needed a few days to recover, but I was a bit worried.'

'I'm fine now. I'd better look out when I'm walking across the sports field in future.'

Mrs Duke appeared in the corridor. 'Good to have you back, Sage. How are you?'

Sage flinched as yellow wisps poured from her, some joining the swirling rainbow above her. As she did, blue wisps appeared.

'Are you sure you're ready to come back to school?' Mrs Duke's smile was replaced by a look of concern.

'Oh, I'm absolutely fine.' Sage fixed a smile on her face.

'Well, let us know straight away if you're not feeling up to it, won't you Sage?'

Sage breathed a sigh of relief as the teacher moved on. 'I'll have to borrow your books to catch up on all the work I've missed, Sophie.'

'Don't worry, I've got copies of all the notes you need in my locker.' Sophie darted to her locker and reappeared by her side with a folder in what seemed like seconds. 'Everything's in here.'

'Thanks so much, Sophie. Anything exciting happen while I was off?'

Sophie spread her hands. 'You'll never guess what Colin did this week! He pinched Loretta Bentley's English essay and gave it in as his! How he thought he'd get away with it...'

By the end of the morning, between Sophie's constant movement and chatter and the growing cloud above her, Sage felt as if her head would burst. It was a relief when they had different lessons just before lunch. Heading outside, she decided to spend ten minutes alone before she looked for her friend.

She sank down onto the grass with her back to a tree and looked at the colourful cloud above her head. Her eyes narrowed as she tried to unravel the mass of colour above her and condense a wisp, but to no avail. With a cry of frustration, she banged her fist on the grass. 'How come she made it look so easy?'

'Because she's had years of practise,' a voice said.

Startled, Sage jumped up and faced a tall, dark haired boy. She had seen him around the school before. He was in the year above her.

'What are you doing spying on me?'

'Evie from the hospital said there was a girl who needed some help.'

'How do you know she meant me?'

He gave a short laugh and nodded at the billowing cloud above her. 'You're not exactly hidden, are you? You need to learn to condense, it's not good to leave a cloud like that on view.'

Sage scowled. 'I've been *trying* to condense!'

He gave a smile and held out his hand. 'I'll help you. I'm Paris, by the way.'

Reluctantly, she shook it. 'Sage.'

'Okay, first you untangle each strand, newer ones are easier to work with than older ones; they can get a bit solid, especially the reds and dark reds...use your eyes to hold one...then grasp it in your hand.' He held out his hand and quickly condensed several of the strands and tipped the discs into her hand. 'There you go.'

'What are these and why can I suddenly see them?' Sage looked at the handful of crystal slivers.

He raised his eyebrows. 'Surely you've already worked out that they're people's emotions? Do you have any family history of Snares at all?'

She shook her head. 'I don't even know what Snares are! All I know is that I was perfectly normal until I banged my head and then...' she waved her arms above her, '...all of this appeared!'

'Oh; you really need to find out about the whole Gifted thing. I have your invitation to Alora for Saturday here...'

As he reached into his pocket, there was a painful shout and Sophie appeared in a bush behind them.

'Ouch!' she cried, peeling the branches from her arms and pushing her way out.

Sage looked up in amazement. 'Sophie, what are you doing there?'

Sophie scowled at Paris. 'You're in year thirteen, aren't you? What did you just give Sage?'

Sage gently opened her hand and looked down at the six coloured discs. Sophie frowned and grabbed her hand, turning it over, causing the discs to fall to the ground. 'There's nothing there.'

'We're Snares, Sophie,' Paris told her as he bent down to pick up the discs.

With wide eyes, Sophie looked at them both. 'Snares? Oh, my life! Why didn't you tell me, Sage? You can see the colours of people's auras and collect them!'

Sage said nothing but Paris nodded. 'That's right. And from the speed you arrived here, I take it you're a Transposer. A beginner by the looks of it.'

'What's a Transposer?' Sage asked, rubbing her forehead.

'A Transposer can move him or herself to another place just by thinking about it,' Sophie explained. 'But I haven't quite got the hang of the landing point just yet. My talents were revealed just last week. We were expecting them—Mum is a Transposer and so are her mother and sister. But my dad and brother aren't and they find it a bit freaky. I've caused a few accidents by jumping at the wrong time or in the wrong place. And since the last accident when Dad ended up in A&E—though the burns weren't too bad, luckily—Transposing at home has been banned. Anyway, enough about me. How long have you been a Snare, Sage?'

'Since I got hit on the head by that cricket ball. I hadn't a clue what was happening to me. I thought I was going mad. I'd never heard of Snares until Paris told me just now.'

'A friend of mine told me about Sage. She needs some guidance and I've brought her the invitation to Alora's on Saturday. She didn't post it as you are living with Non-Gifted, Sage.'

'You've got your invitation! That's wonderful! I got mine in the post the same day my Gift was revealed,' Sophie exclaimed. 'We can go together.'

'Who is Alora?' Sage asked.

'Alora is just one of the greatest witches *ever*!' Sophie said.

'She prefers to be called a Spell Master,' Paris corrected her.

'Gran and Mary told me that Alora can do everything—she can be a Transposer, a Snare, an Animator, *and* cast spells!'

Sage's puzzled look increased. 'What's an Animator?'

'There are two kinds—at level one, an Animator can move objects just by thinking about it and at level two he or she can also bring characters from pictures or photos to life for a short time,' Paris explained. 'The best way for you to understand all this is to see some of them in action. You'll get the chance on Saturday at Alora's.'

'I'll have to check with my grandparents…' Sage began.

'No way!' Sophie cried.

Paris bit his lip. 'I'm afraid you can't tell them about Alora if they're not one of us. Gifted, I mean.'

'I don't want to be deceitful…'

'Paris's right, and anyway, it would scare the hell out of them if they knew about all this,' Sophie pointed out. 'As Non-Gifted, they'd probably just send you back to hospital for tests and things.'

'And it's really important that you learn how to control your talent,' Paris added.

'I know—we'll both come around for you on Saturday morning and you can tell your grandparents you're spending the day with your friends,' Sophie suggested. 'Then you'll be telling them the truth.'

'And in the meantime, here's a list of the colours and the emotions they represent for you to take a look through.' Paris handed her a sheet of paper. 'I'm sure you'll find that you've probably figured out most of them for yourself.'

***

Sophie gave her friend a sympathetic glance in economics that afternoon as Sage was continually distracted by the swirls above her head.

'Sage,' Miss Blake said. 'Could you concentrate on the task in hand and spend less time gazing around you? It looks as if Sophie is having to do the work for both of you.'

Sage clenched her fists and tried to focus on the tablet. 'Give the main reasons for the…oh…I can't do this…'

She pushed back her chair and stood up. All of a sudden, the scene froze around her. Miss Blake was halfway out of her chair; a paper plane was suspended in the air above one of the boys; two girls were smirking over a mobile phone screen, and Sophie was looking at her with her mouth a frozen "O".

A petite woman, who looked to be in her late twenties or early thirties, was walking towards her. She was wearing a long multi-coloured skirt and a bright blue peasant blouse. 'Sage, you're really struggling, aren't you?'

Sage nodded, a tear slipping down her cheek.

'It's hard enough belonging to a Gifted family when you get your Gift, but it's much more difficult when it arrives out of the blue. Don't worry, things will get easier.' She looked around the room at the other students and the cloud above Sage's head. 'Gosh, teenagers have such strong emotions, don't they? First of all, let's see if we can tone down these colours so they aren't so much in your face. Now, think pale…'

Sage frowned and shook her head. 'Nothing's happening.'

'Relax, deep breath, try again. Pale…'

Sage took a deep breath and fixed her eyes on the rainbow cloud above her. 'Pale…pale…hey, it's working.'

'Good, now push them to one side with your eyes. You can leave them there until you get the chance to condense them. Feeling better?'

Sage nodded.

'I'm going to let everything get started again; but I'll hang around for a while to make sure you're managing, okay?'

'Wait,' Sage cried as the woman began to fade from view. 'Who are you?'

There was a soft laugh. 'I'm Alora.'

Sage sat down slowly as everything sprang to life. No-one seemed to be aware of what had just happened.

'Pale…pale…' she murmured as the colourful wisps began to rise up again. With a smile, she tapped the tablet screen and turned to Sophie. 'I can think of three more main reasons for economic growth in scenario one.'

She glanced around her. 'And I've something really amazing to tell you and Paris on the way home'

That night, Sage sat in her bedroom with the sheet Paris had given her. *A yellow glow means happy; red especially dark tones mean anger, hatred. Hmm, the dark colours do feel quite oppressive.* She scanned the list again. *Paris was right, the colours seem to somehow make sense, I would probably have worked out the emotions without this chart—blue for different levels of fear; white for apathy and despair—oh that poor girl in the hospital; green for envy; brown for tiredness and beige is laziness...*

She smiled as she climbed into bed that night. *So, I'm not going mad. And I'm really excited about meeting other—Gifted—people.*

Chapter Four

'Hi, Sophie. And you must be Paris, come in.' Jim smiled as he opened the door on Saturday morning. 'Sage, your friends are here.'

'Are you off anywhere nice today?' her grandmother asked them as they came into the kitchen.

'We're going around to see some friends of mine. They run a sort of youth club on Saturdays,' Paris told her.

'That sounds like a good place to go. There aren't many places for young people in The Valley,' Sage's grandfather commented.

'Yes,' Sophie agreed. She turned and smiled as Sage joined them. 'Are you ready?'

Sage nodded, trying to hide her nervousness.

'Nice to meet you both. You all enjoy yourselves,' her grandmother told them as they set off.

Her husband noticed her rubbing her forehead again. 'Another headache, love? You've got to make an appointment at the doctor's this week.'

'You're right, Jim. I will. I probably need new glasses, that's all.'

***

Sage wasn't quite sure what she'd expected a Spell Master's house to look like, but it certainly wasn't the neat detached house set back on a wide, tree lined road amidst a row of similar houses. An ornately carved sign by the door read, "The Coterie."

As Paris raised his hand to ring the doorbell, the door swung open.

'Come in!' a voice called out. 'Come through to the kitchen.'

Paris led the way to the back of the house into a bright, spacious room. Sage jumped back as two girls and a group of three boys, all dressed in an old-fashioned style, walked through them.

'Is this place haunted?'

Paris smiled. 'They're not ghosts, just memories of people who have been here before. You'll see quite a lot of them.'

They walked into the kitchen where the woman who had visited Sage in the classroom was stirring a large pot. She peered into it and turned it down to simmer. Smiling, she turned to her visitors holding out her hand.

'Hello! You seem to be doing very well since we last met, Sage. Lovely to meet you, Sophie, I'm Alora. We're always pleased to welcome new talent to our community.'

'Where's Jay?' Paris asked, looking around.

'He's visiting his fae family this weekend. He told me you lot are too noisy for him.'

'Do fae live here, too?' Sophie's eyes widened. 'I've wanted to meet one since I was small.'

'Not many fae live permanently in Earth world. Jay's an exception as he's my partner. Some of his relatives visit us from time to time.'

Sage condensed the strands that were accumulating above her head and put the discs in her pocket. 'How come you and Paris don't have colourful auras?'

'We've learnt to conceal them,' Paris told her. 'It's better to keep them out of sight of some Gifted ones.'

'You'll soon be able to do that, too, Sage.' Alora smiled. 'It's one of the first Snare lessons. And Sophie, you're a Transposer, aren't you? I remember your grandmother and your mother coming here when they first got their Gifts.'

Sophie nodded enthusiastically. 'They're both absolutely thrilled I'm finally getting to meet you. They told me so much about you.' Pointing at the large saucepan on the hob, she asked, 'Is that a potion?'

Alora laughed. 'No, it's a bean stew for lunch. I'm just going to make some salad to go with it. While I'm doing that how about you show the girls around, Paris, so they get to meet some of the gang? Animators are on the first landing, Snares on the top floor and down in the basement, Rhandra is putting the Transposers through their paces.'

'Gosh, this place is so much bigger inside than it appears from the outside,' Sage said.

'We let people see what we want them to see on the outside, while we add or lose space according to our needs on the inside. We've been expanding to accommodate all the new Gifted ones who've been joining us these last few months.'

The girls followed Paris upstairs to an open landing. Six teenagers were sitting on the floor near the wall moving their hands and fingers around in strange patterns.

'What are they doing?' Sage asked Paris.

He pulled both girls to one side as a cup, a pen, a notebook, a toy car, a glass, and a plate floated past them towards the opposite wall. 'The Animators are having a race.'

The notebook was in the lead when the pen flipped over and made a clink as it hit the wall.

'Nice one, Brad!' A girl clapped the boy beside her on the shoulder.

'I forgot to use the flip! I could have won that,' another boy grumbled.

'Don't be a sore loser, Sean.' The first girl laughed.

'Merc is right, Sean. It's just a game.' A second girl patted his arm.

'This is practise for the real world, Fiona,' Sean said seriously. 'Who knows when we may have to apply our skills in a life or death situation?'

'Round two! Everyone got a sketch pad?' Brad said. He walked to the items now lying lifeless by the wall and nudged them into a line. 'Pencils over there if you need one.'

'Now what are they doing?' Sophie whispered.

'Just watch.' Paris smiled. 'This is the real fun bit!'

'Ready?' Merc asked the others. 'Shall I do countdown? There were nods and murmurs of agreement. 'Three…two…one…zero!'

Sage gasped with surprise as six cartoon sketches sprung off the pads and began to run towards the items lying by the wall. A super hero ran with a determined expression quickly overtaking a limping figure whose right leg was noticeably shorter than his left. A flat headed figure jogged along beside a female character with long arms that bounced off the ground as she ran.

'The glass, the glass,' Fiona shouted, clenching her fists together as a stickman reached the items.

'Go on, the pen! Pick it up carefully!' Brad hissed at a cartoon cheerleader who had leaped and bounced her way to the writing implement.

'Watch out for Molly and Wilf,' Paris said softly nodding at a couple in deep concentration.

Molly fixed her eyes on the long-armed character. As it reached the plate it swung it high above its head and sprinted back towards her. Wilf's flat headed character balanced the cup on his head and ran back to his creator, tipping the cup into Wilf's outstretched hands seconds before Molly was handed the plate.

There were groans as the limping figure stumbled against Fiona's stickman, knocking the glass from his arms.

'Sorry!' Sean said. His figure tried to rectify the situation but the stickman pushed him away and he overbalanced again, rolling towards the cheerleader who used her pen to vault out of his way, but unfortunately landed in the path of the superhero figure driving the toy car. He spun the vehicle around and ended up heading back towards the starting point.

By this time, Sage, Sophie, and Paris were doubled up in laughter.

'I've never seen anything so funny!' Sage said, wiping her eyes.

'I hope this isn't one of your practises for the real world, Sean,' Molly remarked drily.

'My apologies to all. I must work on my artistic skills; he was a bit lopsided.'

'A great performance, guys!' Paris said.

'Mmm, we've had better!' Fiona shoved Sean playfully. 'Haven't we?'

'Wow! The things you guys can do,' Sage said.

'Are you the two new Gifted Alora was telling us about?' Molly said to them. 'I've seen you two girls around school, haven't I?'

Sage nodded. 'I've only recently discovered I'm Gifted. If someone had told me about all these amazing talents a few weeks ago, I'd never have believed it.'

'So, it's not in your family?' Wilf said. 'That's really unusual.'

'I've heard of Gifts skipping a generation,' Laura commented.

'Well, my grandparents aren't Gifted,' Sage said. 'They don't know I am either.'

'No. It's not good to let Non-Gifted in on our secrets.' Wilf nodded. 'They'd probably treat us like a bunch of freaks and do all sorts of experiments on us.'

'Or burn us at the stake, like they used to,' Molly added.

'We'd better move on guys.' Paris stood up. 'Thanks for the entertainment. See you at lunch.' He turned to Sophie. 'You're not going to be able to see much with the Snares; let's get you down to Rhandra first.'

A black teenager whose long hair was plaited into narrow braids was standing at the side of the room giving out cards to a group of girls and boys as they entered the basement. Each person looked at their card and took up a position around the room. 'When I get to zero, move to the next position on your card. Three...two...one...zero!'

There was a blur as the teenagers jumped to new places. Some were standing, others sitting in various places around the room. One of the girls had crashed into a wall and was rubbing her forehead.

'Not bad, not bad...' Rhandra nodded. 'You okay, Gem?'

'Mmm, just a bit sore.' She gave a rueful smile.

'You know you have to—' Rhandra began.

'—focus on where your feet are going to land; that's what my Gran keeps telling me,' Sophie chimed in.

'Exactly! You're Sophie, aren't you? Alora said you were coming today. Are you going to join us for the next jump?' Rhandra handed her a card as the younger girl nodded. 'Start at position two, then you shouldn't bump into anyone.' She called to the others. 'Is everyone ready? Good. Three...two...one...zero!'

There was a flash of movement, followed by a groan. Sophie was sitting on a sofa on top of a teenage boy.

'So sorry, are you okay?' she murmured as she scrambled off him. 'I really meant to go on the other end of the sofa.'

'Hmm, you need more practice.' Rhandra smiled. 'Jav, you take charge of the others while I work with Gem and Sophie...'

Paris nudged Sage's arm. 'Let's go up to the Snares.'

They climbed the staircase, following shouts and groans coming from a room off to one side. Inside, there was an assortment of armchairs and beanbags around the wall and in the middle of the room four youngsters were racing to condense a large multi-coloured cloud which was quickly diminishing.

'Don't just go for the easy ones,' a young man was telling them. 'Reds earn you more points.'

One of the girls gave an excited shout as the cloud finally disappeared. 'I've got eighteen and two of them are reds!'

'I've got four reds!' a boy countered.

'I've just a load of yellows,' another girl groaned.

'I've yellow and a few blues,' a second boy said.

'Total your scores,' the young man said. 'Who has the lowest? Shelley, mm, yellows are too easy to catch, so you're out. Why don't you do an individual practise in the side room? Rob's already in there.' He gave her a handful of discs and turned back to the others as she left the room.

'Okay, there's three of you left now, I'm going to up the game.' He pulled a handful of discs from his pocket and tossed them up into the air. A wispy cloud of mainly dark colours with plenty of reds appeared. 'Ready? Three...two...one...zero!'

The three youngsters looked serious as they all set about condensing the cloud.

The young man turned to them. 'Hi, Paris. Alora said you've a new Snare with you today.'

Paris nodded. 'This is Sage; Sage this is Casper. He's a Deep, which is a sort of Snare.'

'Please, the official term is a Profound, which *is* a type of Snare, but—at the risk of sounding a little boastful...'

'Which you would never do...'

Casper cleared his throat. 'A basic Snare can visualise and manipulate people's emotions. A Profound can use more than just the sense of sight. We develop our other senses so we can feel, touch, and smell emotions, too. Most of us don't bother with hearing and tasting as they get a bit too much. As you can imagine, tasting fear and hearing excitement can be pretty overwhelming, though there are certain Profound purists who insist on using all of the five senses. Luckily, none of them live around here.'

At that point one of the three teenagers gave a shout, 'I got the last red! And it's a dark one!'

Casper turned back to them. 'So, final scores? Joint second are Bess and Arthur. Ryan you're ahead of the other two by sixteen points. You're today's top scorer.'

'Do you want some condensing practise, Paris?' Ryan asked.

'Good idea. See if you can condense them as quickly as he releases them,' Casper suggested.

Paris rubbed his hands together. 'Okay, bring 'em on!'

The other teenage Snares had joined them and all stood around watching as Ryan opened his hand and two yellow discs disintegrated and rose as wisps into the air. Paris blinked and two discs appeared in his hand. He pushed them into his pocket and steeled himself for the next move.

To Sage it seemed as if Ryan was releasing a firework from his hand as three strands of orange, brown, and green snaked towards the ceiling.

Paris's eyes flashed as he clicked his fingers and pulled the strands into three discs almost as soon as they had formed.

Ryan gave him a grin. 'Ready for the big ones?' As he opened his hand this time, two long dark red strands unravelled.

Paris grinned as they disappeared and he opened his hand to reveal two dark, shiny discs.

'Can I have a go?' Sage asked.

'Sure, let's start with the paler colours.' Ryan took a yellow disc from his pocket and released a pale wisp. Sage quickly condensed it.

He smiled and threw up two more strands which reappeared as discs a few seconds later.

'Not bad for a beginner.' Ryan smiled. 'Try the darker ones.'

Over the next ten minutes, Sage condensed a variety of colours.

'You're a quick learner, well done,' Ryan conceded as she held out a handful of darker discs. 'One last go. Let's give you a challenge.'

He threw up a handful of assorted colours. Sage's frown deepened as the wisps disappeared into her palm.

Ryan's mouth fell open as she opened her hand. 'Casper, Paris, take a look at this.'

'My life.' Casper gave a low whistle as he picked up the multi-coloured disc from her hand. 'How did you know how to blend?'

She looked bemused. 'I just sort of felt it.'

'I'm still struggling with blending,' Paris said. 'Can you release as well?'

'I haven't tried that yet. What do I do?'

Casper laid a yellow disc on her open palm. 'See what you can do. Just go with your feelings.'

Taking a deep breath, Sage closed her eyes. The disc dissolved and a yellow wisp rose into the air.

Casper clapped his hands. 'Condense, release, blend—all on the first day! We've got a rising star here. What's your last name, Sage?'

'Warland.'

'Hmm…interesting name.'

A girl appeared at the top of the stairs. 'Come on, you lot, it's time for lunch.'

Sophie gave her a nudge as Sage joined the others at the kitchen table a short while later. 'Isn't this place just amazing?'

'Hey, can you pass the bread?' Wilf called down to them.

Sophie was about to pick up the basket when Molly, sitting next to her, put her hand on her arm. Picking up a pencil, she hurriedly drew a sketch of two stick men on a pad beside her. She flicked it and the men jumped off the pad and ran to the bread basket. Quickly they hoisted it onto their shoulders and ran down the table, depositing it next to the boy. Sage's eyes widened as the figures scuttled back on to the pad and lay there lifelessly a moment later.

'Nice one, Molly!'

'You're welcome, Wilf.'

Soon afterwards, Alora and Casper joined the others. Two shadowy figures of boys dressed in thin grey short trousers and woollen navy jumpers with several darned patches found a place at the table. Each carried a bowl of stew which they quickly devoured. Alora smiled. 'Edwin and his brother Walter. Food was always scarce at home and they often called to visit us around lunchtime.'

'Are they memories?' Sophie asked Paris who nodded. 'They look so real. Oh, they're just fading away.'

'Talking about memories, can we see your inkwell memory again, Alora?' Wilf grinned. 'I bet Sophie and Sage would enjoy it.'

'Oh, you like to see me make a fool of myself, don't you?'

'Go on, Alora! It's so funny!' another boy urged.

'Pleeease!' several others joined in.

Alora grimaced. 'Okay. Here it is, *Pride Comes Before a Fall…*'

Everyone turned around as a young teenage girl holding a thick leather-bound book entered the kitchen and sat down at a wooden desk. She was dressed in a navy-blue dress with a white collar and long, black woollen socks. As she sat down and opened the book, a boy a few years younger than her appeared in the doorway.

'Hi, Allie. What's that you have there? "Herbs and Potions," mmm.' He pulled a face. 'Rather tedious reading.'

'But we have to learn about them, Matthew. Test's next week,' she replied. 'Name three major masculine herbs and their uses.'

'Oh, come on…'

She tapped the desk. 'This is important basic knowledge, Matthew.'

Her brother sighed. 'Eh, Basil, Nutmeg, and …and…eh…let's have an Animating contest instead! Much more fun!'

He stretched out a hand and began to levitate the book.

'Stop that, Matthew, you can't just practise the fun bits.'

'Face it, Sis, you're the bookworm while I'm the Animating champion of this family.'

Alora stood up. 'I'd like to remind you of my score in last month's Animating test.'

'A lucky accident.' Matthew gave her a cheeky grin as the chair behind her started to rise up to join the book hovering near the ceiling. 'Beat that!'

'Hmm! Large solid objects are easy.'

With her eyes narrowing, his sister turned to face the shelf on the wall opposite. A full inkwell rose up slowly and drifted gently towards her desk. 'Come on, gently does it.'

As the inkwell wavered, she bit her lip. 'Just a little bit further now…'

A flutter of feathers as two quills flew down to the inkwell broke her concentration and sent the glass container hurtling to the floor, splattering her face and clothes with ink before splintering around her feet.

'Matthew, you…' she began as her brother sidled out of the door.

'Alora? What on earth are you playing at?' A tall, thin woman with hair scraped back into a neat bun stood there.

'Oh, Miss Clementine...I was just practising Animating and...'

'You may be a future Spell Master, Alora, but you must remember that even the greatest of the Gifted must learn to walk before they can run.' Miss Clementine waved a hand and the glass container pieced itself together. A second wave reversed the spilt ink until it was back in the inkwell. 'Now, back on the shelf with you.' She turned to the red-faced teenager. 'I'd suggest that for the moment you leave inkwells *well* alone!'

Chuckling at her own humour Miss Clementine left the room. A moment later a bashful Matthew peered around the door. 'Sorry, Sis!' His mouth began to twitch.

Alora scowled, but couldn't hold back her own smile. 'I'll get you for this, little brother!'

Sage and the others laughed out loud as the memories faded away.

'What do you think of *The Coterie*?' Alora asked Sophie and Sage as they ate their meal.

'It's amazing! I can't believe there are so many people like us. And somewhere I can practise openly,' Sophie said.

'Transposing is in your family, isn't it?' Casper said.

Sophie nodded and explained her family background. 'But Dad and Gary are set against it. Personally, I think they are just jealous because it runs through the female side of the family.'

'Or they may be scared,' Molly said. 'One of my NG friends caught me animating a cartoon character in a Maths textbook once. I was getting bored and let my guard down for a moment.'

'NG?' Sage whispered to Paris.

'Non-Gifted,' he whispered back.

'What did you do?' Sophie asked. 'I've nearly been caught a few times already. I always totally deny it and make out that they've got problems.'

'That's one way of dealing with it, but it won't work if you get caught out too many times or if too many people spot your talent,' Rhandra said.

'I agree, it's important not to let down your guard at any time.' Alora nodded. 'But you all must learn how to at least Muddy memories if you *are* spotted. That's a talent you all need to perfect to protect the rest of us, so sign up for at least one of those classes each month. Wilf, you're helping out at those, aren't you?'

He nodded. 'I'm helping out on Tuesday evening. I can do Muddy and Imprint but not Erase yet. Casper is taking the advanced class one day next week.'

'And don't forget, as you get more experienced you may be called upon to use your talent for more than fun or competitions,' Casper said.

'Wow, there's so much to get my head around.' Sage sighed.

'Don't worry, being Gifted is wonderful. And great fun,' a girl said.

'And the competitions are awesome,' a boy added.

'I'm not surprised to hear you say that, Carl. Are we all aware that Carl has reached the semi-finals in the Transposing competition to be held in Birmingham at the end of this month?' Alora smiled as she looked around the table. 'He'll be competing against Transposers from the USA, Spain, and Japan.'

'The girl from Japan will be a challenge,' Rhandra commented. 'You can hardly see her move! You'll need to train hard, boy.'

'No pressure, Carl. But we haven't had a UK win in two years. It's getting embarrassing.' A girl laughed.

'And Casper, have you settled on a team for the Profound mixed match?' Alora asked him.

He nodded. 'And three back-ups. They all know who they are. Don't forget to look at the noticeboard for practise times this month. Animators, have you put your names down for Chester in September?'

'As long as July goes well…' Sean commented dryly.

'What's happening in July?' Sage asked.

'Seventy-year anniversary. The three planets will be aligned and there's a chance *Someone* could open the Portal,' Sean said.

'Sean's being the Harbinger of Doom.' Molly tossed her head. '*Someone* hasn't managed to open anything despite his attempts over the past few centuries, so chances are he won't be able to do it this time.'

'We don't need to be over anxious about it, but Sean's right, we do have to give it some thought,' Alora countered. 'In fact, there'll be a general meeting about the Alignment in the next two months for all Gifted in The Valley, young and old. Everyone needs to be aware of the history of the Portal and how things stand today.'

'And in the meantime, I'm going to be getting in as much Animating practise as possible,' Molly said with a mischievous grin. 'I want to be ready for September.'

Sage noticed that she had flicked the pad on her chair and the two stick men were climbing up the table leg and stealthily making their way towards Wilf. As they neared his plate and hid behind a glass of orange juice, Molly called out:

'Wilf, have you decided what you're going to do for your demo presentation?'

He looked up at her and began to outline his plan, with Molly nodding and asking questions as the stick figures crept forward, picked up a large cookie from the plate in front of him and scuttled back to Molly.

Molly and the two stick men clapped their hands as he looked down at his empty plate.

'Why…you…I'll get you back!'

'Molly, we said no Animating at mealtimes.' Alora shook her head.

After the meal was finished and the table cleared, most of the young people left in groups of twos and threes. Soon there was just Sophie, Paris, and Sage with Alora and Casper.

'Can you three stay for a while?' Alora asked as they were preparing to leave. 'It's pretty hard adjusting to a new Gift even with family support, so it will be even more difficult for you, Sage. Paris told me that you don't know of any Gifted ones in your family but there must be some in your background?'

'I live with my grandparents and they're just ordinary people. My parents died in a car crash seven years ago, but I never saw any sign of Gifts in them, either. In fact, I didn't know anything about any of this until I had a blow to my head a week ago. It's all been a bit scary.'

'Don't worry. You'll soon master your skills. Being Gifted comes with responsibilities, but it is something really special.' Alora smiled. 'And we'll be here to help you.'

'You seem to be a quick learner,' Casper commented.

'You'll need to be,' Alora said seriously. 'You must condense any strands you collect as quickly as possible to keep your identity hidden except when you are among friends. There are other Gifted ones out there who use their talents for selfish and evil purposes.'

Chapter Five

'So, did you have a good time with your friends, Sage?' her grandmother asked as they sat together at tea time.

'Very nice, thank you, Nan.'

'What was the youth club like? What did you do there?'

'It's really great. We played a few games and had lunch there. I met some real cool people. They meet up a few evenings in the week to chat and hang out. It's a great place. I feel I can…be myself…there.'

'Well, that sounds good. Paris and Sophie are very nice. I'm glad to see you finding something to interest you.'

'As long as you keep up with your school work, Sage.' Her grandfather looked serious. 'It's not long until you sit your exams.'

'Oh, don't worry. I'll keep on top of it. What did you and Nan get up to today?'

'This afternoon we went to the library and Mary had two more of Dolores Silver's romances for your Nan and she gave me this book about herbs. It's really interesting. I didn't realise there were so many unusual plants around,' he said, holding up the book. 'I'm going to have a go at growing some of these, though I don't know if I'll be able to find them in the local garden centre.'

'Mary did say she would let you have some cuttings from her own garden, didn't she, Jim? She's going to drop them by later in the week,' his wife said. 'She told me some of their names but I can't remember them now. I hadn't heard of any of them.'

'Some of these sound as if they wouldn't look out of place in a witch's kitchen.' Jim chuckled. 'Listen to this: mugwort—for use in clairvoyance and psychic dreams. The fresh leaves will strengthen divinatory abilities when rubbed on a magic mirror or crystal ball.'

'Do you believe in magic, Grandad?' Sage asked.

'Of course not. It's all just folklore, tales from long ago when people didn't have the scientific knowledge to explain things they couldn't understand.'

'But every now and then there are stories of strange things that can't be explained by science, aren't there?'

'There are usually simple explanations behind these strange stories at the end of the day,' her grandmother pointed out.

'What about Mum and Dad? Did they believe in magic?'

Jim's brow creased. 'I don't know if he actually believed in magic, but your Dad had a great imagination, right from when he was a young lad, didn't he, Ellen?'

She smiled. 'He certainly did. He'd have loved to get hold of a book like that.'

'And Mum?' Sage asked.

Her grandad smiled. 'She was a dreamer, too.'

The young girl walked to the mantlepiece and picked up a photo of her parents on their wedding day. They looked so happy.

'Does my Gift come from one of you?' she murmured.

'Have you any plans for tomorrow, Sage?' her grandmother asked.

Jim looked up. 'Mike and Yvonne's daughter, Harriet, is visiting them for the weekend and we've been invited for lunch. You're most welcome, too, unless you've already made arrangements with your friends.'

Sage tried to mask the look of delight in her eyes. 'Oh, if you're sure, Sophie did say she'd like to meet up again tomorrow.'

'You go ahead. You don't want to spend all your free time with us old folk.' Her grandad winked.

Soon, Sage was chatting on the phone to Sophie. 'I'll see you at the cafe tomorrow at eleven. I've had a text from Paris, too. He'll meet us there.'

***

The next morning, she smiled as she saw Sophie waving to her from a corner table. Paris was seated beside her.

'Hi,' she said as she joined them.

Paris gave an admiring nod. 'No strands!'

Sage held out her hand and grinned. There were six red discs and five other assorted colours.

'And what are we looking at?' Sophie sighed.

'I've condensed eleven wisps since I left home.' Sage smiled. 'I'm really getting the hang of it now!'

'It was amazing at Alora's yesterday, wasn't it?' her friend said. 'I've been practising my landings this morning using some of the tips Rhandra gave me.'

'When did you get your Gift, Paris?' Sage asked.

'Just before my sixteenth birthday last year. Then, like you, Sophie, I got my invitation from Alora. I've been going there about three times a week since then. Whenever schoolwork lets me.'

'There aren't any older people at Alora's are there?' Sage said. 'Apart from some of the tutors.'

Paris shook his head. 'It's a place for the young Gifted to improve their skills, then, when they're about twenty-one, twenty-two, they leave to make space for the next group of developing Gifted.'

'So, we have to work really hard while we have the chance,' Sage commented.

Sophie was frowning at a couple on a table nearby. 'It's a lovely sunny Sunday morning and all they can do is argue!'

Sage watched as several red strands rose from the couple and made their way to curl above her head. She opened her hand as the red discs fell into her palm. Then with a thoughtful expression she pulled out two yellow discs and fixed her eyes on them. Slowly yellow wisps rose and she directed them towards the arguing couple. As she blinked, the yellow strands showered down over their heads.

'Well, I just think...' the man was saying. His expression softened and he spread his hands. 'Oh, why are we arguing? It's a lovely day, why don't we go for a walk along by the river?'

For a moment, the woman looked as if she was going to disagree, but suddenly she grabbed his hand and squeezed it. 'You're right, John. Why are we arguing about nothing? Let's not waste this beautiful day. Let's go!'

Paris smiled as they walked out of the door; John was hugging the woman close to him as she laughed at something he said.

'Nice work, Sage. You're getting good.'

'Did you just change their moods and stop them arguing?' Sophie looked amazed. 'I wish my gift was as useful.'

'I'm sure it is. Anyway, that guy's right.' Paris stood up. 'Let's go outside and enjoy the sunshine.'

The three of them were making their way along the street, when a loud cry made them look behind. A woman holding the hand of a toddler was pointing at a man running ahead of her.

'He snatched my handbag! Stop him!'

Several people looked up in surprise. Suddenly Sophie sprang into action and placed herself directly in front of the thief, grabbing his jacket.

'Give it back!'

For a moment, his eyes widened in shock, but then with a curse, he pushed her over and continued along the road.

Sage and Paris ran towards Sophie but as they reached her, she disappeared to reappear again in front of the thief. She curled herself into a ball so that he tripped over her and sprawled out on the ground. Sitting down heavily on his back, she grabbed the bag from his hands.

'What the...?' he whimpered.

'He stole that woman's bag!' she shouted at a group of youths who were looking at them in amazement. Two came forward and held the thief down as the woman came running up, the toddler crying in her arms. Several other people gathered around.

'I'll call the police...'

'Underhand trick, stealing from a mother with a toddler...'

'You were pretty quick off the mark, young lady...'

Wilf appeared as Paris helped Sophie to her feet. 'I'll sort this out. Get the girls away. I'll meet you in the park by the old oak.'

Paris nodded and the three of them disappeared into the growing crowd of onlookers.

'Well, your gift can be *very* useful,' Sage said as Sophie smiled.

Paris nodded. 'But we must make sure we don't attract too much attention. Let's get away from here.'

Soon after that, Wilf joined them. 'The thief and one of the young guys nearby noticed you, Sophie. I Muddied them both.' He took a deep breath as he sat down. 'Muddying two minds one after the other is a bit tiring.'

'What exactly do you do?' Sage asked.

'I just put a different thought into their heads, so they have a distorted memory of what happened.'

'That sounds like fun,' Sophie said. 'We could use that when our homework is late!'

'Alora is pretty sharp on the correct use of talents.' Wilf grinned.

'Can you give us a demonstration of Muddying now?' Sage asked.

'Okay. Why not?' He looked around; a woman was walking her dog along the pathway. He stood up and went towards her.

'Excuse me. Have you seen a small, black and white terrier coming this way? He's run off!'

The woman frowned as he held her gaze, then slowly she nodded. 'Yes, I've just seen him running towards the main gates. You'd better hurry so he doesn't get onto the busy road.'

Wilf thanked her and signalled for the others to follow him. He laughed as they slowed down near the gate.

'Did you Muddy her memory?' Sophie asked.

Wilf shook his head. 'I had more time, so I went a level above that. There wasn't a dog but I Imprinted a picture of him into her mind and a memory of him running past.'

'That's amazing,' Sophie said. 'I can't wait to learn how to do that!'

'I can do a bit of Muddying, but I'm not up to Imprinting yet,' Paris said. 'It's not as easy as you make it look.'

'You'll all get the chance at Alora's next Tuesday after school. I'm taking the beginners' class,' Wilf told them.

Chapter Six

'Let's eat outside today, Sage,' Sophie suggested as the bell rang at the end of the morning the following Monday.

The two girls were seated on a bench when Paris joined them. Sage looked around her at the other students. Now she had more control over her Snare powers, she enjoyed looking around to view the feelings of those around her. She frowned as her eyes fell on a boy from her English class. Blue and white wisps were rising slowly from him as he toyed with a sandwich. Sophie and Paris were deep in conversation, so she stood up and went over to the boy.

'Hey, Henry, what's up? Where's Bridget?'

'Hi, Sage. Bridget's joined the "in crowd." She's not interested in me anymore. She's in the canteen with Layla and her crowd.'

Sage creased her brow. 'Layla? Why would she bother with that lot? I'm sure she'll come to her senses soon enough, Henry.'

He stood up and tossed his sandwich into the litter bin. 'I'm not that bothered.'

Sage gathered up the blue and white wisps above his head. 'Hmm, you're not?'

Just before they made their way to afternoon lessons, Sage stopped off at the girls' toilets. She was about to leave the cubicle when she heard voices.

'Come on, Bridget. Don't be a baby. It's part of the initiation ceremony. We all had to do it!'

'Except, you, Layla.' Sage recognised the voice of Layla's best friend, Sasha.

'Well, someone has to keep look out, don't they?'

'I don't know...' Bridget said on a quiet voice. 'What if we get caught?'

'We won't. We haven't up to now. And I really need some new Pout lip gloss. This one's nearly finished,' Layla said.

'Can't you just buy some?'

'Have you seen the price? No way I could pay so much for it! Bridget, you do want to come to the party on Saturday, don't you? You do want to be part of the gang?'

'Yes, but…'

'No buts. We'll pop into the shopping centre on the way home today. The bell's about to go. Better get a move on.'

Sage listened to their voices fade as the door closed behind them. Stepping out of the cubicle she drew a deep breath. She had to speak to Henry.

'How do you know which shop they'll be going to?' Henry asked as he, Sage, and Sophie hurried from school two hours later.

'It'll be the new Die For cosmetic shop in the South Centre. Layla is always going on about it being the only place to get decent cosmetics,' Sophie said. 'But I didn't realise she meant steal them!'

'If Bridget gets caught, she could be arrested. And get a criminal record. Why would she take such a risk?' Henry shook his head.

'We have to stop her doing anything stupid,' Sage told him as they entered the shopping centre. She looked at the centre map. 'Die For is on the third floor. Let's hope we're not too late.'

'I'm going on ahead,' Sophie whispered to her. A moment later she stumbled against a woman stepping off the escalator at the cosmetic section. She stood back as the woman gave her an angry look. 'Sorry.'

Layla and Sasha seemed to be listening to a carefully made-up counter assistant as she explained the benefits of the different hair products she sold. Now and again, Layla gave a quick glance towards Bridget who was standing by another counter filled with an array of colourful lipsticks and lip glosses. She had picked one up and was turning it over in her hands.

'Hi, Bridget.' Sophie hurried over to her. 'Are you buying some new lip gloss?'

'Oh, Sophie…I'm just taking a look…'

'I've heard "Pout" is good. It'd better be really good at this price! Hey, Sage, Henry, what a coincidence seeing you here!'

Henry smiled awkwardly and walked towards Bridget. 'Yes, fancy us all meeting up here.'

Bridget's hands shook as she dropped the lip gloss back on to the counter. 'I'm so glad you all turned up…I'd better get going…'

Henry put a hand on her arm. 'I don't suppose you fancy going for a coffee, do you?'

Bridget glanced over at Layla who was glaring at her. 'Yes, I'd really like that, Henry.'

'Ooh, coffee…' Sophie began.

'Unfortunately, we can't join you today, can we, Sophie?' Sage interjected.

'We can't? Oh, no, we can't.'

Chapter Seven

Sophie was really excited as they made their way to Alora's on Tuesday evening.

'I can't wait to learn how to Muddy someone. I'll be able to practise Transposing more at home and just get Dad and Gary to forget it.'

Wilf was surrounded by several youngsters who were setting out tables and chairs in the basement when they arrived at The Coterie.

'Hey, guys! Looks like there's going to be a good turnout this evening.'

Soon the seats were filled and Wilf stepped to the front of the room.

'First of all, glad to see so many of you here. As Alora has already told you, Muddying is a very important skill to keep our talents hidden from NG eyes. I'll run through the basics of Muddying; then you will all have an opportunity to try out a series of tests on virtual targets on the tablet in front of you.'

He lit up a screen that showed a man standing in an empty street. 'We'll go through an example together. Our target here has just witnessed a female Transposer moving at superhuman speed from one place to another. Once you have identified your target and the problem, you must fill your own mind with a mixture of images of the event they witnessed.'

Two bubbles appeared around the central figure, showing a clip of the girl he actually saw and a clip of a female athlete.

'For best and quickest results include one true image; for example, as this NG witnessed the girl moving at superhuman speed, you could include an image of the actual girl followed by another image of a famous female athlete. Then put in images of the scenery, chopping and changing so it becomes disorientating.'

Three more bubbles appeared with a street scene, a running track, and a pathway in a park.

'Now you need to insert these images into the mind of your target. To do this, you must gain and maintain eye contact with him or her for about five to ten seconds, feeding in the images until you can see from their facial expressions that they are feeling confused.'

The face of the central character took on a perplexed expression.

'At this point, reinforce what you want them to believe happened by voicing aloud your ideas—you could say things like, "Hey, that girl can run! She could almost be Olympic standard!" Or, even make a comment about there being two girls, "Did you see those two girls racing by?" Remember, it all has to be done very quickly and without drawing attention from anyone else who might be around. It sounds difficult, but it gets easier as you get the hang of it.'

He smiled. 'Your turn now. You each have a login for the tablets we're giving out. The results will be automatically recorded and you can go through them with myself, Alora, or one of our other tutors. There are ten tests for you to complete, from basic level one up to level ten. Study your target and surroundings carefully before you begin each test. You'll be allowed three attempts at each level. Don't worry if you struggle at first, everyone does. The more you practise the easier it becomes.'

The students exchanged nervous glances as they turned on their tablets and put on their headphones. Paris gave Sophie a wink. 'I only completed three levels at my first lesson.'

Sage was already reading the text outlining the first scenario and frowned in concentration as she studied the target and surroundings.

Wilf and Alora circulated the room stopping to help various students as they did so.

Wilf walked over as Sage put up her hand, taking off her headphones.

'What are you finding tricky?' he asked her.

'I've finished.'

'To level ten?'

His eyebrows rose as she nodded. He leaned over and scrolled through her scores. Looking up, he caught Alora's eye and waved her over. Both stared in astonishment at the screen.

Sage frowned. 'Have I done something wrong?'

'No. Absolutely nothing wrong,' Alora shook her head. 'You've scored one hundred per cent from level one to level ten on your first attempt. I haven't seen that since…well, I've *never* seen that before!'

'A *Gifted* Gifted!' Wilf quipped. 'You'll be able to move on to the intermediate class straight away.'

Alora looked thoughtful. 'You say there's no history of any kind of Gifts in your family?'

Sage shook her head. 'Nothing as far as I know.'

'What's your full name, Sage?'

'Sage Warland. Do you know anyone in my family?' She looked at the page where Alora had scribbled down her name.

The woman blinked as if her mind had been far away. 'Warland does seem familiar.'

***

Sophie was very pleased with herself as they packed up that evening.

'That was such fun; I got to level four on my first lesson! I beat your first attempt, Paris.'

He spread his hands. 'You certainly did. But I finally completed level ten today. I'll be moving up to intermediate level. It's not possible to Muddy a Gifted one, so Alora invites a few NG *volunteers* to come help us out.'

'What here?' Sophie frowned. 'I thought NGs couldn't enter The Coterie.'

'They can if Alora invites them in.' Wilf joined them. 'For those sessions, Alora sets things up so a small group of NGs can join us to help us out. She completely erases any memories of the evening before they leave and they will have no recollection of being here at all. She's hoping to arrange a class quite soon. I hope you'll both sign up for it, Sage and Paris.'

Her two friends looked at her in amazement. 'You've completed all ten levels already?'

She blushed. 'I just seem to have the knack somehow.'

It was raining heavily when they left the building. Sophie smiled as she heard a car horn sound.

'It's Mum. I'm sure she could drop you both off on our way home.'

They quickly bundled into the car.

'Thank you so much, Mrs Wicker,' Paris said.

'Yes, you saved us from getting drenched,' Sage agreed.

Mrs Wicker was very impressed to hear that Sage had achieved level ten on the first day.

'That must be a first. And you say there's no history of Gifted in your family? So unusual.'

Sage's grandmother opened the door when she arrived home.

'When I saw the rain, I thought I'd go and pick you up. But then I realised I didn't know where you were exactly and your mobile was turned off.'

'Oh, sorry, Nan. Anyway, Sophie's mother dropped me off.'

'You must give me the address of this club, Sage. Where did you say it was?'

'It's...erm...oh, Grandad, what have you got there?' Sage looked at a bedraggled, black kitten on his lap. It purred as he gently dried it down with a towel.

'I just heard a tiny meowing sound coming from the garden when I went to close the window against the rain and I found this little fellow shivering outside.'

'What a sweet face he has. His eyes are almost silver...and those ears look too big for him. Can we keep him?'

'Don't get too attached. He looks like a pedigree and I'm sure someone is looking for him. We'll have to ask around here tomorrow morning to see if anyone has lost him,' Ellen said. 'They might be worried about him, especially in this weather.'

'He hasn't got anybody looking for him. He's moving in here with us,' Jim said emphatically.

'We'll make a bed for him for the night and ask around tomorrow,' Ellen said firmly.

'I do hope he can stay with us.' Sage watched as the cat looked up at her grandfather who leaned towards her and whispered, 'That's what he's planning on doing. He says we're a special family.'

His wife raised her eyebrows.

'That's what he said.' Jim met her gaze. 'He's not going anywhere. His home is with us now.'

Chapter Eight

Sophie smiled as she sat down beside Bridget and Henry in the canteen the next day. 'I'm glad to see you two have made up again.'

Henry squeezed Bridget's hand as Layla walked by giving her a cold look. 'Yes, everything's great.'

'Henry told me about your plan to stop me doing something really stupid,' Bridget added. 'I shudder to think what might have happened if you hadn't arrived exactly when you did, Sophie.'

Henry frowned. 'Actually, I was surprised at how quickly you reached her, Sophie. It was almost as if…'

'Hey, Sage! Paris!' Sophie waved her hand. 'Over here. Did Sage tell you about the kitten that her granddad found out in the rain last night? I'm going to go and see him on the way home today.'

'If we still have a kitten.' Sage went on to explain how her grandparents were looking for his owner that day.

***

Sage breathed a sigh of relief as the three friends entered the kitchen and saw the little creature curled up in a box by the cooker.

'We asked around, but no-one seems to have lost him,' her grandmother said. 'We left our phone number with Sala at the corner shop in case anyone does turn up.'

'They won't.' Her grandad smiled as a worried frown crossed his granddaughter's face. 'This is Jet's home now.'

'You can't give him a name and raise false hopes, Jim. Sage will be doubly upset if someone does claim him.'

Her grandfather winked at her. 'But Jet's already told me he's planning on staying with us.'

'Jet can talk?' Sophie raised her eyebrows.

'Well, he doesn't actually *talk* to me, but I know what he means.'

'He's a beautiful cat,' Paris said. 'His face reminds me of the ones you see in ancient Egyptian art.'

'The Ancient Egyptians held their cats in very high esteem,' Jim continued. 'When a household cat died, the owners would often shave off their eyebrows to show mourning. Sometimes pet cats were mummified and buried with their owners.'

'Jet is a very special cat even if he isn't from Ancient Egypt!' Sophie said. 'Surely someone would have put up posters or asked at the newsagent's if they were looking for him?'

'Yes, you would think that someone would be looking for him by now; but we'll leave it until the end of the week before we consider him ours,' Nan insisted.

Jim frowned as the kitten unfurled itself and headed towards his wife. She grimaced and put a hand to her forehead. 'I've a headache coming on again.'

'Perhaps Jet is trying to tell you something…'

'He's a cat, Jim!' Ellen gave him a warning glance.

***

'Jet is a very unusual looking cat,' Sophie told her mother later that evening. 'He has silver eyes and huge ears.'

'And he's black, you say?' Mary gave her sister a look.

Sophie's mother got up and disappeared into the study, coming out a few minutes later with a large, leather-bound book. She placed it on the kitchen table and flicked through the pages. 'Does it look like this, Sophie?'

'Exactly like that!' she exclaimed. 'What kind of cat is it?'

'According to the author, this cat is very special. It's called a Slynk and is only found in regions of the UK that have had strong links with witchcraft over the centuries. In medieval times it was feared as it was believed to be a witch or wizard's familiar.'

Mary began to read out loud, '*A Slynk is a familiar that will choose its lifelong Gifted companion carefully and there will be a strong bond between the two.*

'*The companion of a Slynk will have special skills in communicating with non-human living creatures.*'

'My word, it looks like Sage's grandfather may be a Communicator,' Sophie's mother remarked.

Sophie frowned. 'But he's NG.'

'Or is he?' Mary's eyes narrowed. 'Yet another coincidence, Denise? I told you, the grandparents are definitely our kind.'

'We need to speak to Alora about this,' her sister replied. 'No-one is to say anything to Sage or her family until we've heard what she has to say.'

***

The two women and Sophie sat around Alora's kitchen table the following evening.

'The family name, the coincidence of the house being suddenly available for the second time when they were ready to move, and now the Slynk,' Mary finished telling Alora. 'What other evidence do we need?'

Alora spread her hands. 'It does sound as if Jim Warland could actually be Gifted.'

'And if he is a Communicator, how come Sage is a Snare?' Denise asked. 'Doesn't the same Gift get passed down through a family line?'

Alora stirred her tea. 'The Warlands may be a multi-Gifted family.'

'Wow! That would mean...' Denise looked at Alora who nodded.

'We have a new future Spell Master.'

'Now we know Sage's grandfather is Gifted, can she tell him about her own gift?' Sophie asked.

Alora shook her head. 'No, not until he openly accepts his Gift. A law was passed long ago to protect the descendants of Renouncers from outside magical influences.'

She noticed the puzzled look on the girl's face. 'It's a long story, but when magic was removed from Earth world, there were many Magical and Gifted ones who chose to remain here because they had married mortals and had families or because they felt Earth world was their home. However, as we all know, the persecution of women and men suspected of having magical powers continued. To protect themselves and their families, Gifted ones could renounce their powers. After the Renunciation ceremony, they had to live outside a Crux, that's a place where magical vibes accumulate, such as The Valley. If they returned to a Crux, the Gift could be reignited. But no other Gifted ones can force them to accept their Gifts.'

'Well, that's obviously what has happened to the Warlands since they returned to The Valley!' Mary exclaimed. 'It's only a matter of time before Jim realises what is happening. And if only Ellen knew that blocking her Gift is causing her those awful headaches...'

'Mary...' Alora gave her a warning look.

'No, I won't interfere, I promise. But if I could get one or both of them interested in finding out about their family backgrounds, they could stumble upon it themselves.'

Alora nodded. 'That sounds like an acceptable plan.'

***

'Hi there, it's only me.'

Ellen looked up and smiled as her neighbour waved through the kitchen window the next morning.

'Hi, Mary.'

'I've brought some herb cuttings for Jim. I'll leave them here by the door.'

'Come in. I was just going to make a pot of tea. Jim's gone to get a newspaper. He'll be back soon.' Ellen put two mugs on the table and a plate of biscuits beside them.

'Oh, this is the little kitten Sophie was telling me about, Jet isn't it?' The cat purred as she stroked his head. 'He's a beauty.'

'Yes, he is. He looks like a pure breed and I still think someone might be looking for him. I told Jim not to let Sage get too attached to him just yet.'

'He looks as if he's here to stay. He's making himself at home, isn't he?' Her neighbour smiled as the cat curled up on his blanket by the cooker.

She sat down and pulled a small hardback book from her bag. 'I thought you might like to take a look at this, too. It's a history of The Valley. You might find it interesting now you're living here.'

Ellen flinched as Mary pushed the book across the table to her.

'Have you a headache?' Mary dived into her large bag again and pulled out a small glass bottle. 'This is my own remedy, completely organic from herbs grown in my own garden. Just sit down and close your eyes. This will clear your head.'

Reluctantly, Ellen was backed into a chair and sat quietly while Mary rubbed a pungent smelling liquid into her temples.

'Oh, that does feel better.'

'You're too tense, Ellen. Just relax. What is meant to be, is meant to be.'

Ellen opened her eyes. 'What do you mean?'

Mary looked ready to speak then suddenly sprang up and grabbed her bag. 'Hey, I'll be late for the library.'

The other woman sat bemused as she heard her leave the house. Jim came in a moment later.

'Mary said she'd left me some herbs. Are you okay, love? Is your head bothering you again?'

'No, it's fine. It's just something Mary said. Or, rather, what she didn't say.'

'That's too deep for us isn't it, Jet?' Jim smiled as he stroked the cat. 'We just go with the flow. What's meant to be, is meant to be.'

Chapter Nine

'Hey, move out of the way,' a boy said as he roughly pushed past a younger boy who was putting books into his locker. The younger boy stumbled and his glasses fell to the floor.

'Watch where you're going!'

The older boy faced him. 'Are you talking to me?' He pushed past him to his own locker.

'Callum Hunt is a real pain! He's always picking on people smaller than himself!' Sophie scowled. 'I'd like to teach him a lesson.'

There was a sudden cry of pain from Callum as he stepped back from his locker holding his forehead. 'Who did that?'

Two of his friends looked up. 'Did what?'

'Slammed the locker door in my face. It wasn't funny.'

'There's nobody near you. It must have just closed over.'

'No; someone slammed it in my face. Look.' He showed them a long red welt on one side of his face.

Sage noticed that Sophie was grinning and seemed slightly out of breath. She gave her a questioning look.

'What?' Sophie said artlessly.

'That must have been a very quick jump.'

'My fastest yet, I think.'

'What's going on here?' Paris asked as he joined them.

'Callum has been banging his head on his locker door, for some reason.' Sophie stopped in front of him. 'Beware of karma, Callum. It has a way of making your actions catch up with you.'

Callum scowled at her as she walked away. 'She did this!'

'She wasn't anywhere near you, Callum,' his friend protested.

'I could see from her face; somehow, she did this.'

***

'We have to be careful about using our Gifts,' Paris pointed out as they made their way home. 'Not just for ourselves, but for all the Gifted in The Valley.'

'Yes, but if we can do so safely, why not put them to some good use?' Sophie countered.

By now they were walking through the park where a game of football was being played.

'Hey, it's my old junior school, St George's.' Paris stopped to watch. He gave a grimace as he saw the score marked up on a board nearby. 'They're not doing too well.'

'How can they call this sport? They're all so angry and rough,' Sage commented.

'The spectators are the worst.' Paris gestured towards a group of parents shouting threatening remarks— some aimed at the players and some at the referee.

'Come on,' said Sage, pulling yellow discs from her pocket. 'What have you got there? Let's lighten things up.'

'Are you sure this is a good idea?' Sophie shook her head.

Sage passed Paris a handful of yellow and orange discs. 'I'll collect the reds and you disperse those.'

As Sage captured and condensed the red strands, Paris sent a mist of yellow and orange over the players and spectators and players. Gradually, the parents quietened down, then one by one the players themselves seemed more relaxed.

'Ross, why did you let that kid get the ball?' a woman called out.

'He hasn't touched it once this match, Mum.'

'Hmm. I suppose that's fair enough.'

As a whistle was blown, two players faced each other.

'It's your throw in, mate,' a girl said.

'To be quite honest, the ball did actually touch my foot, so it should be yours, go for it,' the boy replied.

'All sorted?' the referee asked them.

'Yep, it's Anna's throw in, ref.'

'Thank you,' she called out.

'Did you see the goalie let the ball in there?' Sophie frowned a few minutes later.

The team coach ran towards the goalie. 'What are you doing, Kyle? You didn't even try to stop it!'

'It's two all now, coach. St George's haven't had a win all season. I thought we could give them a break.'

The coach blinked, then grinned. 'You're right. We'll manage with a draw, let's give them a break.'

After ten more minutes Sophie began to yawn. 'This is the most boring match I have ever watched. Nobody seems to want to win; they're too busy being nice to everyone else!'

Paris nudged Sage. 'She's right. Competitive sports do need a bit of aggro.'

'Okay,' Sage conceded. 'Let's disperse some of the reds, but not too many.'

She opened her hands and sent a cloud of red mist over the pitch. Soon the atmosphere of the game changed. They smiled at each other as they heard the change of tone as they walked away.

'*Take it down, now, now...what are you playing at?*'

'*Don't let her through...tackle, tackle!*'

'*What's the ref talking about? That was* not *offside. No way!*'

'You've still got quite a few red discs left there,' Paris said as they neared the park gate. 'Have you ever done a high dispersal? It's quiet here, so I'll show you how to do it.'

Sophie sighed as she watched them laughing and joking as they moved their hands through the air. 'I wish I could see what you see.' She glanced around. 'There's no-one around so maybe I'll do a bit of practise myself.'

She looked at a large oak tree a hundred metres away and blinked her eyes. A moment later she smiled as she felt the bark of the tree. Hidden from sight, a shadowy figure stood close by, watching her with interest.

'Let's see if I can do that again,' Sophie muttered to herself. Taking a deep breath, she Transposed herself back to her friends.

'Hey, Sophie.' Sage looked up as she appeared beside them. 'I just saw you over there by the gate. Did you get here in one jump?'

Sophie gave a pleased grin. 'Yep. I've been practising!'

'Impressive!' Paris smiled. 'You'll be the top of your group on Saturday at this rate.'

Chattering happily, the three friends set off for home, unaware of a keen pair of eyes on them. The figure took a sharp breath as she saw Sage's face.

'It's you! At last!'

Chapter Ten

'Are you sure?' The young man raised his head, eyes narrowing as his companion sat on the arm of his chair and ran her fingers through his thick black hair.

'Absolutely. I recognise my own,' she replied, leaning forward so her long blonde hair brushed his face. 'Are you pleased with me?'

He kissed her cheek absently. 'Very pleased, my beauty. Did you find out where she lives? And about her grandparents?'

'I'm going there tomorrow morning. I'll take a look around when she's at school.'

'The long wait is nearly over.' His eyes shone like cold, hard emeralds. 'Everything will be mine…'

'Ours.'

'Yes, of course. Ours.'

***

Pale silver eyes watched as Sage left her home for school the next morning. As she turned the corner, the shadowy figure disappeared to be replaced by a tiny, glowing globe. The light flashed to the front of the house, pausing for a second before it entered the open lounge window. Once inside, the pinprick of light hovered outside the kitchen door where Jim and Ellen were finishing their breakfast.

Jet sprang up, hackles raised, hissing and spitting.

'My word, what's got into him?' Jim said as the cat stood with his back to the door snarling. He bent down to pat him, but the cat bared his teeth and scratched at the door.

'Just let him out, Jim, before he takes a bite out of you!' Ellen looked alarmed.

'He'd never do that. But he does want to go outside in a hurry.' He watched as the cat vanished from sight as soon as there was enough space to squeeze out. 'I wonder what all that was about?'

'Well, we don't really know much about him, do we?' Ellen said. She winced and rubbed her forehead as the tiny light circled the room.

'Is it your head again, love? We need to get back to the doctors' and get it sorted.' Jim looked worried.

'It won't do any good. They've done every test they can think of and they can't find anything the matter with me at all. Ooh, there it goes again!' Ellen clutched her head as the tiny light passed over her. Her expression softened as the light rose up the staircase. 'It's easing off a bit now.'

'I'll get you some paracetamol. You left the packet in the lounge,' Jim said as he headed out of the room.

'It's okay. I'll try Mary's remedy. It worked last time.' His wife walked towards the sink and stopped with her mouth agape as she watched the cupboard door open by itself and the bottle float into her hand.

At the top of the stairs, the light had made its way into Sage's room. The glow lengthened until a pale figure was visible. The woman walked around the room, picking up the photo of Sage and her parents and looking amongst the books that filled her shelves.

She then moved into the second larger bedroom and took a quick look around. Finally, she became a tiny globe of light again and floated away through the window.

'We'll go for a drive and a stroll and clear both our heads,' Jim was saying as he walked back to the kitchen, holding the paracetamol. 'And if that headache comes back again today, we'll go back to the doctors'. And we'll keep on bothering them until they get it sorted...you okay, love? You look like you've seen a ghost. Sit down for a moment.'

Ellen turned towards him. 'Jim...the bottle from Mary...I don't understand what's happening...you're talking to a cat...I just...the bottle...'

'What is it, love?' Jim sat her down and rubbed her shoulders.

'I just thought about the bottle and I...look...' She opened her hand and the glass container floated onto the table.

Her husband took off his glasses and polished them slowly. 'Looks like Jet is right; we are a special family.'

Ellen put her hand to her mouth. 'Jim, this is serious. If people know you talk to cats and that I can do...strange things—they'll take Sage away from us.'

Her husband shook his head. 'I don't think it's just us who have these...talents, love. I think we'll find that The Valley holds quite a few secrets. I've been having a look at that book Mary gave us.'

Chapter Eleven

Sage had a shock as she pushed the door open and walked into the house after school that day. She stopped suddenly, her eyes widening as she looked around the room. 'What the...?'

Her grandfather appeared in the kitchen doorway. 'Hi there. Did you have a good day? Your Nan and I went for a drive out to the Farmers' Market over in Marshfield...'

He stopped as he saw the look on her face. 'What is it, Sage?'

His granddaughter was wiping her fingers across the table top. 'What's this?'

'What's what, Sage?'

Sage looked up at his bemused expression. 'Oh, I just saw something shiny...it must be the way the sunlight caught it...' She gave a laugh. 'It's nothing. Where's Jet?'

'He ran off in a huff this morning,' Ellen said as she came into the room. 'He was in a right mood, snarling and spitting. At nothing at all!'

'Not like himself at all,' her grandfather agreed. 'I'm sure he'll be back soon. Anyway, I'll get the table set, I bet you're hungry, aren't you?'

'I'll just get changed.' Sage sprinted up the stairs. Inside her bedroom her expression turned to horror as she looked around her. With shaking fingers, she pulled her mobile from her pocket and rang a number.

'Oh, Alora! I'm so glad to speak to you! The house...it looks really strange! But Grandad and Nan can't see it. Just me. It's like someone has walked around distorting everything. I don't know how to describe it...'

'Like someone has spread Shimmer over everything?' Alora suggested.

'That's exactly it! Shimmer! And Jet has run off.'

'Jet's here with me. He turned up this morning.' There was a pause. 'I didn't want to explain everything to you all at once, Sage. I was hoping to do it gradually, but it looks as if we're running out of time.'

'I'm quite okay about being a Snare, Alora. I really like being Gifted, you know.'

'There's more than that. Quite a lot more actually. And it would help if we could get your grandparents on board. Look, I'll bring Jet over to your house this evening. Jay will come with me to clear up the Shimmer. We'll be there in about two hours.'

Sage sensed a strained atmosphere as they ate their evening meal and all three seemed glad when she went to her room with the excuse of school work to do. An hour later, she heard the front doorbell and hurried down the stairs to see her grandfather open the door to Alora with Jet in her arms. A tall, slim, handsome blonde man stood beside her.

'Hi Sage, and you must be her grandfather so pleased to meet you. I'm Alora and this is my partner, Jay,' Alora said as the cat jumped from her arms and walked warily into the house, then wound himself around Jim's legs. 'We spotted Jet near the main road and were afraid he would get himself run over. I was pretty sure it was Sage's cat and it looks as if I was right.'

'Hi, Alora, hi Jay.' Sage felt a tingle as the young man shook her hand. She turned to her grandad. 'Alora runs the club we go to.'

Ellen came into the hallway drying her hands on a tea towel. 'Come in. Sage and her friends do enjoy going to your club. It's lovely to meet you.'

'And it's very kind of you to bring Jet home,' Jim added. 'I must admit, I was getting a bit worried about him. He hasn't strayed very far from home since he moved in with us.'

'Sage, put the kettle on and we'll have a cup of tea and some fruit cake,' Ellen said.

'Oh, we don't want to put you to any trouble,' Alora began.

'No trouble at all, come into the lounge.'

Jay followed Sage to the kitchen and gave a low whistle. 'She certainly had a good look around.' He gestured towards the shimmering haze.

'Who? And what was she looking for?' Sage frowned.

Jay shrugged as he pulled a soft, white leather pouch from his jacket pocket and gathered up the shimmering trail with a flick of his wrist. 'Alora can explain things better than I can. I'll take a look upstairs, if that's okay?'

Sage nodded and followed him up, feeling a sense of relief as she saw the trail of shimmer disappear into the leather pouch and the house return to its normal state.

Ten minutes later, they joined the others in the lounge with a tray of tea and cake.

Alora and her grandfather were discussing the possible breed of cat that Jet could be.

'Something royal, I imagine.' Alora smiled. 'He has such a high opinion of himself.'

Jet butted her hand and gave her a long stare.

'Just look at that!' Jim laughed. 'I swear he knows what we're talking about! You know, sometimes...'

'Yes?' Alora prompted him.

Jim waved his hand dismissively. 'Oh, it sounds daft, but sometimes it feels like we're having a conversation together.'

Sage's grandmother gave him a warning glance. 'Jim! You'll have people thinking you're a batty old man!'

'It would be hard to appear batty in The Valley!' Alora laughed. 'There are too many quirky people here already. Some people are Gifted in communicating with animals. We should accept and celebrate our Gifts! What's your Gift, Ellen?'

'Oh...I'm not...' Sage's grandmother began. Jet jumped on to Jim's knee and fixed his eyes on his face. Her husband quietly interrupted her. 'Tell Alora about what happened with the bottle, Ellen. Jet is sure she'll understand.'

Alora smiled at the older woman. 'Did something like this happen?' The teacup on the tray in front of her rose slowly into the air. 'Over to you.'

Ellen's eyes grew wide, then slowly she placed her hand several centimetres under the floating cup and drew it towards her.

Alora beamed. 'You're an Animator! We have a new Communicator and a new Animator in our Gifted community! That's wonderful.'

'There are others like us?' Jim said.

Alora smiled and nodded. 'There's a thriving Gifted community in The Valley.'

'We're not going crazy?' Ellen's voice shook. 'They won't take Sage away from us?'

'No, we'd never let that happen.' Alora stood up and put her arms around the older woman's shoulders. 'We Gifted ones look after our own kind.'

'Sage?' Jim looked at his granddaughter, who gave a huge sigh of relief.

'At last, I can tell you—I'm a Snare! It all happened when I bumped my head...'

'The colours?' Jim asked.

Sage nodded. 'I can catch people's moods—even change some of them. It was scary and very tiring at first, but I'm getting better at it now. And at keeping my Gift hidden.'

Her grandfather shook his head. 'It looks like we have quite a lot to learn about life in The Valley. Are all the folk around here "Gifted?"'

Alora shook her head.

'Then, why are we?' Ellen asked.

Alora tapped the copy of *The History of The Valley*. 'It's all in here. The Valley's Gifted are descended from Hector the Warlock. Tomorrow morning, we are holding a meeting at The Coterie. We have a special presenter to explain to all those in the Gifted Community about our past and about the threat we face in Alignment year every seventy years, which happens to fall this year. Why don't you come along? Everything will be so much clearer to you and you'll get to meet some like-minded people.'

Jim looked at his wife and nodded. 'I think it would be a good idea for us to go.'

Alora stood up. 'We'll leave you and Sage now. I'm sure you've quite a bit to say to each other. See you tomorrow at eleven o'clock. And after the meeting, we could sit down together. I'm sure you'll have more questions to ask me once you've had time to think about everything.'

'You said you had some other things to tell me about my background, too,' Sage said as she showed their visitors to the front door.

'After tomorrow's meeting, I will explain everything to you and your grandparents.'

Her grandfather was flicking through the history book when she returned to the lounge.

'I think I need to read up a bit more about The Valley.'

'There's a bit about a Slynk in chapter six. Jet is a Slynk,' Sage told him.

'You seem to know quite a lot about all this.' Her grandmother spread her hands.

'I've only known for a few weeks. I've being trying to learn as much and as quickly as possible. I hated hiding things from you, but I thought you'd think there was something wrong with me.'

'Well, it looks like it runs in the family!' Her grandfather chuckled. 'So, tell us about The Coterie and what you get up to there. And what about your friends, Paris and Sophie, are they…Gifted…as well?'

Sage nodded. 'Yes, Paris is a Snare like me and Sophie is a Transposer. She got her Gift just before I did.'

She regaled them with the events she'd witnessed on her visits to Alora's house.

'Nan, you'll have such fun when you develop your Animator skills.' She described the competitions and pranks she had seen. 'But there were no Communicators there, Grandad, you must have a rare Gift.'

It was late when Nan yawned. 'I think we'd better be getting off to bed. We've a busy day ahead of us tomorrow.'

'Are you okay about everything now, Nan?'

'You know, Sage, I am. It's all beginning to seem…normal, somehow.' The cups and plates began to rise and, wobbling slightly, made their way to the tray and gently settled on it. 'Not bad for a beginner, eh?'

Chapter Twelve

Alora smiled as she welcomed them into The Coterie the next morning.

'It's so good to have you here. I'm sure you'll recognise quite a few faces in the hall.'

She led them along a corridor and into a large hall.

'I didn't see this room before,' Sage commented.

'The house adjusts to fit our needs.'

'Are there ghosts here?' Ellen shivered as a young girl ran through her quickly followed by a second girl.

'No, they're just Memories. They're silent unless you want to hear them,' their host explained. 'They seem like two happy Memories.'

'Coo-ee!' Mary Goodall was standing and waving from one side of the hall. 'Jim, Ellen, I've saved you seats. Sage, Sophie is over there.'

'I'll see you later. I hope you enjoy the talk.' Alora made her way to the front of the hall. She waited as the last few people found their seats and settled themselves down.

'First of all, I would like to thank you all for attending this Alignment meeting,' she began, facing a large audience from teenagers to elderly men and women. 'Nefarus and Saffron have already made their presence known in The Valley. We weren't expecting them just yet as the Alignment is not due until 25th July this cycle.'

'That means they have just over a month to arrange a plan of action this time,' a man commented.

'Nefarus is getting serious, or desperate,' a woman commented. 'Neither is good news for us.'

'That's why we need to be ready for him,' Alora added. 'But before we think about how we are going to deal with him, as we do at every Alignment meeting, we are going to have a recap on the history of The Valley. And to help us to do that, we have two highly acclaimed Animators. So, I'll hand you over to Avis and Gideon.'

There was a round of applause as an elderly man and woman seated at the front of the room stood up and nodded. The woman sat down again with a sketch pad on her knee while her partner faced those gathered.

Gideon smiled. 'Thank you. It is an honour to be asked to speak to you today. It hardly seems seventy years ago that myself and Avis were sitting where you are now listening to the history of our valley. There's quite a lot to cover today, so we'll get straight into it.

'As we all know, magic has been with us for as long as humans have walked the earth, though most of the stories we hear about magical and mythical creatures are set in mediaeval times with brave knights fighting fierce dragons, and wizards and witches creating havoc.'

As he spoke, Avis's hands flew over the sketch pad and the characters and creatures he described floated from her lap onto the blank wall before them as if on to a cinema screen.

'We have all heard of King Arthur and the Knights of the Round Table who fought so bravely against the invading Saxons. Armed with his enchanted sword, Excalibur, Arthur was able to lead his men to victory.'

The animated scene showed a fierce battle, with horses stumbling, men's faces contorted in pain, and the determined face of the young King Arthur as he galloped through his enemies, striking them down with a long, shiny blade.

'Finally, victory was his and Arthur and his faithful knights settled down in peace in Camelot.'

A shimmering image appeared of a huge castle where knights and ladies strolled together while servants bustled past them with platters of food and minstrels strolled by strumming on lyres.

'By this time, magic was already feared and outlawed throughout the land. Many Gifted ones and even those suspected of being associated with magic suffered cruel deaths. Yet, despite this, Merlin, the greatest magician of all time, became a close friend of Arthur. Merlin was there when the young king fell in love with the beautiful Guinevere and was aware that their happiness was tainted by the jealousy of Arthur's sister, Morgana la Fay—Morgana the fae.'

The audience gasped as Arthur and Guinevere drew together and then were thrust apart by a beautiful, tall, pale woman whose pale eyes narrowed spitefully as she looked at her sister-in-law.

'Defending the king and queen from the malevolent spells and curses Morgana continually tried to cast upon them, Merlin built a close friendship with the king, comforting him when he lost Guinevere to his former friend, Lancelot. After Arthur's death in battle, Merlin took to mourning for many hundreds of years.'

The scene showed battle worn soldiers carrying the body of Arthur up a bleak, grassy hill, while a sad, hooded figure watched them before turning away and walking into the mist.

'From 1300 onwards the fight against Gifted ones, those believed to be liaising with the Devil, was rife and tens of thousands of suspected witches, mainly women, were executed. In 1692 and 1693 at the Salem witch trials in Massachusetts more than two hundred people were accused of practicing witchcraft and twenty were executed.'

A sob escaped from someone as the audience watched an angry mob follow a cart full of terrified women and children up a rough truck. In the background a man stood with a torch held aloft as several others piled logs around a tall stake.

'At this point, Merlin finally emerged from mourning. Seeing the torture and torment of the Gifted community, Merlin created a new world—Aurum—as a place of sanctuary. A Portal was opened so that all the Gifted ones and magical creatures in Earth world could enter and live peacefully in their own territory.'

The blank wall showed a curtain drawn back on lush green countryside flanked by mountains. A river ran through a central valley. A myriad of creatures flew through, dragons soared into the mountains, fae giggled as they ran through the long grass studded with wildflowers, women clutching young children laughed and chattered as they walked towards log cabins nestled at the foot of the mountains. The scene brought a smile to the faces of the audience.

'I wish I was there,' someone murmured.

'Why *aren't* we all there?' a girl asked. 'We're Gifted.'

'Merlin invited all people and creatures touched by magic to enter the new world, but those who had mortal blood in their veins could not enter. Many Gifted ones were married to mortals and had children. They chose to stay here and keep their families together. Some full blooded Magical also chose to remain in Earth world as they felt it was their homeland,' Gideon explained. 'However, there was a certain group, led by the Daemon, Nefarus, who thought once Merlin and the other powerful Gifted ones had left, they could run Earth world as they wished, but Merlin was prepared for this and just before the Portal was closed, cast a spell to protect Non-Gifted Earth world dwellers from their Gifted neighbours. Nefarus was furious when he discovered this. Ever since then he has been seeking someone who can overturn this spell and also open the Portal so he can rule both Aurum and Earth world. He knows that every seventy years, when the three major planets are aligned, the Portal can be opened if the correct spell is cast; and every seventy years Nefarus steps up his search for the one who can do this.'

'Is there someone who is capable of casting such a powerful spell?' a young woman asked. 'A Spell Master, perhaps?'

Alora stepped forward. 'In theory it is possible, but when we take on our roles as Spell Master, we also make a promise not to do so unless directed by Merlin. Nefarus or any other Daemon would have to have a powerful hold over a Spell Master to force them to break that promise.'

'So, we're safe!' A boy gave a sigh of relief.

Alora smiled. 'We hope so, but we must still be on our guard against the Daemons. Their magic is powerful. And always remember...'

'*Never kiss a Daemon!*' An answering chorus came from the room.

'Why would anyone want to kiss a Daemon?' Sage asked.

An elderly woman stood up and cleared her throat. 'Hi, everyone. I'm Daisy. Most of you know me, or know *of* me. You might find it hard to believe, but seventy years ago I was young and beautiful like you youngsters who've just got your Gifts. That thought also went through my head the first time I heard it— how could *anyone* be taken in by a Daemon, especially if you know that if you kiss a Daemon, he— or she—will capture your heart? I remember it as if it was yesterday. The very next morning after the last Alignment meeting, a handsome young man stopped me on my way to work.

'He asked me for directions to a place near my office, so we walked there together. He was so handsome and so easy to talk to. As we cut through the park, he caught my arm and pulled me towards him...those deep green eyes, those full lips...and there was a strange woody scent around him, it made me feel dizzy. I wanted to kiss him more than anything else in the world.'

A second elderly woman joined her. 'But, luckily for Daisy, I was walking through the park at the same time. At first, I wondered what she was doing getting so close to someone who wasn't her boyfriend. I knew she wasn't like that! Then it dawned on me what was happening. If I hadn't been a Transposer, we would have lost Daisy to a Daemon!'

'Yes, the next thing I knew Judy had pulled me from his grasp and we both lay on the ground. Then my handsome young man showed us his true Daemon side! Red eyes, serpent tongue, silver scales…it was horrifying!'

'It was. Somehow, I managed to Transpose us both as far away from him as I could! Then we just ran as if the devil himself was after us!' Judy clutched her friend's hand. Both women were visibly shaken by the memory. 'He could have captured your heart, Daisy.'

Alora nodded. 'A Daemon, male or female, has special seductive powers so we all must be on our guard against handsome or beautiful strangers.'

'Has anyone had their heart captured?' a young girl asked.

A look of sadness passed across Alora's face. 'Sixty years ago, Saffron, a fae, lost her heart to Nefarus. She is still with him today, helping him in his quest to find a Gifted one to open the Portal.'

'If someone's heart is captured, isn't it possible to break the spell and free them? Surely there must be a Gifted one who can do that?' Sage asked.

'Merlin has the power and would happily break the spell—but the captured one must be willing to be freed. Saffron is enchanted and does not wish to be freed from Nefarus. We have all tried to persuade her at some point—even her twin brother, Sylvan, without any luck so far.'

'But we haven't given up on her. If anyone comes across a spell, new or old, they think we can try, please tell us,' Mary Goodall added. 'There's a whole section of Spell books in the Alternative Library Archive that we haven't looked through yet. We've a selection on display by the window. If you want to take a tome home with you, you're most welcome.'

'And if anyone sees Saffron, Nefarus, or any of his kind, report to me immediately,' Alora added. 'Don't try to deal with them yourselves.'

Gideon raised his hands for silence. 'Enough of doom and gloom! Avis and a group of Animators have laid on a snack buffet, if you could just make way for the tables...'

As people stood up and moved to one side, several trestle tables laden with hot drinks, snacks, sandwiches, and cakes floated by followed by the chairs which rearranged themselves around them.

'Please, help yourselves,' Avis urged them. 'And we have some music to lighten the mood.'

A small orchestra of instruments assembled by the windows and began to play a gentle, uplifting air.

Jim and Ellen were happy to find several of their neighbours in the crowd.

'It makes life so much easier when you have a community where you can acknowledge your Gifts.' Mary patted Ellen's arm. 'There are plenty of social groups you can join.'

'Are you into handicrafts at all?' another woman asked. 'The Animators meet here on Thursday afternoons each week. We're always glad of a new face and a new pair of Gifted hands.'

'Axel isn't here tonight. He's a vet—runs The Ark, an animal sanctuary on the north of the river. He's the only Communicator we have here. He'll be really pleased to meet you,' a man told Jim. 'Ask Jet about him.'

Sage and Alora joined them later in the evening. 'Most people will be heading off home soon. Can you stay behind with Sage for another hour?'

Ellen looked at her husband and nodded.

'Sage, take them to the kitchen and I'll be with you as soon as I can.'

Half an hour later, they all sat around the scrubbed wooden table as Jay handed each one a mug of tea.

'I know you've had to take on a lot of information in a very short time, but there are still important things you must know about your family background,' Alora told them. She looked up at a shelf and a large book floated to the table and opened in front of them to reveal a family tree.

'Here is the start of the family tree of one of the most important magic practitioners in the history of The Valley, a man who became known as Hector the Warlock and his wife, Nacra, a Potion Master. All Gifted ones in The Valley are descendants of Hector and Nacra.'

Alora traced a finger over the thin pages of the book until she came to one only half filled. 'Their children married and had children and so on until we come to Sage's generation.'

'In 1790, Hector and his pregnant wife, Nacra, were accused of practising the Black Arts and were condemned to death by burning. Both insisted they were innocent but their pleas fell on deaf ears and they were imprisoned in a cell in the old barracks building. During the night before their execution, there was a fierce storm which caused a great deal of damage. Most of the old barracks was destroyed, but no trace of either Hector or Nacra was found. No-one saw them leave, and magic was believed to have played a part in their departure.

'A Gifted historian recorded that they moved to a small village outside York under the new names of Horace and Nuella Warland. Horace worked as a tailor while his wife was in great demand as a midwife. Despite the high mortality rate of both infant and mother in childbirth at this time, Nuella was famous for never losing a mother or a baby. Horace and Nuella themselves had a son, Bartholomew, and a daughter, Vista, who later married Isaiah Newman. Newman was known to have powers that were almost equal to Hector's. Little is known of Bartholomew except that he married an Irish girl and moved to her family farm in Cork. There are records of his great-grandson living in The Valley at a much later date.'

'Newman was my maiden name,' Ellen whispered.

Alora nodded. 'By choosing each other, Jim and Ellen, you have merged the Gifts of two of the most powerful families in the history of The Valley.'

'So why wasn't our son, Peter, Gifted?' Ellen asked.

'He would have realised his Gifts if he had returned to The Valley. Unfortunately, that chance never came.'

'That means that my mother was the only Non-Gifted one in our family,' Sage observed.

'Actually, your mother was the most powerful of all your family, Sage.' Alora paused. 'She was fae. And that makes you half fae.'

'But I thought that fae are immortal. My mother died of her injuries after the car crash.'

'Let me explain what happened that night.' Alora closed her eyes tightly for a few seconds; taking a deep breath she began:

'Straight after the crash, your parents were taken to Highbane Hospital. They were both in intensive care at first, though your mother was moved to a nearby ward on the second day.'

'I remember that. We were so relieved because it looked like she was going to recover.' Tears shone in the young girl's eyes as she recalled the fateful night. 'They didn't hold out much hope for Dad. He had so many tubes and machines around him.'

Her grandmother squeezed her arm. 'It was awful to see him like that.'

'As Daphne lay in the side ward, she had a visitor. An unwanted visitor. Nefarus,' Alora continued.

'The Daemon that's back in The Valley now?' Ellen's eyes grew wide.

Alora nodded.

'Why did the doctors and nurses let him in? What did he want with my mother?' Sage asked.

'Nefarus froze time so everything stopped when he visited your mother. No-one could see or hear him except for her. He'd heard that she'd married Peter Warland and that his family were descendants of Hector the Warlock and Newman. That meant the child of such a union—that's you, Sage—would hold an extraordinarily high level of power when you realised your Gifts. He wanted to use this to unlock the Portal between Earth world and Aurum.

'Nefarus thought that while your mother was weakened by the crash, he could capture her heart, then take you both with him until your Gifts became apparent. However, he hadn't reckoned on the strength of a mother's love. As soon as she realised what his plan was, she bequeathed her fae powers away so that she was merely mortal and Nefarus could not charm her. But she also knew that by relinquishing her own immortality there was a very strong possibility that she would not survive the injuries from the car crash.'

'Her wounds were healing, the doctors told us,' Jim said.

'But without her immortality, she had only human recovery powers.'

Ellen sniffed and dabbed her eyes with a tissue.

'Who did she bequeath her immortality to?' Jim asked.

'There was a young doctor on duty that night, a Snare. She bestowed it on him,' Alora told them. 'He is now a famous heart surgeon. Already he has saved many lives and if he chooses, he can be around for a long time to save many more.'

'Mum didn't let Nefarus win, and we're not going to do so now!' Sage sat up straight. 'She didn't die in vain!'

'Your parents would be so proud of you, Sage,' Alora said. 'You will need to be strong. More so than other Gifted ones.'

'What do you mean?' Ellen asked.

'With your family background and the fae powers bequeathed by Daphne, Sage is the one chosen to be the next Spell Master.'

'But...that can't be right!' Sage protested. 'I have only one Gift, you have many.'

'You will acquire many more Gifts over time. First of all, your grandparents will teach you their special talents.'

'Once we've got the hang of them ourselves,' Jim pointed out.

'Now you've openly acknowledged them, they will become easier to manage. We always have a few older ones who return to The Valley and need help when they suddenly find they are Gifted. There are two couples coming here tomorrow afternoon. Why don't you join us?'

'And, Sage, you could come and have a chat with me about being fae,' Jay offered.

They talked for another hour until Alora stood up and stretched. 'That's enough for one day.'

There was a thoughtful silence as the three Warlands drove home that evening.

'You're right, Sage. The Warland family is going to stand strong against this Daemon,' Ellen said as she headed upstairs. 'I'm going to get on top of these Gifts.'

Chapter Thirteen

Sage sat with her two friends in the park the next morning.

'Wow!' Sophie said for the third time as she told them about the conversation with Alora the previous evening. 'So, you're part *fae*? *And* immortal? *And* a future Spell Master?'

'I don't know if I'm too happy with it all at the moment.'

'You'll be fine, Sage,' Paris assured her. 'I'm sure Alora will help you along the way.'

'Yes, she told me she would be my mentor. Jay said he would speak to me about being fae. I'm going to see him this afternoon. What are you guys up to?'

'We're going to revise for the Chemistry exam,' Sophie told her. 'Only ten days before we start.'

Sage groaned. 'I've been getting behind with my revision lately. I'll have to get down to it when I get back today.'

'Yeah, we've all been a bit distracted lately,' Paris agreed. 'I think Gift training is going to have to take a back seat until after our exams.'

***

Her grandfather repeated Paris's words as they set out for The Coterie that afternoon.

'I know you've a lot on your plate at the moment, Sage. But I think you need to pay more attention to your school studies until your exams are over.'

'I agree with you, Grandad. The planet Alignment doesn't take place for another month and our exams will be over by then. I'm going to make a revision timetable and stick to it. Like Paris said, Gift training will have to take a back seat for the moment.'

The door swung open and Alora called to them from the kitchen as they arrived at the house.

'So glad to see you again. Jim, Ellen, come upstairs and meet a few more of our late Gifted developers. Sage, you can stay here in the kitchen and talk to Jay.'

Sage felt slightly nervous as she sat down at the kitchen table. Jay smiled at her and put a glass bottle and two glasses in front of her.

'This is the best thing about being fae,' he told her. 'Gifted and Non-Gifted humans absolutely hate the taste, but for us it is nectar!'

He poured a small amount of a pale, pink liquid into each glass. 'Meadowsip, made from the finest herbs and spices of Aurum and brewed to a secret fae recipe closely guarded for over nine hundred years.' He raised his glass to her. 'Don't worry, it's alcohol free and completely organic.'

Sage touched his glass with her own and took a tentative sip. A smile broke out as she felt the smooth liquid on her tongue.

'This is beautiful! I've never tasted anything as good,' she exclaimed. 'It's like drinking happiness!'

Jay nodded in agreement. 'It's perfection in a bottle. A treat for the taste buds and a mood booster in a glass!'

'What other good things can you tell me about being fae?'

Jay sat back in his chair. 'When Merlin created Aurum, any creatures or humans touched by magic chose where they would live—either in Earth world or Aurum— and they would have to remain there, but fae can move from one to the other through the Portal. It is never closed to us. I often slip through to visit my family.'

'Why did Merlin allow that?'

'Merlin decided that it would be cruel to deprive children of the chance to connect with magic while their imaginations are fresh and open. They can be transported to the magical lands in Aurum by fae while they sleep. Of course, the NG parents think the children have just been dreaming.'

'Will I be able to do that?'

'Certainly, once you're able to orb yourself.' Jay noticed her brow furrow. 'Like this.'

He stood up, folded his arms and looking down, closed his eyes. Sage gasped as he shrank into a small glowing orb which flew around the room. After a few minutes the glow settled in front of her. She watched as it lengthened, then Jay reappeared as a transparent image of himself which quickly solidified.

He laughed as she stood speechless. 'Give it a try. Alora tells me you're a quick learner.'

'How do I do it?'

'Relax. Just fold your arms, close your eyes…'

She took a deep breath and felt a vibration slowly ripple through her body. Suddenly she was flying into the air, zipping from one corner of the ceiling to another. She began to giggle.

'Okay. Okay. Return now. Slow down a bit…head for the floor…watch your feet…'

'Ouch!' Sage cried as she found herself sitting down heavily on the kitchen floor.

'Not too bad for a beginner. The first few times I orbed, I returned mid-air—and I had a much more painful landing!'

Sage sat down gingerly at the table again. 'What is Shimmer? Saffron filled our house with it when she visited.'

'It's a way of leaving a message for another fae.'

'I couldn't read anything.'

'No, there are no words, just emotions, warnings, or even threats.'

'Mmm. I did feel there was a kind of threat there. It made me feel uncomfortable. Can I do Shimmer?'

'Only in orb mode. Try again. Let your emotions run free and send me a message,' her companion suggested.

Once again Sage stood arms folded and closed her eyes. This time, the tiny glowing orb rose gently to the ceiling and began to circle the room. A faint silvery effect began to appear, becoming more pronounced over the next few minutes. It stayed hovering in the air as Sage floated down gently and reappeared on her feet in front of Jay.

'What a graceful return! Well done, Sage. You certainly are picking this up quickly.' He raised a hand and gathered in the shimmering strip above his head. 'Oh, we all felt like that when we started out, Sage, even those of us who knew what we had been born into—bemused and slightly confused.'

'You read that from my Shimmer?' Sage asked. 'That's exactly what I was feeling!'

Jay pulled a soft white leather pouch from his pocket and poured the Shimmer into it. Closing it gently, he passed it to the young girl. 'You might want to keep this, your very first Shimmer message.'

As she pushed the pouch into her pocket, her grandfather peeped in the doorway. 'Are you ready to go home now, Sage? You've school tomorrow.'

She stood up. 'I am, Grandad. Thank you so much, Jay. I feel so much better now I'm beginning to know more about being fae.'

'I'm very happy to help any way I can. Just let me know if you have any more questions.'

Sage and her grandfather were in the car when Ellen came out of the house holding a large paper bag. She climbed in beside her husband holding onto it carefully.

'What have you there, Nan?' Sage asked.

'An assortment of rare herb cuttings. Even Mary doesn't have all of them and Ursula told me that these are essential in most healing and mood lifting potions. She's given me a few recipes to try out. How did you get on with Jay?'

'It was amazing!' Sage described what she had learnt that evening.

'I've arranged to go to Axel's rescue shelter on Tuesday,' Jim said. 'He's the only other Communicator around here at the moment.'

'It's been a very productive afternoon for us all,' Ellen commented.

Chapter Fourteen

Sage jumped as she heard a loud crash when she came downstairs the next morning. In the kitchen, her grandmother was standing looking at a broken plate surrounded by slices of toast on the floor.

'Oh dear. I lost my concentration for a moment and the whole lot fell down. Stand back, love,' she added as Sage went to get a dustpan. 'I've got this.'

Taking a deep breath, she turned towards the dustpan and brush. Slowly, they rose in the air and hesitantly headed for the broken plate. Ellen's brow creased in concentration as the brush and pan gathered up the debris and emptied it into the bin.

'There!' she said in triumph. 'I'll put some more toast on *manually*, I think. How are you today, Sage?'

'I had nightmares about the exams. We were all given our English papers and for some reason mine was in Chinese! And Mrs Truman wouldn't let me explain…it was awful!'

'You're just getting exam nerves, that's all. I'm sure one of Ursula's recipes can help you with that. I'll have a go at making some up today. You'll be fine once the exams start. Are you going into school as normal this week?'

Sage shook her head. 'We don't have normal lessons but all the teachers are available for last minute advice. We can book a slot if we want. Me and Sophie have booked one for Maths this afternoon. I'll do my own revision this morning.'

Two hours later, Sage groaned and closed the text book in front of her. 'It's no use! I just can't get any of it to sink in! I'm just going to fail my exams.'

Her grandfather paused outside her bedroom door as he heard her.

'Maybe you just need a break, love. Come and give me a hand in the garden for half an hour. With the rain and the sunshine we've had these past two days, the weeds are starting to take over.'

Ten minutes later she looked with satisfaction at the clear vegetable patch and the pile of weeds she had collected.

'Ouch! That was uncalled for! I was just trying to strike up a conversation,' her grandfather called out suddenly.

'What's up?' she asked.

He pointed to an ant that was scurrying back into a line of its fellow creatures.

'Huh! Did you see the dirty look it gave me? An ant with attitude!'

'Ants don't have attitude.' Sage grinned. 'They just bite if you annoy them.'

'Well, that one definitely has attitude,' Jim said as he rubbed his finger.

'What was all the shouting about?' Ellen said, appearing in the kitchen doorway.

Jim explained about the ant he had tried to befriend.

'Maybe ants aren't that friendly with humans. Anyway, it's time for lunch now.'

Sage smiled as she put her knife and fork on the plate a short while later. 'That was a lovely lunch, Nan. And it was a great idea to have a break this morning, Granddad. I feel ready to take on the Maths revision lesson this afternoon now.'

Her grandmother peered at the table, her brow creased. 'Oh, no! Is that an ant? Have we ants in here now?'

Jim put out his hand and watched as the ant crawled onto it. 'It's okay, Ellen. It's just our little friend from earlier. He says he's come to have a word with me. I'll take him outside.'

Sage and her grandmother listened to the gentle hum of the one-sided conversation as they cleared the table. They looked up when Jim reappeared.

'Is your ant friend with you?' his wife asked.

He shook his head. 'No, he's back at work now. He came to apologise for his earlier behaviour. It's just that I'd upset their routine by removing him and breaking the line which made quite a bit of extra work for them all. So, it should be me apologising really.'

'You weren't to know that, were you, Grandad?'

Her grandfather shrugged. 'I'm a Communicator; maybe I should make it my business to know about the other species on the planet we all share.'

'Ooh, that sounds rather philosophical,' Ellen ventured.

Jim nodded. 'Yes, our ant friend has given me plenty to think about. You know, I was surprised to hear he could Transpose.'

'Wow! It's not just humans who are Gifted.' Sage's eyes widened.

'That was exactly my reaction—which really annoyed him. He pointed out how arrogant the human race is, how we use the planet we all share as if it's our personal property with very little regard for the other species on it.' He grimaced. 'I felt quite ashamed of myself. We're going to continue our discussion when he's finished work this evening. I'm looking forward to it.'

'What is his name?' Sage asked.

'They don't have names. They just call each other "Ant."'

'Oh, that seems a bit sad. Perhaps you could give him a special name and make him feel a bit more valued.'

'How about Adam?' Ellen grinned at her husband. She began to hum a tune which brought a smile to his face. The both laughed at their granddaughter's baffled expression. '*Adam Ant*, long before your time, love!'

'On a serious note, I'm going to see Axel this afternoon and I'll see what he can tell me about the Gifted amongst other species. I can drop you off at school on the way, Sage.'

***

Sage waved goodbye to her grandfather as he drove off a short while later and made her way to the school canteen where she found Molly and Sophie just finishing their lunch.

'He's worse than ever, isn't he?' Sophie scowled across the room at a group of boys who were laughing loudly as they left the canteen. Callum snatched a bottled drink from someone's tray as he walked by. 'That does it!' She jumped to her feet and disappeared, reappearing in the canteen doorway in front of him. 'Give that back!'

Sage winced and looked around. 'I hope nobody noticed that.' The two girls made their way to where Sophie and Callum faced each other. Callum grinned and went to walk around her, but she blocked his path.

'Don't make me angry. Just move.'

Sophie noticed Molly pull a pad from her bag. She put her hands on her hips. 'Not until you give that boy his drink back.'

'Are you getting scared, Callum?' One of his friends laughed.

Callum unscrewed the cap of the bottle and took a deep drink. 'Get out of my way.'

His fists tightened as Sophie held his gaze. Sage stepped forward and took her friend's arm. 'Hey, come on Sophie.'

'Yeah, Sophie, let's go,' Molly agreed. Sophie moved to one side.

'That's more like it. You don't want to mess with me…' Callum began. As he turned back to his friends, he suddenly fell to the floor. The open bottle flew out of his hands and he was covered in fruit juice. 'What the...?' he spluttered as the children around him started to laugh.

'What's up with your shoe laces?' one of his friends said.

Callum looked down to see his laces were tangled together. Beside his feet was a piece of paper with two crudely drawn matchstick men. Cursing, he fumbled with his laces. 'Whoever did this better watch out...'

Sophie leaned down to him. 'I did warn you about karma, Callum.'

He sprang up. 'You did this!'

'It couldn't have been her, she didn't touch your shoes, Callum,' one of his friends said. 'Nobody did. Your laces must have just got tangled up somehow.'

'I *know* she did it! She's weird, I'm telling you!'

'What is happening here?' the voice of Mr Bell rang out as he walked through the crowd of children.

'Callum didn't lace up his shoes properly and he fell over,' a young girl said.

'Okay, the show's over. Callum go and clean yourself up. There's the bell for afternoon lessons.'

Callum gave Sophie a wary look as he walked away.

Mr Bell frowned as he picked up the scrap of paper with the stickmen sketches. There was a thoughtful look on his face as he watched Sophie and her friends leave the canteen.

***

'We must be more discreet with our Gifts,' Sage said to Sophie on the way home that day.

'I know. It's just that Callum really needed taking down a peg or two.' A smile spread over Sophie's face. 'That was a great trick Molly did with his shoe laces.'

Sage smiled. 'I have to admit, it was good.'

She was still smiling as she said goodbye to her friend and pushed open the door to the kitchen. Her smile froze.

Her grandmother was stirring a liquid in a saucepan while on the worktop near her a sharp bladed kitchen knife was quickly chopping a pile of herbs.

'Those go into the second saucepan,' Ellen said, waving a spoon at the chopping board. Once the knife had finished chopping, the board rose and tipped the herbs into a saucepan.

'I'm really getting the hang of this Animating.' She smiled happily at Sage.

'Wow! You certainly are.'

***

Each day, her grandmother increased her animating skills. Sage and Sophie walked into the kitchen on the Friday afternoon to find the knife chopping herbs, a saucepan stirring itself, and a group of matchstick men disappearing through the kitchen window into the garden.

The next minute, her grandfather appeared in the doorway with several matchstick figures pulling at his trouser legs and thrusting pieces of paper at him.

'Ellen, you'll have to slow down. I can't get the herbs they want quickly enough for these little creatures. They're driving me mad!' He sat down heavily on a chair. 'Tell them I'm having a break.'

His wife smiled and raised her hands. Immediately the stickmen flew back and became lifeless drawings on post it notes. She gave one of the saucepans bubbling on the hob a gentle stir. 'I've prepared a pot of Ursula's calming potion in this pot and one of Mary's pain relief remedy in that one. And I found a recipe to help you get a good night's sleep before your exams, Sage. That's the pot with the betony leaves on the back hob. Your aunt's book has some great ideas, Sophie.'

They were all watching as the knife continued to chop the herbs when a voice called out.

'Coo...ee! It's only me! I've just come to...' Ellen's friend, Yvonne, stood in the doorway, her eyes riveted on the chopping knife. 'That...that...knife...'

For a moment, everyone looked towards the knife, then Sage stepped forward and muttered 'Stop' under her breath. She picked up the now still knife and turned to Yvonne. Staring her straight in the eye, she smiled. 'Wasn't that strange? The sunlight caught the knife blade and it looked as if it was chopping away on its own!'

Yvonne's brow creased as she began to speak. 'But it was...I saw...'

Sage's smile widened as she held the older woman's gaze. 'You saw the sun glint on the blade, didn't you? It looked as if it was moving on its own.'

Yvonne gave a short laugh. 'I did, and for a moment I thought my eyes were playing tricks on me.'

'It's hot in here!' Ellen finally found her voice and took her friend's arm. 'Let's sit outside under the tree, it's cooler out there.'

'I'll bring you both out a cup of tea, love.' Jim let out a slow breath as the two women walked outside.

Sophie turned to her friend with a look of admiration. 'You *imprinted an idea* in her mind, Sage! You've only had one virtual muddying lesson and you *imprinted!*'

'You did, love.' Her grandfather patted her shoulder. 'You're obviously very talented. I think you're destined for great things.'

Sage gave a nervous laugh. 'I'm going to spend the summer holidays getting on top of these Gifts.'

***

'And then she *imprinted*, Paris, actually *imprinted* an idea in Yvonne's mind!' Sophie told him as they walked home from school the next day.

He let out a low whistle. 'I've not met anyone like you before, Sage. Your Gifts are coming on fast and furious.'

'Sometimes it's a bit scary,' Sage admitted.

Chapter Fifteen

'I'm so jealous of you, Sage! You've finished your exams!' Sophie said as the three friends walked home together the following week.

'You and Paris have just one more exam to go, Sophie. This time tomorrow it will all be over,' Sage replied.

'Physics!' Sophie sighed. 'The exam I'm dreading the most.'

'Once it's over, we can think about summer holiday plans,' Paris pointed out.

Sophie smiled. 'Yes, the world's our oyster once we get through tomorrow.'

Sage gave a mysterious smile. 'Not just *Earth* world's our oyster; we could have a trip to *Aurum*.'

'You mean *you* can as a fae.'

'Ah, but as a fae, I can take children with me. And as you are both under eighteen, you're technically still children.'

'Oh, man! That is brilliant!'

'Count me in,' Paris added.

'That thought will keep me going for the next twenty-four hours. Paris, would you go over some of the Physics with me one more time this afternoon?' Sophie asked when they reached the corner of her street. She pulled a book from her rucksack, sending the entire contents of the bag to the ground.

'Yes, of course. It'll help me, too.' He reached down to gather up some of the books. 'I can come with you to your place now.'

'See you tomorrow then.' Sage waved as she continued to walk down the road.

She was humming to herself when she heard a soft voice. 'Excuse me, young lady.' Looking up she met a pair of piercing green eyes framed by long, dark lashes. 'Sorry to bother you.'

'Not at all,' she replied, taking in the rugged features of the young man in front of her. Her eyes were drawn to his thick, black hair as he pushed it back from his forehead.

'I'm looking for the town hall. I know I must be near it.' He held up his mobile. 'I'm not very good with map reading.'

'Oh, you're very near, it's just through the park. Go straight ahead to the main gate and turn right.'

As the man smiled, a dimple appeared on his cheek. He touched her arm, sending a shiver of electricity through her. 'Would you walk that far with me?'

She nodded noticing a strange woody scent as still smiling he gently took her hand.

Paris took Sophie's rucksack and put the last of the books back into it. 'Okay?'

'No.' She frowned. 'I've just seen Sage go into the park with some guy or other.'

'It's probably someone from school.'

She shook her head. 'He looked older. I don't like this. I'm going to see what's happening.'

Paris flinched as she vanished and reappeared at the park gate. 'Sage, no!' she screamed as she disappeared from sight. Shouldering their two bags, he followed her as quickly as he could.

Sage was breathing deeply as she leaned forwards. All she wanted to do was to kiss the full, soft lips that were hovering so close to hers when suddenly she found herself flung to the floor with Sophie lying on top of her. 'Sage, wake up!'

Above them, vicious red eyes blazed down. Sophie summoned all her strength and carried herself and Sage out of reach just before red hot flames spewed from a cavernous mouth. With a flash, the figure disappeared from sight.

'Are you both okay?'

Paris's voice seemed to come from far away as Sage blinked her eyes. 'What happened?'

Wincing as she ran a hand along her grazed leg, Sophie nodded at the scorched patch of grass nearby. 'You very nearly kissed a Daemon. That's what happened.'

***

'I just can't believe it, and in broad daylight, too.' Ellen's lip trembled as she watched Alora peer into her granddaughter's eyes an hour later.

'No damage done, thank goodness. If it wasn't for Sophie's quick thinking, it could have been a different story.' Alora took off a thin, plaited bracelet from her own wrist. 'This is the strongest protection spell against Nefarus that I can manage.' She closed her eyes and whispered an incantation as she fastened it around Sage's wrist. 'You must wear it at all times. We must all be extra vigilant between now and the Alignment.'

'Don't worry, I'll be really careful. Anyway, a Daemon can't try to kiss the same person twice, can he, Alora?'

'No. But Nefarus has plenty of tricks up his sleeve. Don't underestimate him, Sage.'

Chapter Sixteen

'Are you sure you'll be okay, Sage?' Ellen asked her the next morning. 'We won't be gone long.'

'I'll be fine, Nan,' she reassured her. 'I'm just going to relax and take a look at the spell book that Mary brought round. You go and get your shopping done and don't worry about me. Jet is keeping me company.'

'She'll be fine, love,' Jim said. 'We really need to pick up some supplies from the supermarket.'

'I'm not too keen on leaving Sage alone at the moment,' his wife continued as they climbed into the car.

'She's probably safer now. As Alora said, a Daemon can't try to kiss the same person twice. And Jet told me he'd keep a special eye on her.'

'Well, so we don't waste too much time, I thought you could get the things from the supermarket while I go to the library.'

Twenty minutes later she hurried back to the car where Jim was waiting for her. As she reached for the door handle, she heard someone give a gasp of pain. A young woman was sitting on the ground nearby clutching her ankle.

'Are you okay?' Ellen asked.

'I will be in a minute,' the woman replied. 'I knew I shouldn't wear these stupid heels into town.'

Jim walked around to join them. 'Can I give you a hand up?'

The young woman grimaced as she pulled herself to her feet. 'Thank you so much. Could I ask you to help me to my car over there? My ankle is very painful.'

She led them to a sleek Porsche sports car. Jim's eyes widened in admiration as he held the door open for her.

'Do you think you'll be able to drive? Can we call someone to come and fetch you?' Ellen asked.

'My husband is out of town at the moment.' The woman winced as she put her foot on the pedal.

Jim and Ellen exchanged glances.

'Perhaps I could drive you home?' he suggested. 'My wife can follow me in our car.'

'Oh, no. I couldn't ask you to do that.'

'Come on,' Jim insisted. 'You get into the passenger seat and I'll drive. I've always wanted to drive one of these.'

With a few weak protests, the woman was finally seated in the passenger seat with Jim beside her.

They drove for fifteen minutes until they reached a quiet road on the outskirts of the town. Large, expensive looking houses could be glimpsed behind high walls and security gates.

Ellen slowed down behind her husband as he stopped in front of a set of large iron gates. On hearing the young woman's voice, a security guard pushed a buzzer and the gates swung open. Jim drove carefully up a wide, gravelled driveway that swept around a marble fountain at the front entrance of a magnificent mansion.

Stepping out of her car, Ellen gazed around her. A beautifully manicured lawn was broken up by flower beds with blossoms of every hue. As she made her way to her husband, who was helping the young woman from the car, a deep voice made her look up. A tall, dark haired man smiled as he came down the steps from the house.

The woman walked towards him with no evidence of her previous injury. 'My plan worked, Nefarus! Are you pleased with me?'

'Very pleased, my lovely.' He nodded, holding out his hand to Jim. 'And I'm delighted to meet you both, Jim and Ellen Warland.'

Ellen grabbed her husband's arm. 'Nefarus? The Daemon?'

Nefarus smiled. 'Exactly. And your granddaughter will also be joining us here, in plenty of time for the Alignment.'

He looked up as two dark, well-built young men appeared. One of them had a deep jagged scar that ran through his left eye and down his neck disappearing into a faded white T-shirt. 'Ammo, move the cars. Lupe, take our guests to their rooms.'

'Hey, wait a minute,' Jim began. 'We aren't planning on staying here, so if you don't mind…'

The scarred-faced man stepped towards them uttering a deep animal growl.

'We do mind.' Nefarus gave a cold smile.

The man with the scar climbed into their car, casting an evil grin at the older couple that made their blood run cold. The second, slightly taller of the two men led Ellen and Jim inside the house. Silently they followed him up an ornate staircase and along a corridor to a spacious, well-furnished suite at the top of the building overlooking the fountain. There was a large reception room with two leather sofas in a bay window looking out over well-tended gardens. A bedroom opened off from one side of the room and on the other side was an opulent bathroom with a sunken bath, surrounded by a selection of toiletries.

Lupe looked abashed as he gave a gesture to take in the room. 'Let me know if you need anything.' With a slight smile, he headed for the door.

Ellen sighed deeply and sank into one of the sofas as she heard him lock the door behind him. 'Oh dear, Jim. What have we let ourselves in for? What about Sage?'

'Let's just wait and see what happens. Sage will contact Alora once she realises we're not on our way home. She'll know what to do. In the meantime, we'd better keep our wits about us.'

'That evil woman! She must be Saffron. I'd like to...' Ellen shook her head. 'How could we be so stupid?'

Jim patted her shoulder. 'We are up against forces that we've never had to reckon with before. And to be fair, you can't really blame Saffron, either. What is she? Just an empty shell, a puppet in Nefarus' hands. Don't forget, if Sophie hadn't come to Sage's rescue, that could have been the fate of our own granddaughter.'

Neither of them noticed the glowing orb hovering outside the window. Saffron felt a pang as she heard his words.

An hour later, Sage frowned as she looked at the kitchen clock again. Her grandparents had been gone for quite a while. She tried to dismiss a feeling of unease.

'They've probably just called off to see some friends, haven't they?' she said to Jet, stroking his silky head. Suddenly, he gave a low growl, his fur bristling as he arched his back.

A glowing orb appeared and settled on the floor in front of her. Sage gave a gasp as it lengthened and Saffron appeared.

'Hello, Sage. We finally get to meet. I'm Saffron. Nefarus sent me.' The fae smiled. 'It looks like we'll be working together.'

Sage jumped up and backed away from her. 'What makes you think I'd want to work with someone associated with a Daemon?'

'Not even if your grandparents' well-being depended on it?'

Sage's face grew pale. 'My grandparents? Where are they? What have you done with them?'

Saffron held up a hand. 'They're fine...at the moment. As long as you cooperate with Nefarus, they will remain safe.'

'What do you mean?'

'Nefarus needs you to help him to open the Portal at the Alignment. He will create a new world with Aurum and Earth world combined. Just think about it, Sage—all Magical and Gifted ones will enjoy a freedom we have never known under Merlin!'

Sage's eyes narrowed. 'Do you honestly believe we can enjoy freedom under Nefarus? You of all people, Saffron. You're completely under his power with no will of your own.'

Saffron looked up sharply. 'You don't know what you're talking about! Come, we must go. You want to be with your grandparents, don't you?'

Sage backed away from her. 'How do I know I can trust him—or you? I'm not going anywhere until I have proof that Grandad and Nan are safe.'

Saffron frowned. 'I will bring proof of your grandparents' safety here tomorrow morning. You must be ready to leave with me then and you must be alone.'

As the tiny globe disappeared into the sky, Sage sank into a chair, cupping her face in her hands. The sound of voices outside the door brought her back to her surroundings.

'Hi, Sage,' Paris said as he and Sophie came into the kitchen. 'Isn't this the best feeling ever? No more exams! No more school work for ten whole weeks!'

Sophie rushed forward as she caught sight of her friend's face. 'What's up?'

'Nan, Grandad...' A sob escaped from her throat.

'Are they ill?' Paris asked.

She shook her head. 'Nefarus has...Saffron was here just now...I'll have to go to them...'

Sophie knelt in front of her and took her hands. 'Slow down, start from the beginning.'

Paris pushed a mug of hot tea into her hands as she stammered out what had happened.

'Nefarus has taken your grandparents hostage so he can force you to help him at the Alignment.' Sophie shook her head. 'You can't just go there.'

'I have to go. They're in danger!'

Paris sat down at the table his hands clasped together. 'No. You're in a more powerful position to help your grandparents here. Nefarus won't harm them before the Alignment, otherwise he won't have any leverage to force you to help him.'

'That's true, Sage.' Sophie nodded. 'We need to speak to Alora; she'll know what to do.'

***

At The Coterie, Alora put a pot of tea on the table as they sat in the kitchen.

'Jay has returned to Aurum to leave an urgent message for Merlin. In the meantime, it's best if you stay here, Sage.'

'Saffron can't come here, so how can I get news of Nan and Grandad?' she replied. 'I need to go home tomorrow morning.'

Alora bit her lip. 'We will have to make sure that you are safe when you meet her.'

Sophie looked alarmed. 'But what if Saffron tricks Sage into joining her grandparents?'

'We'll take steps to ensure that can't happen. Paris is right, Sage. At the moment, you are in the stronger position because without you, Nefarus can't open the Portal. We must play along with him until Merlin gets here. You must be firm, but polite—we can't afford to annoy him. His magic is too powerful for me to manage alone.'

Chapter Seventeen

'So, I have to agree to help Nefarus, but that I will not join him until the day of the Alignment. And I want daily proof that my grandparents are safe and well,' Sage said the next morning.

'That's right, stick with the script we rehearsed, don't let Nefarus' threats worry you. Or at least, try not to show your fear. Insist that your grandparents must be completely unharmed if he wants you to cooperate at the Alignment.'

Sophie checked the wristband that her friend was wearing. 'Don't take this off under any circumstances. Saffron can't touch you while you are wearing it, can she, Alora?'

'It's the strongest charm I could make. While you are wearing that, she can't persuade you go into Nefarus' dwelling place against your will.'

An hour later, Sage sat in the kitchen holding Jet close to her. Her house felt so empty without the presence of her grandparents. He slipped from her arms and hid under the dresser as the tiny glowing orb came through the window and Saffron stood before her.

She held out what appeared to be a large, flat shell. Sage turned it over and smiled to see an image of her grandparents' faces.

'Hello, Sage,' her grandfather spoke. 'Saffron is going to give you this message to prove we are well. They are looking after us. You know what *they* want you to do.'

Sage caught the slight inflection on the word *they*.

'I will help Nefarus, but I'm not going to his house until the day of the Alignment. And I will need daily proof that my grandparents are safe and well.' Sage firmly repeated the words she had agreed with Alora.

'Nefarus is expecting you to return with me today. He will not be pleased with this news. He will be very angry, and your grandparents...' The fae paced the room in frustration.

Sage clenched her fists. 'If my grandparents are harmed in any way whatsoever, Nefarus will have *no* help from me at the Alignment! You can tell him that!'

Saffron massaged her forehead with her fingertips. 'If you don't come today, he will be angry. He can be ruthless when he is angry. It's better for all of us if you come with me now.'

'I don't care how angry he is. I will do nothing for him if either of my grandparents is harmed in any way. And you can tell him that's my final decision so...' Sage stopped as she noticed how Saffron's hands trembled. 'You're afraid of him, aren't you? Why do you stay with him? Let Merlin break the spell and set you free.'

Saffron shook her head as she headed for the window. 'It's not so easy. Sixty years ago, I made a choice...'

'But you didn't make a choice, did you? You were tricked! And now you have no will of your own!' Sage called out. She sighed as she watched the glowing orb disappear into the sky.

***

Saffron felt her body tremble as she stood in front of Nefarus in the wood-panelled office later that afternoon.

'So, you were unable to persuade Sage to join her grandparents today?' His eyes narrowed as he walked towards the window.

'She wouldn't listen to me. And she was wearing a charm from Alora so I couldn't force her to come with me, Nefarus.'

'She is getting too much support from Alora. It will be even worse when Merlin arrives. I *must* have her here before then.' He looked up at the sky, rubbing his chin. 'Tomorrow you will give her a message from her grandparents telling her how afraid they are and how much they miss her. And how much they need her here with them now.'

'But they won't agree to record a message like that…'

'It won't be a real message, but you will convince Sage that it is. Now go and send Ammo and Lupe to me. I need Ammo to help me to collect Diabella and bring her here for the Alignment.'

'Will your sister be bringing her…pets?' Saffron bit her lip.

Nefarus gave a harsh laugh. 'Of course! She doesn't go anywhere without them. Do they make you nervous? Your fae scent makes them hungry! They can be a handful, that's why I need Ammo to help transport them.'

Saffron took a deep breath and leaned back against the door as she closed it behind her.

A soft voice made her look up. 'Are you okay?' Lupe was looking at her with concern in his eyes.

She pulled herself upright. 'Yes, of course I am. Nefarus wants to speak to you and Ammo now.'

She watched as the two men made their way to the Daemon's office. Lupe gave her a kind smile as he followed Ammo. She frowned. It had been so many years since she had been shown any kindness. A smile twitched on her own lips, followed by a sharp pain in her chest, reminding her of the control Nefarus held over her heart.

In his office, Nefarus explained his plan to the two shifters. 'Tomorrow Saffron will bring Sage here and once she is securely imprisoned with the old couple, you will come with me to collect Diabella, Ammo. She will prove invaluable at the Alignment.'

He closed his eyes and gave a deep sigh. 'Soon, I will be ruler of the two worlds. All my plans and dreams of nearly a thousand years will finally come true!' There was a cruel glint as he opened his eyes. 'Anyone who has ever stood in my way will be crushed beneath my feet. And those who support me will be richly rewarded.'

Lupe felt uneasy as the two shifters made their way to the grandparents' rooms later that evening.

'I thought the future with the two worlds united would be a peaceful place where those Magically touched could move freely between Earth world and Aurum. He makes it sound as if we are heading for a bloody battle.'

'Are you really so naïve? Do you think Nefarus is a peaceful man? He's a ruthless ruler, so it's better to keep on his good side.' His companion chuckled and licked his lips. 'I'm all ready for the taste of blood.'

Lupe recoiled at the hungry look in his companion's eyes.

His uneasiness increased as Ammo took up guard duty. His mind was still in turmoil as he set out on a late-night sprint along the deserted beach. Even as he pushed himself to run as fast as he could, Ammo's words and the cruel, hungry look on his face echoed in his mind. Finally, he stopped, panting and sweating. Turning away from the route home, he jogged towards the town along a tree lined avenue. He stood in front of one of the houses, listening for signs of life but there was just the gentle tinkling of a wind chime near the front door. As he stood there, unsure of whether to approach the house or to leave, a shadowy figure appeared in the doorway.

'Lupe. I can't invite you into the house as you are associated with a Daemon, but come and sit in the garden with me,' Alora said, beckoning him forward.

'How do you know who I am?' he asked as he moved towards her.

She smiled. 'I know most things that happen in the two worlds. Sit down.'

He followed her to a long wooden bench and sat beside her.

'You seem troubled.'

He nodded. 'Nefarus promised us a new free way of life if we would help him at the Alignment. We would be able to choose to live in either world and live in peace. But lately he has been showing a crueller, more ruthless side. He's driven by greed and revenge.'

'That has always been a Daemon's way. That is why Merlin limited the control any Daemon or any Magical person could have in Earth world.'

'As you know, Nefarus is desperate to capture Sage,' the shifter continued.

She looked at Lupe, leaning forward so he could see her eyes gleaming in the moonlight. 'She is under my care until Merlin arrives. What about her grandparents? Are they still safe?'

'At the moment they are. But tomorrow Saffron will bring a message from them to Sage to say they are afraid and need her to join them as soon as possible. You must let her know that it's a false message. She must not listen to Saffron. The longer Sage stays away, the better chance her grandparents have of surviving.'

He stood up. 'I must go now.'

Alora stood up and patted his arm. 'Thank you, Lupe. And on the day of the Alignment...?'

'I will stand by Merlin against both the Daemons,' he said gravely. 'Nefarus is bringing Diabella and her pets to join him in the next few days.'

Chapter Eighteen

'So, you've met him before? What can you tell me about the Daemon?' Jim said to a small black speck on his hand the following afternoon. He nodded as he listened to the response.

Ellen joined him on the balcony. 'Oh, is that Adam you're talking to?'

Jim shook his head. 'No, it's…well he calls himself Ant, as they all do. Anyway, he doesn't look at all like Adam. Adam is a darker brown and has a rounder abdomen.'

Ellen peered at the tiny creature. 'If you say so.'

'Ant here was telling me that all the non-human Gifted know that Nefarus is obsessed with becoming the ruler of the two worlds.'

'I think we've gathered that already.' Ellen sighed as she sat down beside her husband.

'Ant also says that many of the non-human Gifted fear what that might mean for all species on Earth world and they would be happy to stand against him. As far as they know, Nefarus is unaware of the Gifted amongst the non-human species. That could be something we could use.'

'Tell Ant that's great news,' Ellen said.

'Oh, but we can't call him Ant. He needs a name, just like we named Adam.' Jim looked down at the tiny creature. 'What do you think, Ant?' Jim frowned as he listened to the reply. 'Well, Adam Ant was a pop singer, famous quite a few years back…hmm, what about Beatle?…no, you're right…that wouldn't work…'

'Elvis!' Ellen suggested. 'The king of rock and roll!'

Jim laughed. 'That does have a certain ring to it. You're happy with that?...well, Elvis it is!'

'How about you and Elvis think about ways we can stand up against Nefarus and his followers?' Ellen asked. 'I'm going to relax in a long, hot bath and see what I can come up with.'

It was beginning to get dark when Jim and Ellen heard a shout from beneath their window. They rushed to the balcony to see Nefarus, Saffron, Ammo and Lupe standing in the driveway below them. Nearby, two goblins looked up from their gardening work to see what the commotion was about.

'You let that *chit* of a girl beat you again?' Nefarus' voice roared out across the grounds. 'I gave you every help and a second chance to bring her here, and you failed miserably!'

'Nefarus, she wasn't convinced. I just couldn't...' Saffron cried.

'You proved yourself totally incompetent!' The Daemon stretched out his hand towards her and twisted his fist with a cruel expression on his face. Saffron sank to the ground, clutching her chest and whimpering painfully. Her cries only brought a cruel smile to his face.

'He's going to kill her,' Jim whispered. 'What can we do?'

Ellen looked around until her eyes fixed on a wheelbarrow at the side of the driveway. The young goblin standing beside it leapt back in surprise as it suddenly began to wheel itself towards Nefarus, rapidly gaining speed. The Daemon looked up in amazement as Ammo shouted out a warning, and threw himself to one side as it narrowly missed him. Pulling himself to his feet, Nefarus cast a venomous look at the young goblin who was stammering his innocence. A blue light shot from his hand, knocking the young gardener to the ground.

'Leave him alone!' Ellen shouted. 'He didn't do anything. I did!' She stretched out her hand and sent the wheelbarrow hurtling towards him again.

Nefarus raised his hand and the wheelbarrow crumbled into a pile of dust. With a malicious gleam in his eye, he reached up towards the balcony.

Ellen stood unflinchingly. 'If you harm a hair on my head, you have lost any chance of getting any help from our granddaughter.'

With a low curse, Nefarus lowered his hand and strode towards the house.

Jim squeezed his wife's shoulders as she gave a sigh and leant against him. 'Perhaps we shouldn't antagonise him too much, love.'

She shook her head. 'He can't ride roughshod over everyone. We have to make a stand.'

Jim peered down into the garden as the second goblin helped his friend to his feet. He was limping as they made their way around the side of the house. The others had already disappeared from view. Jim frowned. 'Where's Saffron?'

His question was answered a moment later when there was a light tap on the door and Lupe entered carrying the unconscious fae in his arms.

Jim rushed forwards. 'How is she?'

The shifter grimaced. 'Not good. She needs somewhere to hide.'

Ellen motioned for him to follow her into the bedroom where he gently placed the fae on a chaise longue; then, peeling off his jacket, he tucked it around her. 'The smell of shifter will hide her fae scent. I didn't think Nefarus would turn against her—they have been together for such a long time.'

'Fear and a magical bond keep her tied to him, not love.' Ellen rummaged through her bag and pulled out a small glass bottle. 'I've only a few drops of Mary's potion left. I don't know if it can help her.' She gently poured a few drops between Saffron's dry lips.

The two men headed back into the lounge area as the sound of footsteps was heard in the corridor. Ammo walked into the room.

Jim nodded at Lupe as if they were in the middle of a conversation. 'Yes, we understand that we are expected to treat Nefarus with respect...'

'...as long as he treats us with the same respect,' Ellen added as she joined them, her mouth a thin line.

Ammo gave her a cold glance. 'Lupe, Nefarus wants to speak with you. He wants you to go and get Sage tomorrow and bring her back here. I offered to go myself, but he thought my appearance might scare her off, so he's sending out the pretty boy.'

Lupe looked back at them as he followed Ammo through the door.

Ellen sat down on the sofa and looked at her husband. 'If Nefarus has all three of us here, we'll all be more vulnerable.'

Jim nodded. 'I agree. I just hope that Sage realises that, too.'

The same thoughts were going around Ellen's head late that night as she sat beside the still figure of Saffron, letting the last few drops of healing potion wet the fae's lips.

'Come on now, Saffron! Don't give up!'

'Any signs of improvement?' Jim asked, appearing by her side.

She shook her head, tears filling her eyes. 'I can't help thinking that this could have been our granddaughter's fate.'

A light tap at the door made them both freeze. Jim made his way across the room.

'Who is it?' he whispered, breathing a sigh of relief as he heard Lupe reply.

Closing the door silently behind them, they made their way to the bedroom where Lupe knelt down by the still figure of Saffron. 'She's getting weaker.'

'Is there anything that can we do?' Ellen asked.

The shifter leant back. 'There is one thing…but I'm not sure if it will work…I could try to give her some of my strength, but I'm shifter and she's fae…I don't know…'

'Anything's worth a try,' Ellen said.

Lupe knelt down and took the two pale cold hands in his own and leaned forwards until their foreheads were touching. Taking a deep breath, he closed his eyes. For a few minutes nothing happened, then slowly Saffron's eyes fluttered as a pink tinge coloured her cheeks.

She blinked and looked around her. 'Where am I? Where's Nefarus?'

Lupe helped her to sit up as Ellen passed her a glass of water. 'It's okay; you're safe.'

She rubbed her chest and gave a painful moan. 'I can't do this anymore. I can't live this life for all eternity. What you said is true—I'm just an empty shell…a puppet with no will of my own. I would rather choose After world than to be bound to the Daemon any longer.'

Lupe nodded. 'We have both made bad choices. I can no longer follow Nefarus either.'

'Merlin will be here soon. If you want, he can break the spell.' Ellen brushed Saffron's hair from her forehead.

The fae lay back against the pillows and pulled a pouch from her pocket, fingering the soft leather. 'I don't know if I have enough time left. I want my brother, Sylvan, to know I renounced Nefarus at the end.' She closed her eyes and pushed something into the pouch. 'Tell him how much I love him and all my family and friends.' With a sad smile, she looked at the three people around her. 'You have been such good friends to me. Forgive me for betraying you.'

'You were tricked, Saffron. Nefarus is the only one to blame in all this,' Ellen said, straightening the covers over the fae. 'Now, save your strength. You'll need it when Merlin comes and we put a stop to the Daemon's ways once and for all.'

A smile spread across Saffron's face as she held out the pouch to her. 'Can you get this message to Sylvan for me? To Aurum?'

'Of course we can.'

They watched as Saffron drifted off to sleep, her breathing seeming stronger than earlier.

'It worked!' Jim smiled.

'For now.' Lupe didn't return the smile. 'Nefarus still has her heart and his power is much more than a mere shifter.'

Ellen put the pouch into his hands. 'We're going to remain positive. You can give this to Sage tomorrow, she'll know how to get it to Sylvan.'

'Yes, about Sage...' Jim's face looked grim.

The shifter nodded. 'We must keep her away from here for as long as possible, in a safe place.' His brow knitted. 'I have an idea. It could protect Sage and help Saffron at the same time.' He went on to outline his plan.

Chapter Nineteen

Sage pushed a handful of books into a hessian bag, glancing around to see if there was anything else that she might add to occupy her grandparents. She frowned as she remembered the conversation she had had with Saffron the previous day. If she hadn't been prewarned, she might have been taken in by the tearful pleas of her grandmother, but she'd looked at it carefully and realised that the words spoken were not the ones her grandmother would use. Saffron's panicked reaction when she was not convinced made her even more certain it was a trick.

She opened the door as she heard the sound of voices. Paris and Sophie were walking towards the house.

'Has Saffron been to see you today?' Sophie asked. 'What are Nefarus' latest ploys?'

'She is late today; that must be her now,' Sage replied as she heard a faint rustle in the garden. She walked towards the window expecting to see the tiny glowing orb that announced the fae's arrival but outside the garden was still and empty.

A light tap at the door startled the three youngsters. Sophie drew a sharp breath as the door was gently pushed open and a dark, well-built young man stood there. He spread out his empty hands as Paris stepped towards him.

'Please, don't be alarmed.'

Sage instinctively felt for the woven band around her wrist. 'Who are you? What do you want?'

The man took a tentative step forward. 'Please, I mean you no harm. I'm Lupe. I spoke to Alora the night before last.'

'You're the one who warned us of the false message?'

A look of remorse crossed his face. 'Yes, I did. I had to…but now Saffron…she's in grave danger.'

'Why should we care about someone who works for Nefarus, who's tricked Sage's grandparents and is now trying to trick her, too?' Sophie spat out.

'And aren't you one of Nefarus' men?' Paris added.

Lupe shook his head slowly. 'I was persuaded to join him with promises of a peaceful future with freedom to roam the two worlds. And now I've finally realised how empty these promises are. Saffron is the least blameworthy in all this. Her heart was captured, taking away her free will. And now she may pay the price with her life. She sent this.'

He pulled the white leather pouch from his pocket and pushed it across the table to Sage.

Shaking out the contents of the pouch, Sage drew a deep breath as she recognised the fae's shimmer. Her frown deepened as she absorbed the contents of the message. 'After world? Oh no! Surely she can last until Merlin is here?' Her voice trailed away as she saw the expression on Lupe's face.

'She's fading fast.'

Sophie grabbed Sage's arm. 'What does it say?'

'Saffron has finally come to her senses. She wants to break the spell that binds her to Nefarus. She said the thought of being with Nefarus for all eternity is so grim that she would rather choose After world.'

'But when Merlin comes here, he can free her,' Sophie pointed out. 'She doesn't have to choose After world.'

'If Merlin arrives in time,' Lupe murmured. He turned to Sage. 'There might be a way to save her. But it could be dangerous for you.'

Sage nodded for him to continue.

'You are part fae, so you can enter Aurum, and as future Spell Master, you should be able to prepare and cast the spell Saffron needs to free her heart if Merlin cannot be found in time.'

Sage bit her lip. 'It could work. It has to be better than sitting around here waiting for news of Merlin.'

'And if you are in Aurum, you'll be safe from Nefarus,' Lupe continued.

'But...Nan and Grandad...' Sage hesitated.

'They are safe until the Alignment. Nefarus knows you won't cooperate with him if any harm comes to them. I'll tell him that you had already gone to Aurum when I arrived here today. If you could leave a letter for him...'

Sage pulled a pen and pad from a drawer. 'This is a written promise to be at his gates four hours before the Alignment, as long as he can prove that my grandparents are safe and well.' She handed Lupe the folded sheet. 'I'll pack a few things and then set out for Aurum straight away.'

'Have you a spare toothbrush, Sage?' Sophie said.

'Make that two,' Paris added, picking up his rucksack. 'These discs I collected may come in handy if we meet any angry creatures.'

'Oh, I don't know...it may be dangerous...'

'You're not leaving without us.' Sophie and Paris faced her with determined expressions.

'Your parents would never agree to this...'

'Jet can ask Alora to explain to them how important this is. For the future of your grandparents. And for everyone.' Sophie nodded eagerly.

Sage softened. 'Well, it would be good to have you both with me.'

After packing a few belongings into a rucksack, she took a deep breath. 'Are we ready to go?'

Lupe stepped forward pulling his jacket off and handed it to her. 'I can't go with you, but this may come in handy to disguise your fae and human scent.'

'Thank you, Lupe. Watch over my grandparents and Saffron until we return with Merlin.'

'I'll guard them with my life.'

'I can't believe we're going to Aurum!' Sophie whispered excitedly as they left the house. 'I wonder what it's like. I used to dream of visiting Aurum when I was younger.'

Paris nodded in agreement. 'It is pretty exciting, but we mustn't forget the reason we're going. We have a serious job to do.'

Sage strode ahead, a frown fixed on her face. She stopped at the corner and looked around her before following the street to the right.

'Where exactly is the Portal?' Paris asked her.

'North from here. I can feel the pull.'

After walking for half an hour, Sage stopped and nodded towards an open field. 'It's just over there.'

Her two friends started to walk forwards but she grabbed their arms. 'Wait! We're near the Portal but we're also getting close to the house where Nefarus is staying.' Her eyes narrowed as she scanned the area. 'We'll go this way.'

Soon they were standing on a hill under the branches of an old oak tree. Sage nodded towards a line of trees below them. The rooftop of a large house was just visible. 'Nefarus is in there. And so are my grandparents.' She bit her lip. 'Okay. Give me your hands.'

A moment later the air grew hazy and a cold mist shrouded them.

***

The three friends emerged shivering from the mist and found themselves on a grassy plateau. A narrow pathway disappeared around the side of the hill into a deep valley. Across the valley was a forest covered hill with an old stone castle at its summit.

Paris pointed. 'That must be Merlin's castle. Let's make our way towards it.'

He led the way with the two girls following. Sophie at the rear was casting anxious glances behind her.

'Did you hear that?' she whispered. Her eyes seemed to glaze over as she looked nervously around her.

Sage shook her head. 'What?'

'That growling noise. Oh no! Quick! Run!'

A pack of small, wild dog-like creatures had appeared further up the hillside and were now running towards them snarling as the three friends stumbled down the rough pathway that wound around the hillside. Paris cried out in dismay as they reached a sheer cliff edge. Below them a river raged as it crashed over jagged, grey rocks.

'Look! Over there!' Sophie pointed to her right. 'A bridge!'

Sage ran towards it and stepped gingerly onto the creaking rope bridge. 'It's okay as long as we don't look down.'

Their pursuers remained on firm land, barking and snapping at their lost prey.

The three youngsters edged their way slowly across the swaying rope bridge until Sophie let out a sharp cry. 'No! What's happening?'

She screamed as the ropes she was clinging to suddenly writhed in her hands and the entire "bridge" unravelled into a hissing coil of snakes. Her panicked cries resounded off the walls of the cliff face as all three plunged into the icy water.

Sage gasped for air as she was swept along by the strong current. A wave of relief washed over her when she spotted her two friends break to the surface.

'We're going over a waterfall!' Sophie spluttered as she once again disappeared from view.

Sage struggled to fill her lungs with air before she too found herself swept along the same route. Flinging out her hands, she clutched on to a tree branch that extended over the river. As her strength ebbed away, she felt someone grab her arms and pull her clear of the water. Paris was standing over her. 'Are you okay?'

Sophie appeared behind him. 'Thank goodness we're all safe.'

The three youngsters lay exhausted on the river bank until Sophie sat up suddenly, her eyes glazing over again.

A wave of understanding crossed Sage's face. She grabbed her friend's arm as she was about to speak. 'Sophie! Don't say anything! *You* are making this story happen! It's all from *your* imagination!'

Sophie shook her head slowly as she seemed to come out of a trance. 'I kept thinking of all the frightening things that could happen here. Well, this is a magical place. And just now I thought…'

'Just keep your thoughts to yourself, *please*.' Paris held up his hands. 'I don't think I can cope with any more of your adventures.'

Sophie gave an apologetic smile. The three friends were silent for a few moments until Sophie pointed into the distance. 'Now, is that real or is it my imagination playing tricks again?' Three figures on pure white horses were galloping towards them. A tall, blonde-haired young man slid from the first horse as they neared the three friends. 'We heard we have some visitors. You must be from Earth world.'

Sage nodded and introduced herself and her friends. He gestured to one of the riders, who nodded at them. 'This is Flora.' The third rider pushed back long, curly red hair and looked at Paris through lowered lashes. 'And I'm Flame.'

'I'm Sylvan.'

Sage's eyes widened as he held out his hand. 'Saffron's brother!' She smiled. 'Of course, you look so much like her.'

'You know my sister? How is she?'

Sage's face grew serious as she pulled the white leather pouch from her bag and handed it to him.

'It's from Saffron.' He grew agitated as he scanned the Shimmer. 'Oh no! Not After world!'

'That's one of the reasons we're here.'

The three fae listened, nodding several times as Sage outlined their plan. 'The best solution would be to find Merlin so he could come back to Earth world now. But if that's not possible, I'll go to his castle and see if I can find the spell to free her from Nefarus' control.'

Sylvan gave a low whistle. 'That's an ambitious plan. I think our best bet is to go to Faeville and find out what's the latest news on Merlin.' He mounted his horse and pulled Sage up behind him. Her two friends were soon seated behind the other riders.

They rode swiftly over a flat, grassy plain and into woodlands. As the horses slowed down, there was the sound of laughter and chattering ahead. They entered a large circular clearing surrounded by small stone cottages. A group of children ran forward as they dismounted, giving the visitors curious glances as they led the horses away.

An elderly woman appeared in the doorway of one of the cottages. She stood looking at them for a while, then rushed forward, and grabbed Sage's hands.

'Oh, my word! Sage! How you've grown—but I'd recognise you anywhere. You're the image of your mother! So beautiful.' She gently stroked her face. 'I haven't seen you since you were a tiny baby at your Name-Giving ceremony.'

'You knew my mother?' Sage whispered.

'Oh, Daphne was like a daughter to me. I was so pleased when she asked me to be your Guidemother.' She put a hand to her mouth. 'Just look at me! Where are my manners? And who are your two friends? Gifted, I see.' She shook hands warmly with them as they introduced themselves. 'It's lovely to meet you. Now come inside and you can tell us all your news while we have a bite to eat.'

She led them into a large, homely kitchen that was filled with the aroma of cinnamon and vanilla. As they ate, Sage once again explained how Nefarus had captured her grandparents and the Shimmer Saffron had sent her. Then she explained the plan she had drawn up with her friends.

'So, even if Merlin is not around until the Alignment, Sage may be able to produce the spell that can save Saffron, with your help, Mercy,' Sylvan added. 'You're so talented in the fae arts and Sage *is* a future Spell Master.'

The old woman raised her eyebrows and rubbed her chin. 'I may be good at what I do, but I'm nowhere near Merlin's level. And have you seen the Spell room in the castle? There must be at least two thousand books there. Even if I cast a categorising charm, it would still be a huge job to find the spell we need.'

She stood up. 'I think the best thing we can do at the moment, is to sleep on it. We've sent another messenger to the castle to see if Merlin has returned yet. Flora and Flame will show you to your rooms for the night.'

Flora led Sage and Sophie to a small, comfortable room with two single beds. As Sophie was closing the door, she paused as Flame showed Paris into a room opposite theirs.

'If you need anything, just let me know, won't you?' she was saying in a flirtatious way.

'Thanks…that's very kind of you…'

'You know, fae and human are a great combination,' Flame added running her hand gently down his arm. 'I could help you to relax.'

Paris gave a nervous laugh, 'I'm flattered, but…'

Sophie pulled open her door. 'Oh, Flame, you're still here?'

'Just leaving,' she replied, giving Paris a wink as she headed back down the corridor. 'My room's just down here on the right.'

Paris looked across at Sophie. 'Erm, she's very friendly, isn't she?'

'Very.' Sophie gave a tight smile.

'Well, goodnight, Sophie,' he said, retreating into his room.

'Did you hear what that fae said?' she began turning to Sage. Her expression softened as she saw the worry etched into her friend's face.

'Do you think Nan and Grandad are okay? How long do you think Saffron can hold out?' her friend asked as she climbed into bed.

'Hey, we're going to do the best we can to get the spell and get back there as quickly as possible.'

After the adventures of the day, it wasn't long before Sophie's breathing deepened as she fell asleep while Sage lay looking at the ceiling, thinking about her grandparents and imagining Sylvan lying in his own room, worrying about his sister. At some point, she finally drifted off until she became aware of a gentle tapping on the door. The sun was filtering in through the thin curtains.

'There's been news of Merlin. Get dressed quickly,' Paris said.

Within minutes, the two girls were dressed and in the kitchen. Flora and Flame were seated at the table next to Mercy who was setting out cups which were being filled by a china teapot. As the teapot returned to the stove, a plate filled with slices of buttered toast landed gently on the table.

Mercy looked up. 'There's been news from the castle.'

Flame nodded as she picked up a piece of toast. 'Merlin left the island and returned to the castle yesterday...'

At that moment, Sylvan came in with a grim look on his face.

'You've heard?' Flora asked him.

He nodded.

Sage looked puzzled. 'But surely this is great news. We can go there immediately!'

Flame sighed and put her toast down. 'Shortly after getting back to the castle last night, Merlin was called to sort out the latest dispute between the vamps and shifters over the boundaries in the Dark Forest.'

'What bad timing.' Sylvan groaned. 'Those discussions can take days!'

'Well, we can go to the Dark Forest and explain everything,' Sophie suggested. 'Surely they won't mind postponing the boundary stuff until later?'

'It's not that simple,' Mercy said. 'Fae and humans are not safe near vampires and shifters here in Aurum. That's why they have their own territory. Only Merlin can enter safely.'

'You mean they would kill us if we went in?' Paris asked.

'Most probably.'

Sage frowned. 'Have they killed fae before?'

'A young girl was injured when she got too near the boundary. It happened nearly a hundred years ago and she still has the scars from her eye right down to her fingertips.' Flame traced a line along her own arm. 'We've all stayed well away since then.'

'So, we have two options—number one, the chance of finding the spell by ourselves to release Saffron in time is almost nil; number two, the chances of surviving a trip to Dark Forest to speak directly to Merlin are slim,' Sage said. She looked at Sylvan's crestfallen expression and put her hands flat on the table. 'I'm ready to take a risk on the second option. Well, no-one has actually been killed yet. I can orb…'

'Vampires can move faster than you can orb,' Flora countered.

'I bet I can Transpose as quickly as any vamp can move!' Sophie stood up. There was a rush of wind as the teapot appeared in her hand. 'See, you hardly saw me move then, did you? Anyone else for another cup?'

'And I've got a whole bag full of colourful discs.' Paris shook his rucksack.

Mercy shook her head sadly. 'You're very brave, but you wouldn't stand a chance.'

There was a tense silence until Sage suddenly grabbed her rucksack. 'I've got it! Lupe's jacket!'

She unzipped the bag and held up the leather jacket.

Flora and Flame jumped up, hands to their mouths and headed for the door.

'Oh, my goodness! Put that away quickly!' Mercy's face took on a greenish hue. She whipped her hand through the rancid air and squashed it back in on top of the jacket as Sage pushed it back into the bag and zipped it shut.

They all breathed a sigh of relief as Flame poked her head around the door. 'Is it safe to come in now?'

Sage gave an apologetic smile. 'Sorry. It didn't smell so strong in Earth world.'

'The animal smell from Earth world is greatly exaggerated here,' Sylvan explained.

'If I wear this jacket, no-one will recognise me in the Dark Forest,' Sage continued. 'I can nip in, find Merlin, explain the dilemma and be back here before anyone notices.'

'Wait a minute.' Sophie shook her head. 'That jacket is *really* smelly…'

'That's the whole point…'

'Well then, it could mask the smell of two, or even three, of us easily.'

'I don't know. It's still very risky…' The older woman frowned.

'I could go as near to the boundary as possible and lure away any vamps or shifters nearby to give you a better chance to get in undetected,' Sylvan offered, his face brightening.

'A great plan. Let's go for it!' Sage and her friends stood up.

Chapter Twenty

Sylvan stopped the three friends as they neared a thickly forested area. 'Look, it's not too late. If you want to back out, if you feel it's too much, don't be afraid to say so. We'll understand and I'll always be grateful to you all for considering to take such a risk for my sister.'

Sage glanced at her two friends. 'Perhaps it is a bit stupid for us all to go in. It might be better if I continue on my own...'

'And we miss out on all the fun?' There was a tremor in Sophie's voice. 'No way!'

'Yeah. We're ready,' Paris added.

Sylvan hugged each of them. 'I'm going to follow the boundary to the left when you're ready. Head for the centre of the forest. The oldest vampire, Delbert, lives there in a huge, white, marble mansion. You can't miss it. That's where they'll be meeting. Good luck.'

With a final wave he headed off to the left. As he drew near to the forest edge, low growls could be heard from behind the trees and bushes. Sophie jumped as a powerful paw shot out of the trees, narrowly missing the fae.

Sage pulled Lupe's jacket from her bag and rubbed herself down with it before passing it to Sophie who did the same with a grimace on her face.

'This really does stink ten times more than it did in Earth world!'

Finally, Paris put his arms into the jacket and fastened it around him. 'Well, at least we all smell equally bad.'

Sage gave a quick smile before leading the others into the forest.

'There's a rough pathway here, let's follow it. Keep together and go as quietly as you can.'

They made their way slowly along the path, pushing their way through the dense undergrowth, stopping at every rustle they heard. Sophie gave a sigh of relief as the pathway finally opened up into a clearing. She was about to speak when Sage put her finger to her lips and pointed ahead. Four young children were giggling and chattering as they rolled around on the grass. Under a tree nearby an old wolf lay watching over them.

The three friends backed up silently and began to skirt around the clearing, keeping themselves out of sight. Beads of sweat broke out on Sophie's brow as the wolf suddenly sat up alert, nose twitching. Paris nodded to Sage as he pushed his hand into his rucksack and drew out a handful of discs. While she gathered up the wisps of darkening blue strands rising from the animal and condensed them, Paris flung a handful of yellow discs to cascade over the wolf's head. As they watched, the wolf relaxed and she settled down on the grass again.

The cries of the children faded away as they continued to make their way into the forest. They had been walking for another half hour when Paris put his hand up and stopped them. Ahead, through the trees a high stone wall was visible.

'I think we're nearly there,' he whispered.

'Thank goodness!' Sophie muttered and began to quicken her pace. Suddenly, with a short cry, she disappeared from view.

Paris and Sage ran forwards to find her waist high in thick mud.

'I'm sinking!' she cried, thrashing around.

'Hold still, Sophie!' Paris called. 'You're only making things worse. Try to relax.'

'You try relaxing as you're being sucked into a swamp!'

'Just listen to Paris, Sophie. We'll have you out in no time.' Sage said softly.

She looked around. There were several long, thick vines wrapped around the tree branches above her head. Pulling a knife from her rucksack, she cut two lengths, tying one around her waist and securing it to a tree trunk and getting Paris to do the same.

'Now, you're going to have to be brave and to trust us, Sophie. I want you to lie back gently on the mud and put your hands out over your head. Paris and I are going to grab you and pull you free.'

Sophie started to cry. 'I can't! I'll go straight under!'

'No, you won't. We won't let you,' Paris said firmly. 'After three—one...two...three—come on, now, gently does it...'

After several seconds, still sobbing, Sophie gingerly lay back. Her friends quickly grabbed her hands and slowly and painfully, she was dragged from the churning mud.

The three youngsters lay panting and trembling on the grass. Paris watched as Sophie dragged a muddy hand across her face and began to giggle.

'What?' said Sophie.

'Your face! It's all streaked with green mud.'

'You can talk!' she replied, a bubble of laughter rising in her throat as she looked at her friend.

Sage rubbed the slime around her own face, smiling. 'Just think, they pay good money in Earth world for facemasks like this.'

Soon the three of them were rolling on the ground, giggling softly. Sage was the first to notice the slight rustling in the bushes nearby and signalled the others to be quiet. They had hardly concealed themselves behind a tree trunk when two thickset young men appeared near the swamp edge.

'I heard something. I smelt shifter, and it wasn't one of our families,' the taller one said, lifting his nose as he looked around.

'I can't smell anything.' His companion shook his head.

'Look, tracks around the swamp. Something crawled out recently by the look of it.'

The first man looked around as his friend peered at the marks in the mud.

'There are several tracks here.'

'Maybe some young trolls?' The first man suggested. 'I heard something, like kids laughing.'

'Well, we can't eat trolls! We'd better re-join the hunt. Come on, it's getting dark.'

Sage let out a slow breath as the two men ran off. 'We were lucky. The swamp mud hid our scent.'

'Or *we* could have been on their menu tonight,' Paris added.

In silence, they began to make their way carefully around the swampland. Sophie gave a sigh of relief when Sage stopped. 'We're right next to the wall. All we have to do is follow it around to the gate.'

'And what do we do when we get in?' Paris asked. 'Just walk up and introduce ourselves?'

'Mmm, that's a point. I hadn't really thought that far ahead.'

As the two of them discussed different options, Sophie sank down onto a flat, grey stone and closed her eyes.

'Well, if I go first and show Merlin Saffron's pouch and my wristband from Alora, that should convince him we're genuine.'

'What's happening? Is it an earthquake?' Sophie clung to the side of the rock as it began to move.

Sage eyes widened as she looked around. 'Sophie, you're sitting on a giant foot! Jump off now!'

An enormous grey figure slowly sat up, making soft guttural noises at it looked down at the girl.

Paris lunged towards Sophie as a huge grey hand lifted the screaming girl into the air.

She screamed even louder as she found herself level with a pair of huge, watery red-rimmed eyes. 'Help me! Help me! Do something!'

Grabbing a large stick, Paris began to whack the leg of her captor, making no impact whatsoever. When the stick broke in two, he seized the tattered tunic of the troll and began to pull himself up onto its arm. 'Let her go!'

With a shout, Sage jumped up behind him, both scrambling towards their terrified friend.

At that point, still muttering to itself, the troll stood up, shaking them off effortlessly. With a painful thud, they hit the ground and watched helplessly as the grey giant drew Sophie towards its slobbering mouth.

Sage pulled herself to her feet and began to jump up and down, shouting and waving her hands. The troll stopped and looked at her briefly before turning its attention back to Sophie who was pulling desperately at the gnarled fingers wrapped around her.

At that moment a young woman appeared. She had golden skin and long black hair that hung in a thick braid down to her waist. Her almond shaped eyes were the same dark brown as the leather jerkin and leggings she wore.

'Hildegard, put her down immediately!' she said sternly.

The troll growled softly and rubbed Sophie against her cheek.

Paris and Sage clung to each other hardly daring to breathe.

'Hildegard, I have a few treats in my pocket…give me the girl and you can have some…'

Hildegard's eyes lit up as the young woman reached into her pocket and drew out a handful of strong smelling, brown biscuits, but still kept a tight grip on Sophie, making her gasp in pain.

'Okay, if you don't want them...' The woman pushed the biscuits back into her pocket.

With a petulant roar, the troll flung the girl to the floor and held out her hand. Paris rushed to Sophie's side and wrapped his arms protectively around her as Hildegard stumbled past.

'Good girl, Hildegard!' The three friends watched as their rescuer poured a handful of the biscuits into the troll's outstretched hand. She stuffed them into her mouth with a gurgle of delight.

At that moment, an even taller green giant appeared.

'Thank goodness you're here, Pognor. Take Hildegard back to the swamp. She shouldn't be allowed to roam off on her own. You know that.'

'Sorry, me and Grogoy were busy sorting out a fight between two of the other trolls and she just slipped away. Come on Hildegard, let's go home.'

Sophie breathed a sigh of relief as the two huge creatures lumbered off through the trees.

The woman turned to Sophie. 'Are you okay?'

Sophie pulled herself to her feet, rubbing at her arms with a grimace. 'Just about. Thank goodness you turned up when you did. I shudder to think what could have happened.'

'Oh, it's easy to distract a troll. I always carry a pocketful of treats when I come this way. They're like toddlers, really.'

'Yeah, just like toddlers—except they're giant and they want to eat you!' Sophie said with a trembling laugh.

'What are you doing here anyway? It's a very dangerous place for you youngsters to be. You're from Earth world, aren't you?'

Before they could speak, a deep male voice made them all look around.

'Mai. What have we here?' A tall, middle-aged man was walking towards them. He was dressed in a black, expensively tailored suit. His skin was almost as white as the shirt he wore. Behind him, a slightly shorter man stood. In complete contrast to his companion, he was olive skinned and dressed in faded jeans and a dirty white T-shirt which accentuated the muscles in his arms and legs. Both men wore sinister smiles.

'Visitors to our territory,' the second man said breathing in deeply. 'Young human blood!' A hungry look filled his eyes as he stepped towards the girls. 'Fresh young human blood…' Sophie drew back as he lifted a callused hand to her face.

Mai pulled the girl from his reach. 'Leave the kids alone, Grey. They're not doing any harm.'

'Hang on a moment, Mai. They're *uninvited* visitors in *our* territory.' The first man stepped forward.

'Exactly! *Uninvited!*' Grey repeated. 'We should be allowed to deal with uninvited visitors ourselves.'

As he reached out towards Sophie again, Sage sprang forward and grabbed his arm.

'Don't you dare touch my friend!'

He laughed in her face. 'And what are you going to do about it?' He called out to his companion. 'Which one do you want, Delbert?'

Delbert stepped forward, his smile showing long white canines. 'Mmm, how about we have a girl each and let the boy make a run for it?'

Paris put a protective arm around Sophie as she let out a soft whimper.

'Enough of your rather tasteless jokes, boys.' Mai held up her hand. 'You're frightening the youngsters. Let's just find out what they're doing here.'

Sage introduced herself and her friends.

'We're looking for Merlin. We need his help to rescue my grandparents and the fae, Saffron, from Nefarus.'

'But Saffron won't let anyone help her. And who are your grandparents? Why are they with Nefarus?'

Sage took a deep breath and explained the situation to her.

'Oh, my word! You're a future Spell Master?'

Grey exchanged a look with Delbert and muttered, 'We'd better watch our step.'

'We'll go straight to the castle. There's a lot to do before we head back to Earth world,' Mai said.

As she held out her hands to the three youngsters, Delbert stepped forward brandishing a rolled-up parchment.

'But we haven't sorted out the boundary yet. It must be decided before you leave, Mai.'

Mai sighed and took the parchment from his hand. 'Okay. I'll take another look and drop this back to you by midnight.'

Once again, she held out her hands and Sage, Sophie, and Paris took them. There was a rush of wind and a moment later they found themselves standing inside the large, stone hall of the castle. Along one wall were three ceiling to floor windows. The top part of each one depicted a scene in colourful stained glass. Above a doorway at the end of the hall was a tapestry showing the English countryside as it would have appeared hundreds of years previously. Extending along the length of the room was a long, wooden table which could seat fifty people comfortably with a line of tall, silver candelabras positioned at intervals. Suits of armour were placed around the walls like empty faced guards. Several long, heavy pennants hung from thick, ornately carved flag standards.

'Wow!' Sophie exclaimed, as the setting sun shone through the windows, bathing everything in a rainbow of light. 'It's so beautiful.'

'Yes, it is lovely to look at, but not very practical on a day-to-day basis,' their host said. 'Follow me.'

She led them through a small door into a stone turret and down a narrow stone, spiral staircase. At the bottom was a brightly painted red door which opened into a modern open plan kitchen and lounge area.

'My living quarters,' Mai told them. 'There are two bedrooms through there, both with shower rooms. You girls take one and Paris you can use the other one. I'll get some supper on; you must be hungry. Oh, and leave your clothes outside your rooms, I'll put them in the washing machine. They don't smell too good! I'll leave you something clean to wear.'

'Is Merlin here?' Sage asked her.

Mai smiled. 'You can speak with Merlin over supper.'

Sage sniffed the air appreciatively as she walked into the kitchen a short while later as Mai was putting a large casserole dish in the centre of the table. Paris, Sophie, and Sylvan looked up as she came in. The fae jumped up and hugged her.

'I'm so glad you're all safe! I was so worried about you. Mercy will be relieved to hear you succeeded in finding Merlin before the vampires and shifters found *you*.'

'Aren't we going to wait for Merlin?' Paris asked their host as she indicated they should start the meal.

She looked around and smiled. 'Let me introduce myself properly. I'm Mai Lin, also known as Merlin.'

Sophie's fork hit the table noisily. 'You're Merlin? But I thought Merlin was…'

'…an old man with a long white beard? Yes, I have appeared in that guise at times, though during most of my earlier life I was disguised as a young man. When I first left my home in China after my parents died, I was only thirteen. I couldn't travel as an unaccompanied young girl; it would have been far too dangerous. That's when I first disguised myself as a youth and adapted my name to Merlin.'

'We've been referring to Merlin as a man and no-one put us right,' Sage remarked, looking at Sylvan.

He shrugged. 'It's up to Mai how she appears to you, so we tend to avoid using he or she.'

'At thirteen, you travelled all the way from China to England alone?' Paris asked Mai.

'Yes, the journey took me several years. I didn't actually set out for England but when I arrived at the court of King Arthur, I knew I would make it my home.' She sighed deeply. 'Anyway, that's another story for another time. Let's talk about the present. Tell me a bit about yourselves. I very rarely get to speak to young Gifted these days. I haven't visited Earth world for several months as there's been so much happening here. It's always the same in an Alignment year—vampires and shifters falling out, ogres complaining about standards of swamps, Dragons dissatisfied with their flying spaces—the list goes on and on. And of course, Nefarus always makes himself known in Earth world around Alignment day. He has been trying to open the Portal for several hundreds of years now, but he has never been able to wield much power. I've grown a bit too complacent, I must admit. Tell me how he managed to abduct your grandparents, Sage.'

'When he realised who Sage was, his first plan was to make her *kiss* him! If Sophie wasn't so quick thinking, he would have succeeded,' Paris told her.

Mai let out a low whistle. 'That would have been the end of our freedom in both worlds! I shudder to think what life would be like with Nefarus as ruler.'

Sophie leaned forward, nodding. 'Well, when that didn't work, he used Saffron to lure her grandparents into a trap.'

'But that was when she was under his spell,' Sage pointed out. 'You can see from her Shimmer that she's a different person now.' She blinked back tears. 'I just hope they're all okay.'

'He won't risk harming your grandparents. He knows that they are the only hold he has over you,' Paris said.

There was a tense silence for a few seconds.

'He won't be so concerned about Saffron's welfare,' Sylvan muttered. 'We have to get to her as soon as we can.'

'Yes, we do need to get back as quickly as possible. I can make up a spell to free her heart now she is willing,' Mai assured him.

'And can you make up a spell to help me to overcome Nefarus?' Sage asked. 'Or at least to protect me and my grandparents from him when I join them at his house?'

Mai shook her head slowly. 'I can give you several different aids to help you to overcome him, but at the end of the day I'm afraid it's going to be up to you yourself, Sage. You will have to use your own powers against him. But we'll all be nearby and ready to help you as much as we can when it is time for the Alignment.' She patted Sage's trembling hand. 'You can do this; you are a future Spell Master.'

Sophie hugged her friend. 'And we'll be there, Sage. We'll be close by.'

'And we'll use all the skills we have been practising these past few months,' Paris added.

'You'll have plenty of friends behind you, Sage,' Mai said as she collected the plates together. 'I have several things to prepare tonight. We'll leave as soon as it is light tomorrow morning. Now, I suggest you all get some sleep as we've a busy time ahead of us.'

Sylvan stood up. 'Yes, and I must get back to Faeville. They'll be glad to hear that you're all safe. Some of the other fae are coming with me to Earth world to make a stand against Nefarus, so we'll see you at Alora's tomorrow.'

They watched as he shrank into a glowing orb and sped off through the night sky.

As Sage and her friends headed for the door, Sophie stopped to look at the parchment Mai had taken from the vampire.

'Is this a map of the Dark Forest?'

'Yes.' Mai picked it up and spread it out on the table. 'I'd better have a look at this first, they're expecting me to give them a new boundary that will keep both vampires and shifters happy—which is impossible!'

Paris peered at the map. 'Is the line in red the boundary suggested by Delbert and the brown one by Grey?'

'Yes. The shifters, quite rightly, think they should have more land as their numbers are growing and the vampires' population has remained the same since Aurum was established.'

'That seems fair enough, doesn't it?' Sage remarked.

Mai spread her hands. 'You'd think so, wouldn't you? But the vampires feel they are being undermined as their percentage of land ownership is falling each time we draw up a new boundary.'

As her hand hovered over the red line it rose and she placed it in a new position and then moved the brown boundary on top of it. 'Mmm, what about if we place the boundary there? Even though the vampires have less land, they do have the shadier part of the forest and still keep their side of the waterfall. Maybe that will satisfy them.'

'But the size of their land does look pretty small compared to what the shifters have,' Paris commented.

'How about you make it the same area but longer, so that it looks bigger?' Sage suggested.

Mai moved the boundary once again. 'Hmm, now their land looks too narrow.'

'Can I make a suggestion? There's really *one* simple solution to suit everyone,' Sophie said.

Mai and the other two exchanged looks. 'There is?'

'Obviously. You just do away with any internal boundary.'

'But what about hunting areas?' Sage asked.

'Everyone would be free to hunt where they wanted to.'

'There is no shortage of suitable prey for everyone,' Mai said. 'That would not be a problem.'

Looking at the map, she nodded slowly. 'You know, Sophie, I think you have solved the problem. It's so simple, I don't know why it never occurred to us before!' She passed a hand over the map and the internal boundaries disappeared. 'And drawing up an agreement over their rights and responsibilities will keep them busy for a while! I'll take that over to them at midnight. In the meantime, I've quite a few preparations for tomorrow. Now, you must go and try and get some sleep.' She looked at the three anxious faces in front of her and clicked her fingers. Three small cups filled with a pale blue liquid appeared on the table. 'These will help you.'

Despite her worries, Sage found herself asleep as soon as her head hit the pillow. It hardly seemed a moment later that she felt someone tugging her arm.

'Wake up. We have to get going, Sage.' Sophie was standing over her. 'Mai and Paris are getting breakfast ready. See you in the kitchen in a few minutes.'

'Were Delbert and Grey happy with the new boundary suggestion?' Sophie asked as they sat around the kitchen table.

Mai gave a short laugh. 'Happy isn't the word I'd choose. The vampires raised a worry about those who sleep during the daytime being disturbed by the shifters when they are at their most vulnerable. The shifters were anxious about the safety of their young with hungry vampires around. I told them these were issues that they'd have to sort out for themselves, and that we'd trial it for a time.' She glanced outside at the rising sun. 'We must leave soon.'

As the others cleared away the breakfast dishes, she bustled around, filling a wicker basket with different sized packages. With the basket over one arm, she signalled for the others to join her in the centre of the room.

'We'll go straight from here to the other side of the Portal,' she said as they linked hands.

Once again, the air grew hazy and a cold mist enveloped them.

***

A few minutes later, Sage rubbed her hands together, enjoying the feel of the sunshine on her face as she looked around at the familiar sights of Earth world.

'Are we going straight to The Coterie?' Sophie asked Mai.

'Yes, once I have taken a look at the place where Nefarus is staying. Wait here for a moment.'

She reappeared several minutes later. 'We'll walk to Alora's now. I want to take a look at our surroundings.' She seemed deep in thought as they made their way back into the town and along the road to The Coterie.

Alora was standing in front of the house when they arrived and gave them a warm welcome. 'I'm so glad to see you all again. And you too, Mai. Come in. Sylvan and five of his friends are in the kitchen. Your parents are there too, Paris and Sophie. Sylvan and Jay managed to convince them that your unexpected trip to Aurum was vital for our success at the Alignment.'

There was a noisy welcome as they made their way into the kitchen. Mai stood at the head of the table and waited for them to grow silent. 'I know you're really pleased to see your young ones back safely, but don't forget, there are still those in danger.' She glanced at Sage and Sylvan who wore troubled expressions. 'I had a look at the place where Nefarus is staying. He's encased it with a Dome. I couldn't penetrate it, but I was able to discern its occupants. Your grandparents are there, as we knew, Sage. They are both in good health.'

'And Saffron?' Sylvan's voice was hardly more than a whisper.

'She's in pain and is weak, but not as weak as I would have expected. I believe she must have taken energy from someone. If Sage gets the spell to her tomorrow, she should make a full recovery.'

'I will, don't you worry, Sylvan.'

'We've had the top international Gifted here with us this week to formulate our plans for tomorrow. If you go to the garden you can talk to them while Mai and I speak to Sage about her role. Before everyone leaves this afternoon, we'll meet up together to go through the final plans,' Alora said.

As the room cleared, she turned to the table where a sheet of parchment was unrolling. 'This a map of the garden that I drew up with Lupe's help. He also told me about the occupants. Apart from Nefarus himself, there is his sister Diabella and her two cats, three shifters, five imps, and eight goblins.'

Mai placed her wicker basket on the table next to her and pulled out a linen package. Gently unrolling it, she shook out a grey suede jacket and a pair of trousers similar to the ones she herself was wearing and spread them out on the wooden surface. A scent of herbs rose from them. As Sage fingered the soft material, it began to change to a light brown until it seemed to fade into the wood.

'Yes, it gives you a natural camouflage,' Mai said as she picked it up and placed it on the back of a red armchair. Sage watched as the suit took on the same hue as the chair.

'As well as providing camouflage, there are pockets to keep your potions and herbs to ward off or discourage a variety of creatures, shifters and goblins included,' she explained. Opening the jacket, she revealed an array of small, almost invisible pockets. 'They'll come in handy in some of the different situations you may find yourself in.'

They looked up as there was a knock on the door and Mary Goodall and Axel came in.

'Hello, I heard you were back.' Mary hugged Sage and then turned to Mai who held out her hand with a warm smile.

'Mary isn't? I'm Mai Lin, so pleased to meet you.'

'It's such a pleasure to meet you too, Merlin, I mean Mai Lin...I...I wasn't expecting you to be a young lady.' Mary stood staring at her for a few moments.

'Yes, I think we both thought that you'd be...' Axel began as he held out his hand.

'...an old man with a long white beard.' Mai smiled. 'Did you get everything, Mary?'

Mary put the large bag she was holding onto the table. 'Yes, yes, I did. Let me show you.' She pulled out a small, grey muslin bag. 'Make sure you keep this to hand! Nepeta Cataria Extremis—for Diabella's two cats—scatter it around them liberally.'

'What kind of cats are they?' Sage asked.

'Persian—when they're not puma,' Mary replied. She pulled out a second brown hessian bag. 'This is Imp Impeder. Toss it straight into the face; it stops them from biting you. And this,' she pulled out a small blue glass container, 'if you *do* get bitten, rub it straight into the wound. Now, I know Alora was told that most of the goblins with Nefarus are ready to stand with us against him, but I thought as a precaution, in case there are one or two unfriendly ones, I'd include this.' She put a green bag on the table. 'Goblin Grief. Again, just toss it straight into the face. And finally, the red bag contains a powder that will slow down a shifter for two minutes, but it won't stop him or her completely.'

Sage gave a loud sigh. 'How am I going to remember all this?'

'Oh, you don't have to. The jacket will do that for you. Put it on.' Mai helped her into it and Mary pushed each bag into a different pocket. 'Now imagine one of Diabella's big cats is racing towards you. Which potion do you need?'

'Cats!' Sage cried and found the grey bag in her hand. 'Wow! This is brilliant!'

'Yes, it will come in useful, but the hardest thing, dealing directly with Nefarus, is something we don't have a potion for, I'm afraid, just advice,' Mai said solemnly. 'Can you explain the plan you have made, Alora?'

She nodded. 'This is what we have planned so far, if you want to add any further suggestions, please do. Tomorrow, Mai and I will accompany Sage as far as the main gate to Nefarus' property. He will create an opening in the Dome for you to enter. I will cast a "Foot in the Door" spell to prevent them closing it completely. This spell will only last for two hours, then the dome will seal over again so we will have to move quickly.'

Mai put her hand over Sage's. 'The crucial point is all on your shoulders, I'm afraid, Sage. To harness your powers, Nefarus must be in contact with you at the Alignment time. Maybe he'll put a hand on your shoulder or hold your hand or even brush against your arm—if he's in contact in any way, he will be able to join the two worlds. If he can achieve this, he will be ruler of both worlds.'

Sage looked worried. 'If I can orb, I can move out of his reach, but I can't do that if he is holding on to me, can I?'

Alora looked at Axel. 'I believe you have a solution to this problem, don't you, Axel?'

'I do indeed.' He opened his hand. An ant appeared from his sleeve. 'We have a volunteer.'

'Adam, is that you?' Sage asked and smiled as she heard his reply.

Axel nodded. 'He volunteered to help out. Keep him hidden in your sleeve as the Alignment time approaches. As you pointed out, Nefarus is going to make sure that he is in contact with you. A bite from Adam, the Gifted Ant, at the right moment will cause Nefarus to jump back...'

'That will give me the chance to orb and get away from him. If I'm really quick.'

Alora squeezed her arm. 'You can be. But, Adam, leave it until the last possible moment so that Nefarus loses the chance to open the Portal. Once we see you orb, Sage, we'll enter the Dome. Our first task will be to get your grandparents to safety. Deft and Race, our top Transposers, will take care of that.'

'Nefarus has proved himself to be a bigger threat then we had ever imagined.' Mai looked grave. 'Tomorrow we must imprison him and make sure he does not reappear with a new plan in seventy years' time. I will set a *Minima Circle* here in front of the fountain. We must lure him into it. Once he touches the ground inside the circle, he will be reduced in size and I can lock him into this.' She held out a small crystal capsule in the palm of her hand. 'Then I will launch him high into the atmosphere where he can orbit the planet and think about his misdemeanours for the rest of eternity!'

'A great plan, as long as I prevent him from opening the Portal,' Sage said weakly.

Alora hugged the young girl to her. 'I know you can, Sage. You're a future Spell Master.'

***

Sage felt nervous as she sat at a table with Mai and Alora in front of the rest of the assembled Gifted later that day and listened as Alora outlined the final plans. She had brought up a map of the grounds on to the wall in front of them and explained how they would be able to gain entrance to Nefarus' property as soon the Alignment time had passed.

'Casper and the frontline Transposers and Snares will be waiting nearby and once they have the signal from us, they will join us as we make our way into the grounds.' Alora nodded towards Mary. 'Our Potion Master will also accompany us with her remedies for injuries. She has also mixed up a very useful entrance mist which she will disperse as the gate opens, giving us an initial advantage. Mary will position herself and her team over here near the wall in the orchard; it's a sheltered spot where she can look after any injured. As soon as we are inside, Deft and Race will carry Sage's grandparents there.

'Now for our opponents.' She clicked her fingers and a list of names, headed by Nefarus himself, appeared next to the map on the wall. 'As we all know, Nefarus is the most dangerous of our enemies. He can appear in human or Daemon form as a giant serpent. His sister Diabella is also a force to be reckoned with, especially as she is always accompanied by her two cats which shift into pumas. There are four human shifters, including Lupe who is the only one on our side. Ammo—recognisable by a deep scar running down his face—is the most ruthless of them.

The five imps are tenacious and hungry for blood. Lupe has gathered that most of the six goblins are disillusioned with Nefarus, but are also afraid of him, so we can't count on their support.'

There was silence as she finished speaking and Mai stood up.

'Once Nefarus realises he has lost the opportunity to open the Portal this time, he is bound to try to capture Sage and get her away from us so that he can use her at the next Alignment in seventy years' time.' She looked at Sage's aghast expression. 'But don't worry. We're not going to let that happen. We have seven fae whose job will be to watch over Sage at all times. If Nefarus or Diabella get too close to her, they will lead them away with a false fae scent until we are ready to trap the Daemon in the Minima Circle. We need to disarm as many of his followers as possible before this so they are not able to interfere with our success.' She clicked her fingers at the map on the wall and a second list of names appeared. 'Our frontliners are to work in pairs, for safety. Alora and I will not be visible until the final showdown; we will need about an hour to set up the Minima Circle. This is the biggest battle any of us has had to face for a very long time. The future of both our worlds is in the balance. Good luck to you all. If there are any questions, just ask myself or Alora; otherwise find your frontline partner.'

There was a gentle murmur and people began to seek out their frontline partners. As Mai stepped down from the platform, she was faced with Sophie and Paris.

'Our names aren't on the list, Mai,' Paris said.

Mai shook her head. 'You don't really have enough experience to join the frontliners tomorrow. We think it's best if you stay here at The Coterie with the rest of the Gifted.'

Sophie's mother put a hand on her daughter's shoulder. 'What were you thinking, Sophie? You've only had your Gift for a few months.'

Paris's father joined them, nodding. 'She's right. Neither of you are ready to take on Nefarus and his people tomorrow. Not many of us are, and we have more experience as Gifted.'

Mai gave a smile and patted Sophie's arm. 'It really is better if you both wait here tomorrow.'

Sophie shook her head resolutely. 'No, Paris and I *need* to be there for Sage! We three have already been through so much already. We've seen off ogres, gone through swamps, faced up to vampires and shifters together…'

Her mother's eyes widened. 'I don't think we've heard the full version of your trip to Aurum up to now.'

'Sophie.' Her father stepped forward. 'It's best if you stay with us at The Coterie. You two would probably end up just getting in the way if you were there.'

'With all respect, Sophie's right,' Paris interjected. 'Sage *needs* us there as moral support for her, even if we're not as powerful and experienced as the other frontliners.'

'Sage may be the next Spell Master, but she's only a teenager. We're her closest friends and tomorrow she will *really* need her friends nearby…' Sophie pleaded.

'We can give her the strength to keep going,' Paris added.

Alora turned to Sage who was standing to one side. 'What do you think, Sage?'

She bit her lip. 'I would not like my best friends to be put in danger.'

'So that settles it then…' Sophie's mother gave a sigh of relief.

'Sage, you *know* you need us there. And Paris and I can't just sit around here when we could be in there with you…' Sophie insisted.

'Or at least, somewhere where you could see us and feel our support,' Paris interrupted. 'Couldn't we go as Mary's assistants? And keep ourselves out of danger?'

'Mary, you could use some help, couldn't you?' Sophie's eyes lit up.

Her aunt sighed. 'Mai, I think these two youngsters may be right. Sage's going in there to save her grandparents, the only family she has. She might well be the next Spell Master, but she is also just a young girl who really does need the support of her closest friends.'

Mai and Alora exchanged looks.

'Okay, if you promise to stay well back and do everything Mary tells you to,' Mai finally said.

Mary nodded sternly. 'That goes without saying.'

The three friends hugged each other.

'We're in this together to the very end!' Sophie said firmly.

Chapter Twenty-One

The following morning, Sage, Mai, and Alora looked across at the heavy metal gates flanked on either side by a tall, dense hedge that completely surrounded Nefarus' property. Towering pine trees lined the driveway that led up to the large, imposing mansion, curving around an ornate fountain that sparkled and played near the entrance to the house.

'Do you see the statue at the centre of the fountain?' Mai asked Sage who nodded as she looked at the white marble figure holding a conch shell aloft. Water cascaded over her hands into the pool beneath her feet.

'I will set the Minima Circle three paces from the fountain wall, lined up with where she is facing. That is the spot where we can entrap Nefarus.'

Sage nodded again.

'It's time for us to go now but we won't be far away.' Mai gave her a reassuring smile.

Alora hugged her and whispered, 'We'll be with you again soon. Together we will succeed.'

The two women stepped back into the shadows as Sage walked up to the gates. There was a gentle tickle on her wrist. Looking down, she saw Adam's head appear. She let out a slow breath and drew herself up tall as the gates swung back and Lupe appeared with a second man at his side. From the jagged scar that ran down his cheek, she realised he must be Ammo.

'Welcome, Sage.' He gave her a cold smile. 'Come this way.'

'Where are my grandparents?' she asked, keeping back from the gateway.

He pointed towards the house where she could see her grandparents standing on the balcony.

'Nan! Grandad!' she cried, her spirits lifting at the sight of their familiar faces.

She followed the two men up the driveway, glancing around to take in her surroundings. On one side of the house, bordered by an avenue of trees, a wide, well-tended lawn led down to a small copse. On the other side, French windows opened on to a garden of herbs and flowers and small shrubs.

As they made their way to the wide entrance steps, several goblins who were working silently around the grounds gave her quick, curious glances. Nefarus appeared in the doorway and held out his hand. 'Sage, welcome.'

She hesitated before holding out her own.

'I'm sure you're anxious to be reunited with your grandparents. Ammo will take you to their suite now. You'll see they have been well cared for, as I promised you. We have just under four hours until the Alignment. I will send for you shortly before that time for the final preparations.'

Sage followed the shifter up the winding central staircase and along a corridor. She held her breath as he unlocked the door to her grandparents' rooms.

'Nan! Grandad! How are you? I've missed you so much!' She rushed forward to embrace each in turn. 'How have they been treating you?'

Her grandfather smiled at her. 'We're both fine. It's so lovely to see you, Sage,'

'It would be even better to meet up in different surroundings,' Ellen added.

They sat on the sofa and began to make desultory conversation, aware of Ammo standing nearby.

'How about a cup of tea?' Ellen said, looking across at the bored shifter.

He scowled. 'I'm only here to keep an eye on you, not wait on you.' Looking out of the window he saw a goblin nearby and shouted down to him. A short while later, there was a knock on the door and the goblin entered, followed by Lupe.

'They want me to be babysitter and waiter,' Ammo grunted as he motioned to the goblin to put the tray on the table.

'Diabella wants someone to tend to her cats. If you want to volunteer, I'll take over guard duty,' Lupe offered.

Without a moment's hesitation, Ammo left the room. The atmosphere changed as the door closed behind him.

'Where's Saffron?' Sage asked, pulling a small package from her jacket.

She followed her grandmother into the bedroom and gave a gasp when she saw the fragile fae. Kneeling down beside her, she unwrapped the package and placed a purple stone on Saffron's chest. Slowly a pink light flowed from the stone into her body. As the warm glow spread, the fae's eyes fluttered open. She took a deep breath and placed a hand on her chest.

'My heart, it's free; it's free!' she cried as she pulled herself up. She blinked and looked around her as Lupe and Jim appeared in the doorway. 'Thank you all so much!'

'Let's just be glad we were in time,' Ellen said with a wide smile.

'Now we know that you're safe, Saffron, we must talk about the Alignment while we still have the chance.' Sage quickly gave an outline of the plans Mai and Alora had drawn up. 'And here's the one who is going to get things started,' she added, pulling back her sleeve to reveal the tiny ant.

Jim gave a short laugh. 'Adam! I should have known you would want to be part of the action.'

He held out his hand and the tiny creature scuttled on to it.

'Race and Deft will take you to a sheltered spot where Mary will be stationed,' Sage continued. 'She is going to tend to any wounded.'

Ellen nodded. 'I can make myself useful there.'

'I wonder if Axel is able to use any of the Gifted non-human creatures?' Jim mused. 'Hey, how about I take you to meet Elvis, Adam? He's out here on the balcony. Perhaps we can get some ideas together.'

'I'll be watching over you, too, Sage, with the other fae. And Sylvan will be there. I can't wait to see my brother again!' Saffron said.

'Nefarus and Ammo think I am still on their side, so I will be in a good position to watch them carefully and keep you all safe,' Lupe said, looking around the room, his eyes lingering on Saffron.

A loud rap at the door brought them all to their feet. Saffron disappeared into a glowing orb while the others hurried back to the lounge.

'It's time! Nefarus is waiting,' Ammo announced.

Sage gave her grandparents one last hug. Jim winked as Adam scuttled up her sleeve. Then, taking a deep breath, Sage followed Ammo down the stairs.

When they reached the garden, Nefarus was already pacing backwards and forwards beside the fountain. His eyes gleamed brightly as they fell on the young girl.

'Over here, Sage.' He raised a hand and beckoned her towards him. She walked slowly, her eyes taking in the expectant faces of the creatures positioned around the grounds as far as the metal gates.

'I need to have my grandparents where I can see them,' she insisted as she reached him.

'Lupe, bring them forward. Is everything to your satisfaction now, my dear?' he asked with a cold smile.

She nodded briefly, exchanging a quick glance with the shifter who had stationed himself behind Jim and Ellen.

Her palms felt clammy as she felt the heavy hand of Nefarus grasp her shoulder.

'Not long to wait now...' he whispered, his breath deepening as he gazed into the clear, blue sky.

Sage moved her arm until her sleeve brushed against his hand. She could feel the slight tickle as Adam readied himself and forced herself to keep her eyes raised.

'A minute to go...' Nefarus continued. His brow creased briefly as he flicked at his sleeve.

Time seemed to freeze as Sage watched the small black speck knocked to the ground. 'No! No!' she murmured. Her attempts to pull away from Nefarus only made his grip on her arm tighten.

Lupe frowned as she threw him a silent cry for help. 'Something's not right!' Saffron's voice whispered beside the shifter's ear.

The next moment, Nefarus grabbed his head with a painful cry as a bright, glowing sphere struck him in the face. Seizing her chance, Sage folded herself into an orb and quickly put a distance between herself and the Daemon.

Within moments, the air was filled with loud cries as the gates were flung open to reveal Mai Lin flanked by her followers. They dispersed around the grounds, shouting and scattering a colourful mist as they went.

'What the...? The girl! Don't let her escape!' Nefarus bellowed, still clutching his face. 'Seal the Dome!'

Immediately, Diabella raised her hands and the gates clanged shut. She ran to her brother's side. 'Nefarus, what happened?'

'Saffron! Kill her! Kill all the fae—except for the girl. We need her.' He pulled his sister close to him and dropped his voice to a whisper. 'We can't let her escape. We must capture her and get her away from here. Somewhere where we can hold her for the next seventy years. I *will* be ruler of the two worlds!'

Diabella nodded. 'I'll have my car at the ready.' She looked around, taking a deep breath. 'Let's find the girl. Follow the scent of the fae.' A puzzled look crossed her face. 'There are several fae trails.'

Nefarus tutted angrily. 'I'll take this one; you take one of the others.'

At the same time, high in the treetops, Sage watched as they set out in different directions. A painful cry alerted her to a commotion nearby. A young Snare had been set upon by two imps. With a shout, she jumped into their midst.

'Imp!' she cried. The snarls of the two attackers turned to painful yelps as she released the Impede charm into their faces.

'I'll take him to Mary,' a deep voice said. She turned to see Race behind her.

'Nan and Granddad, are they...?'

'Safe and sound!' he replied with a smile as he picked up the wounded Snare and disappeared from sight.

Hearing a soft whimper, Sage crept forward and spotted a small figure crumpled on the ground.

'Saffron!' Sage rushed to her side. As she bent over her, she felt the hairs prickle on her neck. She turned slowly around to see a large, grey wolf edging its way towards them.

'It's Ammo! Saffron, you must orb, quickly!'

The fae shook her head. 'I can't, I'm too weak.'

Before she could carry Saffron to safety, the huge animal lunged towards them. As he sprang into the air, a second wolf appeared knocking him aside. The two animals began a vicious struggle.

'Lupe!' Saffron cried as they watched the vicious struggle. 'Do something, Sage!'

Sage held the shifter potion in her hands, but shook her head. 'I can't...I might get the wrong one.'

At that moment, Molly appeared and took in the situation.

'Molly, we must stop this fight!' Sage cried.

The Animator glanced around at the fountain. Her brow creased as she held out a hand to the marble figure that stood there. Still holding the conch aloft, the figure stepped gracefully from her plinth onto the ground and walked towards them. When she reached the snarling wolves, she upturned the shell, sending a cascade of cold water over them. The wolves were instantly thrown apart. Slowly they transformed into their human form and lay panting on the ground, wounded and bloody. Lupe had a deep gash across his chest.

Saffron knelt down beside him. 'Oh, Lupe!' She looked up at Sage. 'We must get him to safety.'

Sage frowned. 'He's too heavy for me to carry.'

She breathed a sigh of relief as Sylvan appeared. 'I knew it was your voice I heard, Saffron!' The two fae embraced briefly as Sage explained the problem.

Sylvan shook his head. 'I am not strong enough to carry him but I'll take you first, Saffron, and we can find someone to come for him.'

'We'll watch over him, Saffron,' Molly reassured her as her brother picked her up.

Under the apple trees, Ellen fussed around as Sylvan placed his sister on a makeshift bed a few minutes later. 'We heard how you came to Sage's rescue at the last moment, Saffron. You were so brave but my word, you have some nasty bruises there. We must put something on them immediately. Sophie, can you hand me the Arnica poultice, please?'

Saffron struggled to sit up. 'Someone must go and get Lupe straight away. He's badly injured.'

'It's okay, Saffron,' her brother told her. 'Deft has already left.' He pushed her hair back from her face. 'We have so much to talk about later but now I must return to Sage.'

'How is Sage?' Ellen asked.

'She's fine. She's with Molly. The young Gifted are a force to be reckoned with.'

'Wait! I'm coming with you,' a breathless voice called as the fae turned to leave. Jim hurried towards him, carrying a cardboard box. 'Elvis' idea. A pretty good one, too!'

Sophie looked at Paris. 'We should be out there with Sage, too.'

Paris frowned. 'But we promised that we'd stay to help Mary. They wouldn't agree to us going out there.'

'Ellen and Mary have enough helpers here. They won't notice if we just slip away. We'd never forgive ourselves, if something happened to Sage and we could have saved her.'

'You're right. We would *never* forgive ourselves.' He picked up an injured Snare's rucksack and glanced at the discs inside. 'These may come in handy. Let's go.'

Glancing around to make sure no-one noticed their departure, they followed Jim and the fae.

Meanwhile, Sage watched as Deft disappeared carrying Lupe. She looked up as Molly tugged her arm. 'I think Ammo is coming round.'

The shifter was pulling himself up with an evil smile spreading slowly across his face. He pointed behind them. 'Diabella has sent her pussy cats to deal with you!' he chuckled, wiping a hand across his blood-streaked face.

Sage pushed Molly behind her as the two pumas edged their way towards them. 'Cats!' she whispered and a grey muslin bag appeared in her hands. With trembling fingers, she pulled open the lace that secured it and scattered the dried herbs on the ground in front of them. Each animal sniffed the air, then as if in a trance, pushed their heads onto the herbs, with loud guttural sounds of pleasure.

Ammo shook his head in disbelief. 'What the...?'

"Nepeta Cataria Extremis"—also known as Catnip! But an extra strong version!' Sage opened her hand to show a second package. 'And I've something here for you, too!'

With a curse, the shifter fell back. 'We'll get you yet! Nefarus *won't* lose!' He limped out of sight as a shrill voice sounded.

'What have you done to my cats?' Diabella strode towards Sage, her fists clenched.

Quietly, Molly animated the fountain statue and guided it towards the furious Daemon. Just as it raised the conch above its head, Diabella swung around. With a flick of her wrist, the marble figure shattered and fell to the ground in a thousand pieces. Then, she continued her steady pace towards the two girls, forcing them back towards the driveway. She smiled as she heard the soft hum of a car engine as it pulled up behind the girls and a tall shifter climbed out of the driver's seat.

From the shrubbery, Sophie and Paris peered out at the scene. They listened as Jim whispered something to the fae beside him and stepped out onto the driveway placing the shoebox on the ground.

'Something for you, Diabella,' he called out.

Her puzzled look was replaced by horror as ants swarmed from the container and headed towards her. Soon she was covered in the tiny red insects. With a shriek, she turned and dived into the fountain pool, swiping them from her. Spluttering angrily, Diabella pointed towards Sage.

'Leave me! Get *her*!' she screamed at the shifter who was running towards her. 'Put her in the car!'

Sage pushed Molly behind her and once again summoned the shifter charm. As he neared them, she opened the muslin bag and threw the dust into his face. With a look of astonishment, he gasped for breath before collapsing to the floor. Her relief was quickly replaced by fear once again as Diabella clapped her hands and two imps appeared, snarling as they made their way towards the girls.

'I've no more charms. We must use our own Gifts, Molly.' Sage grabbed the swirls of yellow and red that poured from the imps which only marginally slowed their pace.

Running forward, Paris tossed several white discs into the air over the imps. However, Diabella's shouts of rage soon dispelled their feelings of apathy and clouds of red and orange quickly replaced the pale wisps.

'I've only one white disc left, Sage!' Paris shouted as he watched the two imps move menacingly towards them.

'Don't throw it!' Sage shouted. She pushed a handful of red and yellow discs into his hands. 'Mix whatever discs you have left. Blend then disperse!'

'I can't...I've never managed to Blend successfully...'

Sage continued to pull the red and yellow strands from the air. 'It's our only option! Just do it!'

Paris stood, frozen to the spot as the imps drew closer.

'No!' Sophie screamed and threw herself in front of the nearest Imp as it hunched down ready to pounce on him. The Imp stumbled and fell, the red wisps rising from him taking on a darker hue.

The movement seemed to bring Paris to life. Grabbing a handful of discs, he fused them together before throwing them over the creature, concentration etched on his face. Without waiting to see the result, he grabbed a second handful and dealt with the second Imp. He continued to compress and toss the blended discs until the bag was empty.

Bemused expressions flickered over both their faces as they felt so many conflicting emotions spin through their minds at the same time. Clutching their heads in their hands, they fled from their tormentor.

Jim ran forward and helped Sophie to her feet. 'Let's get you kids somewhere safe.'

A loud bellow made them all freeze.

'What incompetence is this?' Nefarus strode into their midst, glancing at the fallen shifter. He turned to his bedraggled sister as she pulled herself from the water. 'You let a handful of kids and an old man reduce you to this?'

'They have the sorcery of Mai Lin on their side!'

'Get the girl into the car, we're leaving now!' Nefarus waved a hand at a large, grey wolf standing behind him.

With a growl, the beast edged forward, forcing Sage nearer to the open door of the car.

'No!' her grandfather shouted. But as he moved towards her, Nefarus raised his hand and sent him flying backwards to land heavily on the ground.

'I can't touch her, but I can decimate the rest of you!' the Daemon snarled turning towards Sophie and Paris.

Suddenly his arm was enveloped in a yellow flame.

'Stop right there, Nefarus!' said Mai, as she and Alora appeared in front of him.

With a howl of pain, Nefarus drew himself up, his eyes wild. 'Mai Lin! You won't stop me this time!'

His body grew and lengthened until he became a glowing red serpent towering above her. Mai's mouth tightened. She clenched her fists at her side and bowed her head. Slowly her body was enveloped in a strange yellow light. Taking a deep breath, she threw back her head and let out a roar. Sophie clung to Paris's arm as they watched the young woman's face take on a yellow hue. Her nostrils flared and widened, her shoulders and arms thickened, her fingers curled into long, sharp claws. Finally, she was transformed into a giant, golden dragon. There was a crackle of lightning as she leapt into the air making the serpent recoil from the plume of flames that shot from her mouth. Soon the sky was filled with red and golden flashes of light as the two creatures fought furiously.

Alora ran towards Jim, who still lay motionless on the ground. Signalling to the youngsters to help her, she pulled him away from the battle that raged above them. Hardly aware of their presence, Diabella stood nearby, her eyes fixed on the creatures. A smile spread over her face when the sky turned blood red which was replaced by a look of fear when a golden hue took over. At times, the air was filled with an orange glow as both opponents seemed to be equally matched.

Sage looked at Alora and tried to read the emotions on the Spell Master's face. 'Can we do anything?'

She shook her head. 'It's between the two of them now. We can only keep the Minima Circle free.'

'Mai will win, won't she?' Sophie asked.

Paris squeezed her hand. 'Of course, Mai will win. She's a Sorcerer. The Daemon doesn't stand a chance against her!'

Sage noticed that Alora made no comment. At that moment, Jim opened his eyes. 'What in the world…?' he muttered, pulling himself up.

'Mai Lin is teaching Nefarus a lesson!' Paris exclaimed.

Sage took a sharp breath as the red glow spread further and the golden light slowly diminished.

For the first time, Diabella turned to face them. 'Ha! It looks as if your mighty Sorcerer has finally met her match!'

She gave a shrill cackle as the yellow light grew smaller and the human shape of Mai became visible, her eyes closed as she drifted slowly towards the ground. With a triumphant roar, the serpent rose up in the sky.

'No! No!' Sophie screamed and buried her face in Paris's chest. He stood still, a look of disbelief etched on his face.

'Alora! We must do something!' Sage tugged at her arm but she merely shook her head and gave a strange smile.

Tears stung Sage's eyes as Mai silently twisted and turned in her downward journey. The serpent gathered himself together and lunged towards her. Then, to everyone's surprise, just before she touched the ground, Mai's eyes shot open and she flung herself to one side leaving Nefarus to crash to the floor. Leaping to her feet, she held out the crystal capsule and gave a cry of joy as the diminished Daemon was trapped inside.

'No more will you spread evil and terror on Earth world!' she cried, holding aloft the now scarlet capsule. 'You are going to a distant place, where you will have all eternity to gaze down on us and reflect on your misdemeanours!' She flung the crystal high into the sky where it crashed through the Dome and continued its journey upwards. The air was filled with a soft grey ash that gently floated down to the ground.

Diabella clutched her chest and looked around wildly. Ammo and the other shifter were scrambling into the car and several imps jostled each other aside as they also struggled to climb into the vehicle. She pulled Ammo out and climbed into the driver's seat. 'My cats!' she screamed. 'Get my cats!' Tyres screeched as she pushed her foot down on the accelerator, only slowing down to allow Ammo to bundle himself and the two Persian cats into the back of the car, before they sped off through the open gates, with people jumping aside as they left.

As the sound of the car engine faded away, silence descended. Slowly, a soft murmur rose as people headed towards the fountain where Mai stood.

'We did it.' She smiled. 'Together, we defeated the Daemon.'

A shout of triumph ran through the crowd.

Casper pointed towards the open gate. 'But, Diabella and the others! They've escaped!'

'Let them go,' Mai said. 'I expect they'll hide away in her hilltop home and lick their wounds for a while. By the time they're ready to start any trouble, I'll have a few new restrictions in place. Now, I think it's time we returned to The Coterie and our friends waiting for us there. Can you organise Transposers to carry the injured back, Mary? Casper, we'll need a team to Muddy any NG witnesses around here since the Dome is no longer there to hide everything, can you sort that out?' She turned to Alora and Sage. 'We can deal with the clean up here.'

Alora smiled as Sage drew a deep breath, looking at the devastation around her. 'Don't worry, there's a spell for it. I'll show you.'

As she raised her hand, Jim rushed forward. 'Wait! I must find Adam. You were standing about here Sage...'

He looked down at a small speck on his hand. 'You may be right, Elvis, but I'm going to check, anyway. And if...the worst...has happened, I'm going to take him back to bury him in our garden, where we spent so many happy times...' He frowned as the ant commented. 'Maybe it *is* a human thing and it *is* pretty pointless, but that's what I'm going to do!'

He bent down and began to search the gravel driveway. 'Adam! Can you hear me?' A smile crossed his face as Elvis jumped from his hand onto the ground. 'You've found him!' He spread a clean white handkerchief out on the ground and watched as Elvis pulled the injured ant onto it. 'That leg looks painful...well, let's not look on the bad side, Elvis, let's see what Axel can do for him.'

He walked slowly away, carrying the handkerchief carefully in his hands.

'I do hope Adam will be okay,' Sophie commented as she and Paris followed him.

'Me, too,' Sage said as she watched them walk away. 'He means the world to Grandad.'

'If anyone can save him, Axel is the one.' Alora patted her arm. 'Now for the clean up.' She pointed towards the fountain. '*Fractis rebus melius.*' As she said the words, Sage's eyebrows rose as the statue was slowly rebuilt until she stood tall, holding the conch high above her head. With graceful steps, she took her place back on the marble plinth before freezing into a lifeless statue once again.

'How about you finish off out here while I tidy up inside the house?' Mai suggested.

An hour later, the three of them joined Casper at the gate. He was chatting to an elderly couple.

'It is a pity that the place has stood empty for so long, isn't it? It would be nice to see it occupied again.' He turned and smiled at Mai. 'Mr and Mrs Jenkins and I were just saying what a lovely quiet area this is.'

'It looks very peaceful.'

They watched the couple walk back to the adjoining house. Casper winked. 'Our work here is done. Let's go back to The Coterie.'

Chapter Twenty-Two

There were cheers as they walked into the hall of The Coterie. A long table laden with food and drinks was set out along one wall. A glass of wine floated into Mai's hand and she raised it in a toast.

'To all the Gifted and Magical members of Earth world and Aurum,' she proposed. 'We have saved our two worlds from the hands of the Daemon, Nefarus.'

There was an answering cheer and a clinking of glasses.

'However, this battle has opened my eyes,' Mai continued. 'It's time that some adjustments were made. The two worlds are isolated from each other except to the fae who can move from one to another easily. I know there are some Earth world dwellers who would like to make their homes in Aurum…' She paused as the goblins looked at each other and nodded and Lupe looked hopefully at Saffron who was standing by his side. 'Over the next week, I will be listening to them and I will hold a meeting with the leaders to make some changes to the way we live now.'

A murmur of excitement ran through the room.

'But now, I suggest we forget all our worries and celebrate today's victory!'

Sage slipped away to join her grandparents as Mai was quickly surrounded by young and older Gifted of The Valley. Ellen hugged her. 'What a time this has been! It'll be so nice to sleep in our own home tonight. Jim's already taken Adam home. Axel is going to have a look at him.'

There was a squeal, and Sage found herself embraced in a tight hug by Sophie. 'We did it! We defeated the Daemon!'

Paris stood behind her, grinning. 'We certainly did. There's no stopping The Valley Gifted!'

Soon they were joined by other youngsters, some with stories of their part in the battle, while others who had remained at The Coterie listened in awe.

It was after midnight when Alora stepped into the kitchen and found Mai standing at the open French windows looking up at the full moon. A young couple drifted past, arms entwined around each other.

'It's a night for romance, isn't it?' Mai sighed. 'I can remember nights like this.'

Alora squeezed her shoulder. 'It's been such a long time, Mai...'

The other woman fingered the gold cross that hung on a chain around her neck. 'Yes, it has been a long time. But I will find the second cross no matter how long it takes. Vinnie heard of a new lead in Winchester.'

'Vinnie's been spending more time in Earth world lately, hasn't she?' Alora commented.

'Yes, she wants more than life in the Dark Forest with the other vampires and shifters. There are a few people from Aurum who have seemed unsettled lately. It's definitely a time for change. I'll have to spend less time on my own quest and pay more attention to our two worlds in future.'

At that moment, the sound of voices drifted in. A couple appeared and sat down on a bench nearby. They sat close together with their hands intertwined.

'I can't believe I'm sitting here with you now, after all those long, lonely years. I still can't believe I'm so lucky,' the woman said.

'Hey, I'm the lucky one,' her companion replied, pulling her closer to him. 'First thing tomorrow, we'll speak to Mai about making a home in a neutral territory, away from where the shifters and fae live. It might be hard at first, but it'll be worth it.'

'I know it will be.' As she leaned towards him, Sylvan and Sage appeared on the scene.

'Hey, Saffron, I've been looking…' Sylvan's words faded away as he shook his head, frowning. 'What is this?' Grabbing his sister by her arm he pulled her to her feet. 'Get away from her!' he shouted at the man.

'Sylvan, wait!' Saffron pulled herself free. 'I'm in no danger from Lupe!'

Lupe raised his hands, stepping backwards. 'Yes, just let us explain…'

'I don't need any explanation from a shifter who's getting far too close to my *fae* sister!' Sylvan retorted, lunging towards him, fists raised.

Sage grabbed his arm. 'What are you doing?'

'Stop, Sylvan!' Saffron cried out. 'Lupe is not going to harm me. Just listen for a moment, will you?'

In the kitchen, Alora stood up and moved towards the French windows, but Mai shook her head and signalled her to be quiet. 'Let's see if they can sort out this problem on their own.'

Saffron stood in front of her brother. 'Lupe and I love each other. We are going to be together.'

The fae shook his head. 'No, that's impossible! What are you thinking of, Saffron? It can't happen. Has he bewitched you like the Daemon? He's obviously up to no good!'

'Your sister is telling you the truth, Sylvan. I would never harm a hair on her head. I love her. I want to spend the rest of my life with her.'

Sylvan gave a harsh laugh and turned to his sister. 'What? Fae and shifter together? What a joke! Come on, it's time we left.'

He made a grab for her hand, but Saffron drew away from him and stood beside Lupe who put his arm around her protectively. 'No, Sylvan. We're serious. We're going to be together.'

Sylvan looked at his sister with pleading eyes. 'We lost you to a Daemon for sixty years, and now, instead of celebrating your freedom, we are to lose you once again, this time to a *shifter*.'

'You haven't lost me, Sylvan…'

With a wave of his hand, her brother dismissed her claim. 'Of course, we have. Have you forgotten how fae and shifters are sworn enemies? Have you forgotten the fate of any fae who dares go near shifter territory? How long do you think you'll last? Make your choice, Saffron.'

Her face crumpled as her brother's eyes burned into hers. She looked from one man to the other. 'No, no…I can't bear this…'

Sage stepped forward and held up her hand. 'Sylvan, you can't force your sister to make such a choice! We need to discuss this calmly and on a practical level.' She looked at Saffron and Lupe. 'Where do you plan to live? Will your fae family be able to visit you safely?'

Lupe explained their idea of setting up home in a neutral territory in Aurum. 'There must be others like us, who don't fit neatly into one category.'

'It sounds like a good solution. Fae and shifter could visit you easily,' Sage said.

'Hmm, but would fae be safe in a place where shifters can freely come?' Sylvan's mouth hardened.

'Maybe it's time to start building bridges between shifters and fae,' Sage continued. 'If these two can live together, why can't others see eye to eye?'

'Because shifters *kill* fae, that's why!' Sylvan threw up his hands. 'We all know about the fae who got too close to a shifter and ended up with a scar…'

'…that ran from her eye to the little finger on her right hand? Yes, but have you ever met this fae yourself, Sylvan?'

'No, but…but…*everyone* knows this story…'

'Everyone knows the story!' Sage raised a finger. 'But no-one has *actually* met her. She's probably just a myth.' Once again, she turned to Lupe. 'Speak truthfully now, how many of your kind have harmed fae?'

He frowned and scratched his head. 'I never met any fae where I grew up. Saffron is the first one I've met but I never felt I wanted to harm her; I just thought how beautiful she is. There were always stories going around about shifters that had caught fae, but no-one I knew had caught one themselves.'

'So, perhaps shifters and fae aren't such enemies after all,' Sage said.

'Ammo, a *shifter*, definitely tried to attack Saffron. You came to her rescue, Lupe,' Sylvan pointed out.

'Hmm, Ammo. Well, he'd eat *anything*, I mean *anything*. Even roadkill. It was really horrible to watch.'

'So, we *do* have some kind of basis to build up a peaceful relationship between shifters and fae, don't we?' Saffron offered, casting a pleading look at her brother.

'I don't know. Things between us go back too far, too deep…'

At this point, Mai stepped through the French windows, smiling. 'And it would take brave people to try to bridge the gap, wouldn't it?'

Alora joined her. 'I think you're right, Sage, the division is based more on rumours and hearsay than on actual facts.'

'Some of the vampires and shifters enjoy their reputations as creatures to be feared,' Mai agreed. 'It's definitely time we took a long hard look at life for Gifted and Magical in both worlds and made a few changes. Things have been the same for centuries.' She turned to Lupe. 'I like your idea of setting up home in a neutral territory. You are right, there are quite a few Gifted and Magical ones who don't fit into one particular group.'

'You're holding meetings with our Earth world dwellers this week; you could set up similar ones in Aurum when you return there,' Alora suggested.

'Yes,' Mai nodded. 'I've plenty to think about when I get back to Aurum.'

Alora smiled. 'Anyway, it's late now, it's been a long day, I think we all need some sleep.'

Saffron lay a hand on her brother's arm. 'Try to be happy for me. Please?'

Chapter Twenty-Three

Six days later, Mai once again stood at the front of the hall in The Coterie and looked around at the assembled Gifted.

'This has been an incredible week. I didn't realise just how many of you would like to visit Aurum and to see what life is like over there. Some of the goblins are very keen on moving there permanently, aren't you?'

A female goblin stood up, nodding vigorously. 'Yes, we do. We want to live in a land where we can raise children to be proud of their green skin. We're tired of hiding away from our human neighbours.'

'Rina's right,' her partner, Verdan, agreed. 'Some goblins think that the riches they make from the mines in the mountains compensate for everything, but for us, our freedom is priceless.'

'And Saffron and Lupe, you want to set up home in Aurum, too, don't you?' Mai continued.

'Yes, we do,' Saffron said, smiling at Lupe.

A murmur ran around the hall as they stood up, holding hands.

A pained expression passed over Sylvan's face, but he gave a weak smile as Sage gently squeezed his arm.

'Yes, I can see many of you are surprised,' Mai nodded. '"*A shifter and a fae?*" you're thinking. There are so many tales—shifters eat fae, don't they? But don't listen to all the stories. Don't forget, there was a time when fae and human partnerships were frowned upon, but today it's very commonplace. You may be the first, Saffron and Lupe, but I imagine there will be many other mixed relationships. We need to work on breaking down prejudices between our different people in both worlds. In a few days' time, I am returning to Aurum. I'll be talking to the people there and collecting their ideas so we can begin to forge stronger links between the two worlds. I am going to set up a system so that our people can spend time in both of our worlds, if they wish to. I will be back to speak to you all about it in the next few months. In the meantime, Alora will keep you all up to date on our plans.'

Sage turned to Sylvan as Mai finished speaking. 'Will you be returning to Aurum soon?'

He nodded. 'I promised Saffron I'd help her set up her new home there. They want to set up home on The Plains, which is an expanse of grassland west of Faeville. She's a bit nervous of meeting up with family and friends in Faeville again after all these years. And now with Lupe as her new partner...'

'He seems like a nice guy. Are you going to put in a good word for him, Sylvan?' Paris asked.

Sylvan shrugged. 'I suppose so; he is my sister's choice.'

'I wish we could be there, too,' Sophie said.

Sage's eyes widened. 'We could go with you. We could help Saffron and Lupe settle in.'

'Oh, that would be great!' a voice agreed. They looked around to see Saffron and Lupe walking towards them. 'Do you think Mai would agree?'

Mai was pleased with the idea. 'You three hardly had time to look around Aurum on your last visit so we could remedy that this time. And there's the Annual Festivities next week, events not to be missed. See what your families think of the idea. You could leave with me on Friday.'

***

'I can't believe we're getting the chance to go to Aurum *again*!' Sophie could hardly contain her excitement as they arrived at The Coterie with their bags a few days later.

Her mother frowned. 'And this time, there are to be no close encounters with ogres or vampires.'

'Don't worry. I'll make sure they don't get into any trouble this time.' Mai smiled as she met them at the door.

Behind her, Saffron and Lupe appeared, each carrying a large carpet bag. Six goblins followed them, holding similar bags.

'Don't forget this!' Mary hurried up to Lupe, holding out a glass bottle that contained an orange liquid. 'The others will get away with it, but as a shifter, you'll definitely need to disguise your natural scent until you adjust to Aurum if you don't want everyone running away from you, especially fae! Take a spoonful every morning for the first three weeks. I've washed your clothes in a separate potion so they should be acceptable.'

'The scent of the jacket you gave us was pretty strong in Aurum,' Paris said. The three friends smiled as they recalled the fae reaction to Lupe's jacket.

'And don't let your imagination run away with you this time.' Sage nudged Sophie's arm.

***

Her words echoed in Sophie's mind a short while later when they found themselves once again standing on the plateau in Aurum.

'There's nothing to be afraid of,' she muttered to herself as she glanced around her. 'No wild dogs, no snakes...'

Noticing her nervous expression, Paris took her hand. 'Hey, don't worry. I'll look after you.'

She smiled gratefully as he pulled her closer to him. She blushed as she remembered clinging to him just before Mai had captured Nefarus and wondered what he thought about it. Suddenly, Saffron gave an excited cry.

'Look, Faeville!' She pointed to the stream of colourful shadows and shapes that rose in the sky in the distance.

'They're rehearsing for the Faeville dance,' Mai told them. She pointed to a bright green copse. 'And over there is Goblin Glen.'

A wide smile spread over Rina's face. 'And our new home.'

'And there are The Plains,' Mai indicated, 'bordered by those two settlements and The Dark Forest—home to the vampires and shifters.'

'The Plains would be a good place to set up our new home,' Lupe said.

'We'll go down to Goblin Glen first so you goblins can meet your new neighbours,' Mai continued.

Soon the excited party stood in front of a wide gate that led into a lush green copse.

Saffron drew a deep breath taking a tentative step through the gate. 'It's such a long time since I've been here and it hasn't changed a bit.'

'There are so many shades of green,' Sophie marvelled as she followed her through an arbour of trees and plants.

'Goblin colour,' Sylvan told her. 'Do you remember how we used to play here as children, Saffron?'

There were sudden squeals of excitement as many of the surrounding "plants" burst into life and a crowd of giggling goblin children jumped down in front of them.

'Oh, my life!' Mai clutched her heart, laughing. 'I had forgotten how good you goblins are at camouflaging yourselves.'

'Come on! Come on!' several of the goblin children urged them, grabbing their hands and pulling them forwards.

'Jaden, Smaragda! Take it easy with our visitors.' An older goblin appeared on the pathway. 'I hope they haven't scared you too much.'

Saffron and the older goblin stood and looked at each other.

'Olivia?' Saffron whispered. 'It is you, isn't it?'

The two women embraced. 'We were so relieved when we heard you were free of the Daemon's curse. You haven't changed a bit in sixty years! Not like me; I'm a grandmother now.'

She turned to the others. 'Welcome to you all. Mai let us know that we'd be having some new neighbours from Earth world. We want to know all the news of the goblins over there.'

Rina smiled and patted her bag. 'I have some letters here.'

The two women chattered happily as they neared a long wooden building.

'Are there regular Gifted ones like us living here?' Paris asked as he looked at a group of teenagers eyeing them curiously. 'They don't look like fae or goblins.'

Mai shook her head. 'There are witches and elves here in Goblin Glen and in Faeville. There are a few witches in the Dark Forest, too.'

'Are the witches dangerous?' Sophie asked.

'No, any magical ones with evil intent were not allowed to join us here in Aurum.'

They had arrived at a long wooden building. A carved sign over the doorway proclaimed it to be *Pine's Diner.*

'If you need anything as you settle in, Pine is the one who knows someone who can help you,' Olivia told them.

A tall, slightly stooped goblin appeared in the doorway leaning on a carved walking stick. His green hair was flecked with grey. 'Mai, so good to see you again. And welcome to you all. It's a great pleasure to have newcomers in our midst. Come in and have a cup of tea and meet some of the others.'

'Moss, it's so good to see you again.' Mai clutched the old man's hand as he led the way inside. 'Pine's cooking smells as good as ever!'

A short, rotund goblin hurried towards them, wiping floury hands on her apron.

'Mai! Stranger! Where have you been? It's been months...' she cried as she pulled the younger woman into a hard embrace.

'It's Alignment year, Pine. You know how busy Mai gets...' Moss pointed out.

'Of course, I do. And we were all so glad to hear you defeated the Daemon and we're safe for another seventy years.' She waved two waiters over to attend to their guests. Soon the table was filled with teapots and plates overflowing with pastries and cakes in different shades of green. As they tucked in, another woman pulled up a chair to join them.

'Hi, I'm Pine's sister, Fir. We're all so excited to have newcomers joining us. Once you've had some refreshments, I'll take you on a tour of Goblin Glen and show you the homes available. We've two new family homes near the centre of town and a student apartment for you two, Lichen and Brassion. I hear you're going to start courses related to the Brunswick mining company.' She turned to Saffron and Lupe. 'And you're the new couple causing such a stir in Faeville. Have you been up there yet?'

Saffron shook her head. 'I'm going to go there once we've set up our new home on The Plains, then there'll be a place for my family and friends to come and visit us.'

'Hmm, the fae/shifter thing is going to be a tricky one,' Moss commented.

Lupe took Saffron's hand and held it firmly. 'And it's one we are going to deal with.'

'Goblins aren't afraid of shifters, are they?' Paris asked.

'No, nor vampires. They're not tempted by our green blood.' Pine chuckled.

Fir shook her head. 'Though I sometimes worry about Peridot.'

'Why are you worried about me, Fir?' a tall, slim girl asked as she entered the room. Her skin was a pale green while her hair, piled up on top of her head, was a dark green. In her hands she held a sketchpad.

'I do worry when you wander out of the Glen all alone to do your drawing and painting.'

'I'm fine, really.' Peridot smiled as she opened her sketchpad and picked up her pencil.

'Now if everyone has had enough to eat, let's start our tour of Goblin Glen,' Fir said, pushing back her chair. 'I've the farm carriage waiting outside.'

'And I think it's time we made our way to The Plains to set up your new home,' Mai added turning to Saffron and Lupe.

'I'll come with you,' Peridot said. 'I could do some sketches of your design ideas. Here, you can have this as a house warming gift.'

She carefully tore a page from her sketchpad and gave it to Saffron. Her expression softened as she looked down at the picture of herself and Lupe looking into each other's eyes, clearly deeply in love. 'Oh, this is beautiful.'

Mai bit her lip as she looked over her shoulder. 'Peridot, this is amazing! Did you sketch this just now?'

Peridot nodded. 'I saw the look they exchanged and wanted to capture it.'

'You certainly did that.' Lupe smiled.

'Do you get asked to do many portraits?' Mai asked her.

The young girl shrugged. 'No, it's more of a hobby really. I qualified in Gem and Precious Metal Design last year and now I'm working in Uncle Brunswick's business, designing jewellery and costumes.'

Pine smiled broadly. 'It's a great opportunity. Brunswick's is one of the most important suppliers of ceremonial robes and precious artefacts in all of Aurum.'

Mai turned back to the portrait of Saffron and Lupe. 'You are a very talented artist, Peridot. I would like you to do a portrait for me if you would.'

'It would be a great honour, Mai.'

Sage stood up. 'Can we come to see your new home being created, Saffron?'

'Yes, I'd love to see a complete house being created from nothing but magic,' Sophie said.

For the next few minutes, there was excited chatter and bustle as the party split into two groups.

The two goblin couples and the boys climbed into an open carriage pulled by two green Shire horses. Fir flicked the reins and the horses trotted forwards.

'We'll see you later.' She gave them a wave.

As the carriage drew away, Sylvan tapped Saffron's arm. 'I'm going to Faeville, to get them used to the idea of my new...brother-in-law. I'll tell them you will be joining us this evening.'

Saffron hugged him before he left. 'Thank you so much, Sylvan.'

Mai turned to the others. 'Are you ready to go? There's a particular spot on The Plains which I think will be a good site for your new fae/shifter home.'

***

A few moments later, they found themselves on a flat grassy plain with Goblin Glen lying below them.

'Wow, what a view,' Saffron said as she spun around. 'And from here, we can see Faeville over there and The Dark Forest on the other side.'

Lupe nodded. 'It's the perfect location.'

Mai smiled. 'Now we have the site, how do you picture your perfect home?'

Peridot picked up her sketchpad as Saffron furrowed her brow. 'I was thinking of a cottage, similar to the ones you find in a typical English village. Oh, I don't suppose you know what an English cottage looks like, do you?'

Peridot smiled. 'I do. Vinnie brings me books and magazines from Earth world. I can sketch you an English cottage.'

'It must be big enough for a family,' Lupe added.

Saffron leaned in closer as Peridot began to sketch, 'Just make the windows a bit wider...that's better.'

'I like the garden but can you include a shed in it?' Lupe added.

As the pencil flicked across the page, they both nodded. 'Perfect.'

Mai smiled with approval as she looked at the finished design. Sophie's mouth fell open as a shimmering outline of the house appeared and settled into a solid brick construction before their eyes.

'Let's take a walk around inside and make sure that's what you had in mind, too,' Mai said.

Peridot sat with her sketchpad as the others stepped through the front door. She was lost in thought and it was several minutes before she realised that Sage was speaking to her.

'You've drawn another house. Who is this one for?'

Her face flushed a deeper green as she laughed. 'This place is where I often come to sketch. It's so bright compared to The Glen. I've designed my dream studio— light and airy.'

'So, why don't you ask Mai to build it for you?' Sophie suggested as Mai and Saffron appeared in the garden. 'Show Mai your design, Peridot.'

'We could set this up right now,' Mai said. She spread her hands and a shimmering image appeared, which solidified into a small stone building. 'Let's take a walk around and fix it up inside exactly as you want it.'

With a wide smile, Peridot eagerly followed her into the building.

'I'd like a glass conservatory at the back, to catch maximum light. And I'll need a wet area...' she began.

'We'll make that a shower room and we'll put a kitchen over here. You'll need to eat something if you're here all day,' Mai added.

'Oh, I hadn't planned on two storeys,' Peridot said peering up a narrow staircase.

'If you work late, you might want to sleep here,' Mai said beckoning her to follow her upstairs.

There were two good sized bedrooms and a small bathroom.

'Everyone needs a guestroom,' Mai explained.

Peridot walked to the window and gazed out at the view. 'This is the perfect place to live.' She seemed torn. 'Well to work, anyway. My aunt and uncle wouldn't be pleased if I moved out of Goblin Glen and they have done so much for me already. They hope that I will live with them until I settle down with someone from the Glen and we have our own family home there.'

'Is that what *you* want, Peridot?' Sage asked her.

She shook her head. 'Not really. I'd like to have my own place to live for a while. I'm in no rush to find a partner.'

'How about you take it slowly,' Sophie suggested. 'Start off by spending your working days here, then add an overnight stay, then gradually increase the nights you spend here.'

'Yes, then they'd have a chance to get used to the idea of you living independently,' Sage agreed.

'And we'll be neighbours!' Saffron grabbed Peridot's hands. 'It'll be so good to have you nearby.'

'Hopefully, before long, others will come to live here on The Plains. It could be the start of building bridges between the different kinds of people of Aurum.' Mai looked around her thoughtfully. Her brow cleared as she clicked her fingers in three different directions. There was a low rumbling sound, then three paved roads appeared, leading away from the new homes towards Goblin Glen, Faeville, and The Dark Forest.

'Now you can visit them or they can visit you easily by carriage, or even walking, it's not far.'

The sun was beginning to set as Sylvan appeared on the new road from Faeville. After admiring both new homes, he turned to Lupe. 'Are you ready to meet the family?'

With a nervous nod, Lupe took Saffron's hand and they set off towards the lights that sparkled and glowed above Faeville.

Peridot sighed. 'And it's time for me to tell my uncle and aunt about my new studio.'

'I'll come with you,' Mai said.

Sage slipped her arm through hers. 'Don't forget to tell them how beautiful it is.'

'And what great designs you'll be able to create there,' Sophie added.

'And point out that it's just a short walk from Goblin Glen itself,' Paris concluded. 'Especially with the new roads.'

Mai smiled as she followed them down the hillside.

They were making their way along one of the town's narrow streets, when a shout made them look up.

'Paris, girls! Come up and see our new home!' Brassion called from a window above them.

'Go on.' Peridot patted Sage's arm. 'We'll see you in The Square later on.'

The front door opened and the three youngsters climbed the stairs to be met by Lichen, Brassion, and two other goblins.

'Welcome to our new home.' Brassion spread his arms. 'And these are our neighbours—Herb and Reed.'

'Wow, this is a great place,' Paris said as he looked around the apartment.

'Yes, it's great and only a fifteen-minute walk from the college, too,' Lichen said. He carried in a tray of mugs and set them down on a small table.

The youngsters chatted together for a while until Herb looked out of the open window.

'Everyone's heading for The Square.'

'What's happening there?' Sage asked.

'The start of the Annual Festivities,' Lichen told her. 'Come on, it'll be standing room only soon.'

The sound of chatter and laughter grew louder as they reached the main square. It reminded Sage of the Parisian scenes she had seen in films. There were several cafes and restaurants with tables and chairs spilling out on to the pavement. Groups of small children ran in and out of the crowds. Two old men sat playing chess on a large board with several others recommending different moves and strategies to win the game. In one corner, a band was tuning up.

'Hey, let's get some ice cream before the dancing starts.' Herb led them to a barrow. There was a selection of ice cream tubs arranged in hues from a pale lime green to a dark bluish green.

'I'd recommend the Pampas Fonds if you like something sweet. Or the Blue Grass if you prefer a savoury taste.'

'I'm going for…' Lichen began.

'Cottage Borders—you always do!' Herb laughed.

'They're all shades of green,' Sophie noted. 'Do you have vanilla or strawberry?'

Lichen and Herb exchanged looks and let out peals of laughter. Herb patted her shoulder. 'You're so funny!'

'I take that as a no. Okay, let's be adventurous; I'll have a Dusk Pine.'

The three visitors were tentatively tasting the new flavoured ice creams when Peridot joined them.

'I see you're enjoying Sweet Pea's creations. What do you think?' she asked as she ordered a cone for herself.

'Delicious.' Paris nodded.

The talk moved on to the reaction of Peridot's relatives to her new studio.

'Mai was wonderful. She persuaded them to see the benefit of me having a bright and airy studio as a designer for the business.'

Lichen clapped his hands as the crowd suddenly moved into a large circle around the edge of the square. 'The dancing's about to start.' He grabbed Sophie's hand and paired her up with another young goblin, then did the same with Paris while he partnered Sage himself.

One of the bandsmen held up a flute. 'Let's go!'

Paris looked alarmed, but the young girl partnering him smiled. 'Don't worry. Just follow everybody else.'

Soon the whole circle was moving around in a lively dance similar to the country dances Sage remembered from her primary school. It involved a lot of skipping, twirling, and clapping. After each movement, the females moved on to a new partner and repeated the sequence.

As soon as the first dance ended, the band launched into a second one. This time the male dancers were the ones to move to a new partner after a series of complicated steps with each partner. Sophie caught Paris's eye and grinned as he stumbled trying to copy the steps.

After a few more lively dances, the band started to play a slower tune. Couples began to move around the floor in a dance that reminded Sage of a waltz, but with extra moves. After several minutes, she felt she had mastered the dance. Sophie seemed confident as she glided past with her partner but Sage spotted Paris spreading his hands and standing back to let another man take his place with his partner who was rubbing her foot.

Just after midnight, the band played the last dance and people began to make their way home. Sage made her way towards Mai who was talking to Brunswick.

'It's time we made our way back to the castle,' Mai told Brunswick. 'We've a busy day tomorrow. I want to show our guests as much as I can of Aurum this trip.'

'We'll see you at the Dragon Races on Sunday, won't we?' said Peridot.

'We wouldn't miss it for either world!'

'Dragon Races?' Paris asked.

'Yes, it's an annual event. A bit like the Grand National on Earth world but with dragons instead of horses. Now give me your hands…'

***

A moment later, they found themselves in the Great Hall of the castle.

'Tomorrow I'll take you on a full tour of the castle and its grounds,' Mai told them as they made their way to her apartment. 'Sunday it's the Dragon Races and on Monday there's the Faeville Dance.'

'This summer holiday is the best one ever!' Sophie exclaimed as the three friends reached their rooms.

Sage frowned as she caught sight of Paris's face as he turned towards his own room. 'What's up? Didn't you enjoy today?'

He sighed. 'Today was great. Except for the dancing. I was so useless. I trod all over poor Leaf's feet in the final dance. She was polite, but she looked really relieved when someone else took my place. You and Sage seemed to find it easy. And now I hear there's more dancing!'

'We were given the option of ballroom dancing in PE lessons last year. The last dance was a bit like a waltz,' Sage told him. 'It's easy, look...' She began to step up the corridor. 'One, two, three; one, two, three—that's the waltz. Now the goblin version is one, two, three and then two more little jumps, four, five. See?'

Paris scratched his head.

'Take my hand,' Sophie instructed, 'and put your other hand on my waist. Good. Now, slowly, one, two, three—move your other foot, that's it. Now face left and jump. Then face right and jump. That's it. Let's do it again...'

After ten minutes, Paris began to relax. 'Hey, I can do this! Oops, sorry, one, two, three; jump, jump...'

They continued to slowly dance up and down the corridor, finally stopping at a large, curved window seat. Both of them collapsed into it, giggling.

'You'll be ready to sweep the ladies off their feet at the next dance,' Sophie quipped as she pulled herself to her feet. She gave him an arch look. 'Handsome and a great dancer—what a catch!'

Paris blushed and looked away. 'I bet you say that to all your dance partners.'

Chapter Twenty-Four

The two girls were already there when Paris joined them in the kitchen the next morning.

'Good morning Paris.' Mai smiled. 'We're just planning a tour of the castle. We're going to start at the Great Hall and take a look around the old living quarters first of all.'

Paris sat beside them with a mug of tea. Sophie pushed a plate of toast towards him.

'I bet there's a great view from the battlements.'

'There is.' Mai nodded. 'We'll end our tour there. I've a surprise for you three.'

'A surprise?' Sophie looked up eagerly.

'Yes, I'll tell you all about it later.' She stood up, pushing back her chair. 'Now, let's go.'

Soon they were climbing the narrow, stone staircase.

'These steps are really worn, as if thousands of feet have trodden them,' Sage commented as they made their way upwards.

'I was thinking of a medieval castle where I lived for a while in Earth world many years ago when I designed this. I included as many features as I could recall.'

'Do you use the hall sometimes?' Paris asked as they entered the room.

'Not at the moment. Come and take a look at the armoury. Of course, we don't need to defend ourselves in Aurum now, so these are really just items of historical interest.'

After a brief look around the armoury, Sophie walked on ahead into a narrow corridor. She pushed open a wide wooden door. 'This must be someone's bedroom.'

A woman was polishing a mahogany desk which stood near the window. She nodded to them.

Sophie ran her hand over the embroidered curtains held back from the four-poster bed. 'This place is fit for a king!'

'Maybe it will house a king one day.' Mai smiled wistfully.

'Well, it hasn't for several hundred years,' the woman commented. 'That's how long I've been keeping this place ready.'

'And you will do so for another few centuries, if that's what it takes, Flavia.' Mai gave her a sharp glance.

Sophie had picked up a silk shirt that was hanging on a stand near the bed. There was also a jacket and a pair of leather trousers. On the floor was a pair of old-fashioned leather boots. 'It looks as if they are ready for someone to put them on.'

Mai put the shirt to her cheek. 'Everything is ready. The shirt is of the finest silk from the East. The trousers are the softest chamois from France. The boots, handmade in Italy.'

'Ready for what?'

There was a *tsk* from the woman. 'Exactly! Ready for what? I think—'

'Please, don't tell me again what you think,' Mai interrupted.

'What's through this door?' Sage grabbed Sophie as she sensed an argument brewing between the two women. Paris quickly followed them. They found themselves in a second larger turret. Stone steps took them up to a circular room. In the centre was a scrubbed wooden table. There were dark stains on its surface as if hot plates or containers had been placed on it over time. One half of the wall was covered in thick, wide shelves which held thousands of old leather-bound books. The remaining half was covered in crosses of every shape and size, from tiny ones that would decorate a necklace to larger ones that would not look out of place in a church. Some were gold encrusted with precious gems, some were plain metal, others were simple wood while others had intricate carvings.

'I've never soon so many crosses,' Sophie gasped. 'There must be hundreds of them!'

'Seven hundred and eighty-six, to be precise,' Mai said stepping into the room.

'It's a pretty impressive collection,' Paris commented. 'How long have you been collecting them?'

'Just over a thousand years. Ah,' she turned to Sage who was gently taking a book from the shelf. 'You've found my favourite spell book.'

Sage placed the book carefully on the table and opened it up. 'A spell book from the fourth century.'

'Yes.' Mai gently stroked Chinese characters written in ink on the old vellum. 'It was a present from my first teacher, a Wushi in the village where I grew up.'

'A Wushi?' Paris asked.

'A wizard or sorcerer. Apart from his sister Suyin, no-one else knew of his powers. He was considered an academic and sometimes taught the sons of some of the better off people of the area. Only boys were thought worthy of learning in those days. It was very unusual for girls to be educated as it was considered a waste of time. But he recognised my future powers long before I knew of them. He taught me to read Chinese and to speak and read Latin and explained the mysteries of numbers to me. But it was all done in secret. I would go with my mother each day to cook and clean for him and his sister and then we would spend an hour poring over his books. It was a happy time.'

'How old are you, Mai?' Sage asked her. 'And how did you end up in England?'

Mai smiled and shook her head as if awakening from a dream. 'Oh, that's a long story, for another time.'

Sophie placed another book on the table. 'This one is in English—well, old English.'

'This one is in hmm, Greek or maybe Russian,' Paris said as he looked through another book.

'And is this Arabic?' Sage asked, opening another. 'Can you read all of them?'

'It's a sorcerer's responsibility to read the great works from around the world. And I met many great teachers on my travels.'

'What about your collection of crosses?' Sophie asked. 'Did you collect these on your travels, too?'

A look of sadness washed over Mai's face. She shook her head. 'No, that's yet another story for another time…'

She closed the book she was holding and placed it carefully back on the shelf. 'Come on, you must see Flavia's kitchen and her gardens. She has made up a picnic basket for you. I won't be able to join you but Sylvan has offered to take you on a tour today and he's sure to find the best place to have your lunch. I have an appointment with Saffron and Lupe this afternoon. They have agreed to manage the visitors' applications between the two worlds and we have a number of issues to sort out before I meet with the area leaders in two weeks' time.'

Flavia seemed to have recovered her good mood when they reached the kitchen.

'I love the modern gadgets in the new kitchen, but there's nothing like preparing food and baking in a traditional kitchen like this one,' she told them, taking a tray of bread rolls from a large cast iron oven. A plate of cakes was laid next to it on the table. She took a wicker basket from a shelf. 'While I make up some sandwiches, you can pop outside and pick yourself some salad. And collect some eggs from the coop out there on the right.'

'Your garden is lovely,' Sage remarked as they came back with their selection of salad and eggs. 'And you have a beautiful display of flowers, too.'

'There is such a wide variety of crops growing in the fields nearby. Do you grow all this just for your family and Mai?' Sophie asked.

'Oh, no. We produce enough food for most of the communities around here. Every day, at least one cart will arrive to collect what their folk need. The crops are always ripe, there is no winter season here in Aurum, so there is plenty for everyone.'

'Where do they pay for everything?' Paris said.

'We don't have a need for money here,' Mai told them. 'If you contribute to life here, your needs will always be met.'

'It sounds like an ideal world.' Sage sighed.

'It's time for your tour.' Mai stood up. 'Sylvan should be on the battlements any minute now.'

Thanking Flavia and taking their carefully packed picnic, they followed Mai up to the castle roof.

'Ah, here they come,' Mai said, shielding her eyes and gazing at two growing specks in the sky.

Sophie's mouth fell open as the shapes approached. 'Dragons?'

'Yes, you're going to tour Aurum on Abraxas and Mimosa, two of our oldest and most gentle dragons. Don't worry, Sylvan is an experienced dragon flier—he's actually a jockey in the Dragon Races tomorrow.'

The two giant beasts slowly circled above them and then gently landed on the wide parapet, their long claws clattering on the stone. Sylvan jumped down from one of them.

Both creatures crooned softly as Mai began to pat their long snouts. She made a soft clicking noise with her tongue and pulled a handful of treats from her pocket.

Sylvan slapped the neck of one of them. 'This is Abraxas, our finest Greenback. And over here we have Mimosa, a Midnight Blue.' The second dragon ruffled her electric blue scales and gave Paris a curious sniff.

'Are you going to race one of them tomorrow?' he asked nervously.

Sylvan laughed. 'No, these two are not built for racing. If they were horses, they'd be more shire than racehorse. Here, give her a treat and pat her. Let them get to know you before we set off.'

Paris stepped forward and took a handful of treats from Sylvan. 'Here you are, girl.' He gingerly held his hand out to Mimosa and slowly relaxed as the huge mouth nibbled gently at his palm. He stroked the broad blue snout of the creature. 'She's beautiful. Just look at how her scales shine in the sun.'

Sage stepped forward as Sylvan gave her a handful of treats. 'Here's some for you, too, Abraxas. Ha, his tongue feels rough, just like a cat's. Come on, Sophie. Come and pat him.'

Sophie hesitated a moment as he pushed his face closer to her then slowly put her hand on his long neck. 'He feels so soft and warm.'

'Now that we're all introduced, you're ready to get going,' Mai said. She looked into Abraxas' large, slanting eyes. 'Look after our guests, won't you?'

Sylvan helped Paris on to Mimosa. 'Hold on to her collar if you need to. Now, Sophie, you sit in front of him; that's it.'

Once they were seated, he mounted Abraxas and helped Sage up in front of him. 'Are we all ready? Let's go.'

Sophie drew a sharp breath as she watched the waving figure of Mai diminish beneath them and clutched the collar tighter. 'I hope we don't fall off.'

Mimosa followed Abraxas upwards in a gentle, circular trail. Behind the castle the rolling plains gave way to a light mist.

'Is that the lake that Mai was visiting?' Sage asked Sylvan as she caught a glimpse of a sparkle of water.

'Yes, that's Mai's special place. We'll head over to Faeville now.'

Soon they were approaching the colourful lights and shapes above Faeville. There was the sound of gentle piped music which came to an abrupt stop as a loud voice cried out.

'No, no, no! Weren't you paying any attention for the past two hours?' They peered down into a clearing where a slight figure stood in front of a group of dancers.

'Benigno!' Sylvan laughed. 'He was one of the most famous dancers in Faeville. Now he's retired, he coaches the young hopefuls. He's a hard taskmaster.'

Sophie forgot her fears of falling as she smiled to see the dancers backing away from the tiny formidable coach as he continued his tirade. 'Now. From the beginning of the second act. Remember your new positions. And...two, three, four...'

'He doesn't sound very benign, does he?' Paris laughed.

By now they were flying though the main street of Faeville. Several people looked up and waved as they flew overhead. The stone cottages at the outskirts of the town had given way to larger buildings. There was a row of shops and a community hall flanking each side of an open green. Parents watched and gossiped as young children played on swings and slides nearby.

Sage read the sign above a group of low, stone buildings. '*College of Fae and Magic.* My mother must have studied there.'

'Yes, she would have. All fae attend the college from fifteen to eighteen. Some stay there for longer, depending on their particular skills,' Sylvan told her.

'Where is the school for the younger children?' Paris asked him.

'Fae, witches, and elves go to the school with the goblins in Goblin Glen until they're fifteen, then they follow their own education.'

As they left the town, they flew over a wide avenue with several exclusive properties standing in large grounds screened by tall pine trees.

'This is where the older fae live. The ones who didn't bequeath their immortality,' Sylvan told them.

'It looks like they're pretty rich,' Sophie commented.

'Yes. Some of the ones that live here have been around for over a thousand years, so they have acquired quite a bit of wealth. Most fae decide to bequeath their immortality and grow old with a partner, especially when they start their own families.'

'It would be a bit weird to have parents the same age as you, wouldn't it?' Sophie commented.

Sage pointed to the area bordering Faeville that was shrouded in a purple mist. 'What's in there? I thought I saw something moving.'

'Ah, that's Lilac Brae, home to the mythical creatures. Many of them are shy and stay hidden from sight, such as the unicorns and the wood nymphs. But the centaurs and satyrs can often be seen in Faeville and Goblin Glen. In fact, the satyrs can be quite mischievous.'

'I'd love to see a unicorn.' Sage sighed.

'Me, too!' Sophie agreed.

'Now we're crossing The Plains, heading for Goblin Glen,' Sylvan announced as the dragons veered to the left, crossing a wide expanse of grassland. 'The Plains extend from the castle all the way to the Portal between Earth world and Aurum.'

'I can see Saffron's and Peridot's houses down there,' Sophie said pointing downwards. 'And isn't that Mai talking to Peridot in her garden?'

'Yes, she said she was going to speak to her about the portrait she wants her to do for her.' Sylvan nodded as Mai and Peridot looked up and waved.

'That's where the young goblins jumped out at us,' Sage pointed out. 'And there's Pine's Diner.'

Several goblins looked up and waved.

They passed over the main street in town and turned into a wider road. There were flashes of gold and sparkles of different colours.

'This is the Jewellers Patch,' Sylvan explained. 'The streets aren't exactly paved with gold, but the shops are decorated with gold, silver, and assorted precious jewels. Quite a spectacular sight.'

'Wow,' Sophie uttered. 'Can we go down and take a closer look?'

'We could have our picnic on the hillside over there and afterwards we could take a walk down Gem Street, if you like.'

Paris groaned and rubbed his thighs as he dismounted onto the ground beside Mimosa. 'I don't know how you can be a dragon jockey, Sylvan.'

Sophie stroked the dragon's muzzle. 'But it wasn't at all frightening. I really enjoy riding a dragon.'

While the two dragons stretched out in the sunshine, Sylvan pointed out different landmarks of Goblin Glen while they ate their picnic.

'There's the First School, which all goblins and fae attend until they're fifteen. The tall building behind that is Goblin College and on the nearby hillside you can see the entrance to the mines.'

Once they had all eaten, they packed up the picnic basket and, leaving the dragons to sleep in the sunshine, made their way down to Gem Street.

Sage's eyes widened as she ran her hands over a bejewelled shop front. 'Are these real diamonds and rubies?'

'Of course, goblins don't do paste.'

'Fancy having your name spelled out in precious jewels,' Sophie said as she looked up at the dazzling sign above a shop.

'It is a little bit showy, isn't it?' someone whispered behind her.

She looked up. 'Peridot! Is this where you work?'

'Just across the road. I'm putting together some ideas for a costume for one of the elder fae for her nine hundredth birthday party next month. Come in and have a look.'

A liveried goblin opened the door of a small shop as they crossed the road. A sign above the window read *Ruby's Emeralds*, each word decorated with the appropriate stones. In the window itself was a single ruby necklace displayed on a green velvet background. Inside the shop there was a hushed, reverent atmosphere.

'Here are our visitors from Earth world, Mint,' Peridot told an older goblin woman who came forward to greet them. 'They're going to have a look around the studio.'

She led them to a small room where a desk held a pile of papers. Next to it stood an easel with several sketches. There was an open cabinet containing trays of different jewels nearby.

'Our client has sent me pictures of the costumes she wore at the last five celebrations. She wants something completely different this time. I've also been advised that it must not look anything like costumes worn by the other elder fae at their celebrations,' Peridot told them.

Paris flicked through the papers which were pictures of different fae wearing elaborate gowns. 'It must be hard to come up with something completely different to all of these.'

She turned to the easel. 'Well, all these gowns have one thing in common—they're very ornate. I thought I'd go for something simple, but expensive. I've made a few sketches. What do you think?'

Sage stepped forward as she spread out her designs. 'That one is lovely. I prefer the simpler look with fewer jewels.'

Sophie frowned. 'If it's all about telling everyone how wealthy you are, I don't think she'll be satisfied with that.'

'That's what Brunswick said.' Peridot sighed. 'Perhaps I should be going for the over-the-top look. It's not very original though and I really want to make my own mark on the design front, not just copy other designers' ideas.'

'Hmm, you can make gold thread…is it possible to weave the actual dress from spun gold?' Sophie suggested.

'You might have something there, Sophie. Then the design can be both simple and also appear very expensive.' She picked up a spool of gold thread from the cabinet. 'This is too thick, but if we can get a finer thread which is strong enough…I'm going to go down to the workshop straight away and see what they can come up with. Brunswick's new secret weapon!'

'We'll fly over the Dark Forest next,' Sylvan told them as they mounted the dragons a short while later. 'Most of it is quite dense, but you can make out a few interesting features.'

'There's Delbert's home.' Paris pointed out the marble mansion in the centre of the forest.

Sophie shuddered. 'That dark brown area must be the swamp I was stuck in.'

'Are there any…pretty…places in the Dark Forest?' Sage asked.

'It's no good asking me that.' Sylvan smiled. 'As you know, fae don't venture into The Dark Forest. Anyway, it's time to get you back to the castle, now. Abraxas and Mimosa will need a rest tonight as they're transporting the goblins to the races tomorrow.'

Chapter Twenty-Five

'The Dragon Races are one of the highlights of the year here in Aurum,' Mai told them at breakfast the next morning. 'Sylvan came in fifth in his race last year. From his training times, he's expected to do much better tomorrow but he's up against some formidable fae and goblin champions. I think he'll have quite a few people betting on him this year.'

'If you don't use money here, how do you bet?' Sophie looked puzzled.

'Everyone is given ten pieces at the gate. You choose how to place them—you can put them all on one race or on a couple or spread them over all the races. At the end of the day, the person who got the biggest returns gets their name on this year's board alongside the winning jockeys' names. Some of the older goblins take their bets very seriously. Brunswick had his name up there for three years running. He was knocked off by Mercy last year, so he's been keeping a very close eye on the race training sessions this year. We'll leave here in about an hour so we have time to chat to everyone before the races start. Wait in the Great Hall and we'll leave from there.'

***

The three friends could feel the excitement in the atmosphere as they arrived just outside a stone gate set into a long stone wall that disappeared into mist on either side. Above the gate was a large carved statue of a dragon.

'Mai!' The goblin gatekeeper shook her hand warmly. 'And you've Earth world guests with you today. It's a pleasure to meet you all. I hope you enjoy today.'

'Haraa, it's lovely to see you, too. How are your wife and children?'

'They are all very well, thank you. Our eldest, Rush, has her first ride today in the fourth race. She's been training hard these past few months. Sylvan's been giving her some tips.'

'Let's hope she does well.'

'Here are your programmes and pieces.' Haraa handed them each a muslin bag. 'Oh, here come the two goblin carriages. It's going to get busy.'

Sage looked around as there was a loud rush of wings. Abraxas and Mimosa were landing gently on the ground nearby. Each one pulled a long carriage filled with goblins. Amidst the green faces, she spotted Lupe waving at her. Soon he stood beside them.

'Where's Saffron?' Paris asked him.

'She orbed with Peridot. They told me to wait here for them. Ah, here they are.'

Once everyone had been issued with a muslin bag, they made their way inside. They were now in a flat, sandy area with small canvas booths set up between the first gate and a second stone wall. The place was packed with goblins and fae and the air was filled with laughter and chatter. At every few steps Mia was stopped by someone. She gestured for the others to go on ahead.

'Before we do anything else, we'd better get in line to bet on the first few races,' Saffron said, ushering them towards one of the booths. As she spoke to the fae teller, Sage turned to Peridot. 'Are you fae on your mother's or father's side?'

'Mother's,' she replied. 'Brunswick is my father's brother.'

'You're half fae?' Sophie's eyebrows raised.

'Isn't it obvious from my skin? And from my name?'

'Peridot is a green stone, isn't it?'

'Yes, but look at the first part of the word…'

'Oh. *Peri*! I see the link now. So, you can visit Earth world when you want, can't you?'

'I'd love to, but it would be hard to fit in with green skin. And I wouldn't like to have to stay out of sight like the Earth world goblins.'

'Maybe there's a magic spell that can help you with that,' Sage suggested.

'I haven't heard of one yet.'

'Has everyone placed their bets?' Saffron said as she and Lupe joined them, both holding several paper slips.

'I've bet on the first three races. I want to speak to Mercy and Brunswick before I place any further bets,' Paris replied.

'Everyone ready? Let's join them in the arena.' Peridot led them towards a large entrance in the inner wall. It was shaped like a dragon's head, with its yawning mouth the entrance to the tunnel. Huge emerald eyes gleamed down on them as they entered the tunnel which itself was encrusted with rubies and diamonds.

'This is amazing,' Sophie whispered, overawed by the dazzling display.

The tunnel opened out onto the top steps of the arena which reminded Sage of an ancient Greek or Roman theatre. Tiers of stone steps were arranged around an oval pool. Brunswick and Holly, his wife, waved them over to the other side of the arena where several silk cushions were arranged on the marble steps. Holly patted one of them. 'Make yourself comfortable. The first race will be starting in about half an hour.' She turned to the woman sitting next to her. 'This is Vera, her daughter Cora is taking part in the dragon races for the first time today. Vera, these are the youngsters from Earth world we were talking about, the ones Cora was so keen on meeting.'

Vera sighed. 'Cora is always thinking about the next dangerous thing she can do—ride dragons, visit Earth world...' I wish she could get it all out of her system and just settle down happily.'

Sage looked at the woman. She was tall and thin with pointed features. Dressed in a tailored grey trouser suit with her black hair pulled up into a tight bun, she had an air of severity about her. 'Well, it's good to be ambitious, isn't it?'

Vera pursed her thin lips. 'I can only hope it's a phase she's going through.'

As they settled themselves down, Holly hugged Saffron to her. 'It's so good to have you back, we've missed you so much.' She gave Lupe a nervous handshake. 'And lovely to meet your young man, too.'

'What's happening up there?' Sage asked Holly as five bright orbs circled above their heads.

'They're marking out the course and the starting gates.'

'And those others are setting up the posts,' Brunswick continued. 'Each jockey has to collect one of their own flags on each lap.'

'Why is there a pool?' Sage asked her. 'Do they have to swim, too?'

Saffron giggled. 'No, that's to make a soft landing for the riders who fall off.'

Paris moved into a seat beside Brunswick and they were soon engrossed in a discussion on the merits of the riders and their mounts.

Hearing someone call her name, Sage looked up to see Mercy arrive with Flame and Flora. She noticed the look of annoyance that flashed across Sophie's face as Flame managed to squeeze herself in between Paris and Lupe.

'Here come the dragons and their riders!' Peridot pointed to the four dragons emerging from the cloud above them. The largest one was a bright orange colour; the smallest was a mixture of dark blue and purple. The two others were a mixture of greens and yellows. As they flew around the arena, the crowd began to whistle and cheer, many of them waving scarves in the colours of their chosen jockeys.

'There's Cora, on the yellow dragon,' Holly pointed out.

A deep voice sounded out over the arena and everyone fell silent. 'Competitors to the starting gates.' There was a pause as they lined up behind their gates. 'Prepare. Three, two, one, go!'

The gates flew upwards and the jockeys urged on their mounts. The beat of huge wings and flashes of fire filled the arena. There was a cry of dismay from a group of spectators as one of the riders slipped from her dragon as she reached for her first flag. She plunged into the pool as her riderless dragon soared upwards and disappeared into the clouds. Vera gave a gasp and stood up.

'Cora!'

A head bobbed up from the pool and two assistants helped the young girl climb out. She laughed and gave her mother a wave as she made her way to the changing rooms.

Meanwhile, the other three dragons were continuing in a tight huddle. The tension mounted in the final lap as the smallest dragon began to pull ahead of the others. The jockey on the orange dragon urged him on. The crowd rose as the two beasts neared the finishing line. With a shout of triumph, the blue and purple dragon shot over the finishing line seconds before his larger rival.

'My dragon won!' Sophie jumped up and down, waving her betting slip.

'He was a complete outsider.' Brunswick shook his head.

'There are always plenty of surprises at the Dragon Races.' Mercy grinned.

The crowd began to settle down again as the fae marked out the new course and set up the flag posts.

'Here come the riders,' Saffron said, standing up and waving a yellow scarf at her brother who gave her a wide smile as he flew by towards the starting gates.

As the gates flew upwards, Saffron and Mercy stood up, clutching each other's hands.

'You can do it, Sylvan, you can do it,' Mercy muttered to herself. 'Gently does it with the flag…perfect!'

There were disappointed murmurs from their group as two of the dragons surged forward, leaving Sylvan and the other jockey behind.

'Come on, Sylvan!' Paris shouted as they sped past. 'One more lap to go!'

Sylvan leaned forward and whispered into his dragon's ear. The beast gave a shiver, then letting out a long plume of fire, gave a powerful thrust of his wings. Slowly, he began to draw level with the dragon ahead of him. With half a lap to go, he pushed himself forward until he was nearing the first dragon.

By this time, Sage and Sophie were standing, motionless.

'Go! Go! Go!' Lupe whispered.

The two dragons were neck and neck as they reached the finishing line. With a loud cry, Sylvan's rival spurred his dragon on to finish a nose ahead of him.

'What bad luck!' Mercy shook her head.

'He came second, that's pretty good,' Lupe said.

Saffron smiled. 'Yes, he did well. He told me that he'd be pleased if he could just improve his performance on last year.'

They settled themselves into their seats as the riders appeared for the next race.

'That's Rubio on Firemaker,' Brunswick told Paris, pointing to the largest dragon, a red-scaled beast. 'I've my money on him. He's the most experienced of the fae jockeys.'

'He has to be, on Firemaker,' Mercy commented. 'I don't know how anyone can handle that creature!'

The four dragons were standing behind the starting gates when Firemaker began to buck and snort. Rubio leaned forward, patting his neck and murmuring softly until he calmed down. The countdown ended and the gates shot upwards. Off they went, a compact group until they reached the first flag. The goblin on the smallest dragon reached over too far and went tumbling downwards, catching Firemaker with his heel as he passed by. The red dragon reacted by rearing up and tossing his rider off before he turned his attention towards the goblin jockey. The crowds held their breath as the dragon eyed the terrified goblin who was pulling himself from the water. As the young jockey began to scramble to his feet, Rubio orbed and reappeared on the back of his mount.

The voice of the starter came across the arena, quietly urging the spectators to silence as Rubio patted the head of Firemaker, whispering in his ear once again. They watched, trembling as the stream of smoke from his nostrils slowly dwindled away. White faced, Rubio steered his dragon high into the clouds above them, where they disappeared from sight. The other jockeys brought their dragons down to the ground and helped the still shaking goblin to his feet.

The entire crowd seemed to let out a gasp of relief as the jockeys were taken from the arena in a small carriage and soft music filled the air. Sage listened to the snatches of conversation around her:

'...too highly strung...'

'...a danger to the public...'

'...tighter controls...'

'...only Rubio could have pulled it off...'

The voice sounded out again. 'Thank you for your cooperation. We're going to take an earlier break than usual today and continue with today's races in just over two hours' time. Refreshments are available at the gateway.'

Sophie clutched Sage's arm. 'That was so scary!'

Mai appeared by her side and patted her shoulder. 'Yes, it doesn't usually get that exciting until the last few races.'

'Remember last year?' Flame said to Flora, as she and Paris joined them, her arm tucked firmly in his.

'The clash in the sixth race? One of the young dragons broke her wing.'

'Yes, we used up all the healing potion supplies we had here and had to send for extra supplies from Faeville,' Mercy added. 'Luckily, she made a good recovery.'

'Let's hope that's all the excitement we'll be getting today!' Holly said.

Brunswick said, 'I don't know about you, but I'm ready for some of those fae cakes.'

'And a glass of Greenade,' his wife added.

Mercy looked at Flame and Flora. 'Come on, you two. I've spotted a Meadowsip stall.'

Flame looked torn for a moment, but let go of Paris's arm and hurried after her. 'Keep me a seat for the second half,' she called out as she left.

Mai smiled and shook her head as Paris let out a sigh. 'Flame—she's a bit too hot, isn't she? We'll get her a seat by Brunswick for the second half and you three can sit together.'

'Unless you'd prefer to sit with your new girlfriend?' Sophie raised an eyebrow.

'She's not my girlfriend, no way!'

'How about we go somewhere a bit quieter for the break once we've placed our bets for the second half?' Mai suggested. A short while later, she drew them to one side and said, 'Give me your hands…'

***

The three friends looked around at their new surroundings. They were standing on a grassy hillside that sloped down gently to a lake. Above them, the grassland gave way to rocky outcrops that rose high into the sky. Opposite them was deep green forest-covered mountain. On their left a white, marble plateau stretched as far as the eye could see, while on the right snow-covered peaks could be glimpsed through a drifting blue mist.

Suddenly, Paris pointed to a movement in the mists. 'I just saw a dragon over there.'

'Where?' Sophie cried, peering into the distance. 'Oh, I saw something move, over there in the forest.'

'And there are two down there in the lake!' Sage added excitedly.

'You'll see lots of dragons around here,' Mai told them. 'This is Dragon Land, the part that visitors rarely see.'

'It's made up of so many different kinds of landscapes,' Paris commented.

'Yes,' Mai agreed. 'When we first created Aurum, we had to accommodate the many different species of dragons that exist. Not all dragons like the same environment, so we created the ideal surroundings for each kind.'

Suddenly the ground trembled and an orange mist rose from behind the mountain range opposite them.

'What was that?' Sophie shivered and moved closer to Paris.

'Nothing to worry about,' Mai reassured her. 'Over there is the volcanic region. Some dragons like the heat and the fire.'

As they watched, a dragon landed on the mountainside opposite and a figure slid down from its back and patted the long, red, muzzle.

'There's Rubio, taking Firemaker home. It looks as if he's calmed him down.'

The dragon soared into the air and dived down into the red mist. Rubio disappeared from view, then reappeared as a bright orb nearby.

'Rubio,' Mai greeted him as the fae materialised.

'I thought it was you, Mai, and our Earth world visitors. Are you taking a break from the races?'

'I'm just giving our friends a taste of Dragon Land,'

'You've chosen the right time. I spotted Flax heading for the marble caves as I flew Firemaker home.'

'The marble caves…so it might be today?' Mai's eyes lit up.

'Indiga is guarding the higher cave, so there could very well be a hatching today.'

'A hatching?' Sage gasped. 'You mean a dragon hatching from an egg?'

'Can we go and see?' Sophie said excitedly.

'We can watch from this side, but Indiga isn't going to let us anywhere near the cave,' Mai told them. 'And we'll have to be very quiet. Follow me.'

They followed her around the hillside until they were standing opposite a slate grey mountainside where several cave openings were visible. A dark blue dragon appeared at one of the cave entrances and let out a long stream of smoke. Mai held out a hand and blew across her palm. Sparkles of silver drifted across and landed gently at the dragon's feet. She raised her head and peered around until she spotted the small group.

'I've let her know we're not interfering, that she has nothing to worry about,' Mai explained.

The dragon settled down outside the cave as a young goblin climbed up the hillside towards her before the two of them disappeared into the cave.

'She's not scared of him, is she?' Paris said.

'No.' Rubio shook his head. 'Flax has been friends with Indiga since he was not much more than a toddler. His father would bring him with him on his rounds when he was the warden here himself. Once he was old enough Flax took over his father's job. Indiga will be glad of his company today at the hatching of her firstborn.'

For the next few moments, pale blue and yellow flashes were visible inside the cave and a thin grey trickle of smoke filtered into the air. Then all was still. Sage could hear her own breathing in the silence as the minutes seemed to stretch out. Suddenly there was a low guttural rumbling sound. Flax appeared at the cave entrance with a broad smile. He waved across to them and held up two thumbs before disappearing from sight once more.

Mai beamed at them. 'A new dragon today. The first new-born in fifty years!'

'Will we get to see it?' Paris asked.

Mai shrugged. 'Some dragon mothers will let us catch a glimpse...others can be rather overprotective. Let's wait a few minutes and see...'

Their eyes were fixed on the cave as the low guttural noises continued. Sage gripped Sophie's arm as a shadow became visible in the mouth of the cave. Indiga appeared, moving slowly with a tiny figure half hidden beneath her. With a soft mewl, the newly hatched dragon stumbled forwards, blinking in the bright sunshine. The new mother swept up the little one and began to groom it with her tongue, her soft calls mingling with its high-pitched squeals.

Sophie let out a long breath. 'Oh, my life; a new-born dragon!'

'Amazing,' Paris whispered, while Sage could only nod her head.

After several more minutes, Indiga rose up and taking her young by the scruff of the neck, retreated back into the darkness of the cave.

'Well.' Mai broke the silence. 'You've witnessed a very rare occasion today. There will be an announcement of the new arrival after the final scores are read out this afternoon. We'd better rejoin the others. But we're not allowed to say anything until the official announcement. We'll have to keep this to ourselves for the time being.'

***

Flame pouted at Paris when they reached their seats shortly afterwards. She patted the seat beside her. 'Where have you been? We couldn't find you anywhere.'

'I took them for a walk.' Mai smiled, slipping into the empty seat and continuing before she could protest. 'You three, sit down over there. The next race is due any minute. Who's in this one? Ah, I've bet on Grassia. I'm sure she'll come first in this one. She did so well last year.'

'I've three pieces on Bracken.' Brunswick tapped the programmes in his hand. 'It was only a fluke of luck that gave Grassia first position last year.'

'My pieces are on a fae—Zephyr, to be precise,' Mercy added.

'No, no. Not this race. Not on these dragons.' Brunswick sat back and began to expand on his ideas. Soon there was a heated debate between the two of them.

'I put my piece on Puck because it's such a pretty name,' Sage told Sophie.

'I wonder if it's male or female.'

'Female.' Sage pointed to her programme. 'Look, she's seventy-five—quite young for a fae jockey—and she's…'

'No. Not the jockey. The…'

Paris put his arm around Sophie's shoulders and pulled her close to him. 'Some things you can't talk about.'

'Oh, my goodness. Of course. My lips are sealed!'

Flame shot an angry look as the two huddled together but her attention was diverted as Flora pointed to the dragons heading for the starting gate.

All four dragons were a dull, green colour and were of a small, stocky build. The two goblin jockeys gave each other a high five as they lined up. One of the two fae riders smiled and waved to an excited group of supporters who were standing holding a large banner bearing "Puck" in the jockey's colours.

'Both you and Saffron have backed the same jockey in this race,' a voice said near Sage. She looked up as Sylvan sat down between her and Saffron, pointing at her betting slip. 'Puck has a strong following.'

He laughed when Lupe told him she had chosen her just for the name. 'There they go! Puck has more experience than the others in the race. The new jockeys tend to start off too quickly and can't keep up the momentum. See, Puck doesn't seem too worried to be left behind in the first lap.'

Flame and Flora were cheering on the second fae as the riders sped past them. Their cheers grew quieter as Zephyr started to fall back in the second lap with Bracken and Grassia moving ahead.

Brunswick stood up as Bracken pulled into the lead, but a frown soon darkened his brow as Puck began to build up speed and draw close to him.

'Go on, girl!' Sage whispered, clenching her fists.

Saffron clasped her hands together and watched silently.

'Come on!' Brunswick cried. 'Keep your lead! Don't let up!'

A minute later he gave a howl of dismay as Puck crossed over the finish line a neck ahead of Bracken. 'Today's definitely for the fae.' He shook his head and turned to Mercy. 'It won't be my name up there this year.'

'It won't be mine either. Even if your team, Gold Sands, win the relay, Sylvan, I won't have enough points. But I'd still like to see you win.'

'I'll do my best, Mercy,' he answered, preparing to orb. 'Wish me luck!'

Saffron kissed his cheek. 'We're all behind you.'

'How many jockeys are in each team in the relay?' Paris asked Brunswick as they watched the new lanes being prepared.

'One per team,' Brunswick explained. 'It's not exactly a relay as you would imagine it to be. There are four dragons and four jockeys. But there are also four fixed riders—they're trainee jockeys who actually stay with the same dragon in this race. It's a flat, four lap race this time, with a loop at the end of each lap. During the race, Sylvan and the other three jockeys have to move from dragon to dragon, tying their colour to each dragon collar, then get back to their own dragon before they cross the finishing line.'

'What happens if two jockeys end up on one dragon at the same time?' Sage said.

'The first one is disqualified and must dismount— either orb or dive into the pool,' Mercy told her.

'Here they come,' Mai said, looking up as four dragons appeared from the clouds and made a lap of the arena amidst much cheering and waving. Sylvan smiled as Saffron waved her yellow scarf.

'The relay dragons are short-winged with longer, more slender bodies compared to most of the other racing dragons,' Brunswick pointed out to Sage and her friends. 'They tend to glide, too. That makes it easier for the riders to bring them closer together for the changeovers.'

The arena grew quiet as the dragons lined up behind the starting gates. The voice called out the countdown and the gates flew upwards. At the back of each dragon, the jockeys crouched ready to leap to the next animal.

'He's done it!' Flame cried as Sylvan jumped onto the dragon on his right a second after its jockey had left it. She smiled as he tied a streaming yellow scarf to the dragon's collar.

'He'd better get a move on,' Mai muttered as she watched another jockey readying himself to leap onto the same dragon.

Sylvan stumbled as he jumped just before the next jockey landed, holding on to the tail of his intended mount.

'Pull yourself up! You've the first loop coming up!' Mercy called out. She gasped as Sylvan inched his way up the dragon's neck, clinging tightly as it dived into a neat loop. 'Oh, that was *so* close!'

'That's two scarves,' Flame said. 'Two to go. The fixed rider should be getting them closer to the one on the righthand side, not that one, surely?'

'No, the rider's right,' Brunswick argued. 'The jockey over there is undecided about his course. Sylvan might jump and miss the dragon entirely.'

'I can't see how they know which way to jump,' Sage whispered to Sophie.

She nodded. 'And those loops! How do they stay on?'

'Three scarves for Sylvan!' Lupe cried.

'The blue jockey has tied three scarves, too,' Sophie commented. 'Keep going, keep going, Sylvan!'

Saffron peeped from behind her fingers as her brother steadied himself before jumping with his last scarf. 'I know you can do this Sylvan!'

The fixed rider was shouting to the blue jockey as he steadied himself to leap onto the neighbouring dragon. Before he could jump, a second jockey had joined him.

Cheers and groans rose up as the blue jockey orbed.

Unaware of the developments, Sylvan tied his last scarf and looked around to see where his own dragon was. After a brief exchange with the fixed rider, the dragon made its final loop and twisted and turned until it was level with his original mount. The jockey tying his scarf on to its neck urged his rider to move out of reach, but Sylvan and his rider were not to be outmanoeuvred. The rider guided the dragon into an upward movement until it was hovering over the original mount. Sylvan slid to one side and dropped down onto the dragon a minute before the unsuspecting jockey knew what he had planned. With a sad shrug, the goblin jockey dived gracefully into the pool.

Sylvan raised his arms in victory as his dragon flew over the finishing line well ahead of the jockey in second place.

The crowd stood and cheered as the dragons disappeared into the clouds.

'What excitement!' Mercy said, fanning her face with her programme. 'It's a good job it was the final race, I couldn't sit through that again.'

'Look, they're putting up the announcement board,' Flora commented. 'The final scores are in.'

'I hope Gold Sands has done well,' Saffron said, her eyes fixed on the hovering screen as words and numbers formed.

The voice sounded out over the now silent arena. It began to extol the virtues of each jockey and the great sportsmanship each one had displayed.

'Just tell us who won!' Flame muttered.

'For speed and agility, the following scores were awarded,' the voice continued, reading out a number after each team. 'Points gained for perseverance are as follows...' It listed the four scores. 'Imagination and intuition scores as you can see from the display are very close this year.' There was a pause. 'And finally, with the total scores we have in fourth place Purple River; Blue Haze in third place; Grey Mist is second so that means Gold Sands is our overall winner!'

Cheers rose up again as the four teams emerged from the clouds and rode their dragons around the arena.

'And our betting champion this year is a surprise outsider. Congratulations to Paris, our visitor from Earth world.'

'Your name will be up there right next to the winning team!' Sophie shrieked giving him a hug.

As the excitement died down and the dragon riders disappeared up into the clouds again, the voice called for silence. Staff were circulating amongst the tiers, handing out glasses of Meadowsip and Greenade.

'We have a very important announcement to make...Ladies and Gentlemen, we are delighted to announce our first dragon hatching in fifty years! Please raise your glasses to the safe arrival of our new-born!'

A picture of Indiga and the blurred outline of her young one peering from beneath her body was shown on the screen.

'We saw it! We *actually* saw it!' Sophie cried excitedly.

'Really?' Mercy asked. 'Is that where you were during the break?'

'We just happened to be in the right place at the right time.' Mai beamed. 'A really lucky coincidence.'

'Rubio saw Flax heading for the caves and we were able to find a spot on the hillside just opposite. After a few moments, Indiga came out with her young one,' Paris continued.

'What a wonderful thing to happen on your holiday from Earth world,' Saffron said as the others gathered around Sophie and Paris. She moved closer to Sage and put her hand on her arm. 'As you're feeling in such a good mood, I wonder if I could ask a big favour?'

'Of course.' Sage smiled. 'If I can help at all.'

Saffron moved her away from the crowd. 'I've been invited to supper with Grey and his family in the Dark

Forest tomorrow. Lupe is so pleased. He says they're all looking forward to meeting me so much.'

'That's great news, isn't it?'

Saffron played with her hands. 'It is, I know that…it's just…I can't tell Lupe; I don't want to offend him or his friends…but…'

'You're nervous, aren't you?'

Saffron nodded. 'For nearly a hundred years I have listened to tales of the fate of fae at the hands of shifters and vampires. And now they've invited me to dine with them.'

'Mai said it's all talk with the vampires and shifters and there is no record of them ever harming a fae. I'm half fae and I survived our last trip into the Dark Forest,' Sage reassured her. 'Would it help if I came with you?'

Saffron gave her a hug. 'Oh, Sage! That's exactly what I was going to ask you. Would you do that?'

Sage took a deep breath. 'Well, the Dark Forest is the only place we haven't visited officially, anyway. I wonder if Paris and Sophie would come, too?'

Paris moved towards them. 'Did I hear my name mentioned?'

'Actually, we were planning a bit of an adventure for tomorrow…in a place we haven't visited this trip…' Sage began.

Saffron gave him details of their conversation.

'Oh.' Paris looked at the ground for a while. 'Okay. Count me in. That's two of us.'

'Hey, you two aren't planning on going anywhere without me, are you?' Sophie said, joining the group.

'You want to come, too?' Paris asked.

'For sure. I'm not being left out!' she retorted. 'Where are we going anyway?'

'I'll explain on the way home.' Sage smiled.

Chapter Twenty-Six

'I wonder what tomorrow will be like,' Sophie said to Sage as they made their way to the kitchen the next morning.

'Are you having second thoughts about visiting the Dark Forest?'

'Not at all; I'd hate to be left out of an adventure that you two were going on.'

'Even if it's dangerous?' Paris added.

'I told you that I wouldn't let you go there if there was any danger,' Mai said as they entered the kitchen.

'I wish you were coming with us,' Sophie said.

'I'm afraid I can't cancel my appointment but luckily Vinnie has just arrived back from Earth world and she said she'd love to look after you today.'

Seated next to her was a tall, slender, pale girl of about their age.

Sage noticed how cold her hand felt as it briefly brushed her own. 'Sage isn't it? And you must be Sophie and Paris.'

'Vinnie lives in the Dark Forest at Delbert's house,' Mai told them.

'I thought I could give you a tour of the Forest before supper at Grey's. I'm sure Malbeam would be happy to bring Delbert's coach here earlier than arranged.'

'That would be interesting.' Sage nodded. 'We've only seen a small part of the Dark Forest up to now.'

Vinnie raised an eyebrow. 'Yes, Delbert told me about your first meeting.'

Sophie sat down at the table and pulled a cup towards her. 'Anyone else want a cup of tea?' she asked, picking up the teapot. She poured cups for the two others and looked at Vinnie.

'Yes, please. One sugar. Thank you.' She pulled the cup towards her and began to stir it.

Mai shook her head. 'What are you doing, Vinnie?'

'Sorry. It's a habit from spending so much time in Earth world. It's a *blending in* trick. I never actually drink it.'

'Whereabouts in Earth world were you, Vinnie?' Paris asked.

'On this trip, I started off in Winchester, then the trail took me to Rome and on to Istanbul, where I found what I had been looking for.' She smiled and patted an open package on the table in front of her.

'Can I have a look?' Sage asked. She unwrapped a small gold cross. On the back was a Latin inscription. 'This is beautiful.'

'Are you going to put it up with your collection?' Sophie looked at Mai.

'Oh, I hope not!'

Sophie, Sage and Paris exchanged puzzled looks.

'I heard rumours of another selection smuggled out of England and into France in the ninth century. I could follow that up. If need be.' Vinnie patted Mai's hand.

Mai nodded. 'If…if…yes, please follow up any leads…until we find the…' She bit her lip and walked over to the window. 'It's a beautiful day. I think a tour of the Dark Forest is a great idea. Can you speak to Malbeam, Vinnie? You could leave straight after lunch.'

***

That afternoon, they stood waiting for her on the castle parapet.

'Here's Vinnie and Malbeam,' Mai said as a black coach appeared in the sky.

There was a clash of steel on stone as the hooves of the two jet black horses landed on the wall. The coach driver gave a shout, pulling at the reins as the coach landed heavily behind them. He was dressed in a sombre black suit. Stepping down, he raised his top hat to reveal dark green hair tied back in a low ponytail. He held out a gloved hand to Mai with a slight bow.

'Good day, my lady.'

'Good day, Malbeam. This is an honour, Delbert's personal driver and coach.' Mai smiled, shaking his hand.

'Yes, I managed to persuade him that we deserve the best coach and horses,' Vinnie added as she stepped from the coach and stood beside him.

Paris gave a nervous laugh. 'The horses seem very lively.'

As if to underline his words, one of the horses pawed the ground and reared up on its hind legs.

Malbeam patted his neck and gave a laugh. 'Easy there, Midnight, you'll frighten the youngsters.'

The second horse laid back its ears and snorted as Vinnie stepped forward and stroked its nuzzle. 'What a crosspatch you are, Darkness.'

'Let's get going.' Malbeam held open the coach door. 'I'll need to have the coach back by sundown to take Delbert to Grey's house this evening.'

As soon as they were all seated, Malbeam gave a loud shout and flicked the reins. The three friends found themselves flung back against the seats as the coach rose into the air.

Vinnie laughed at the look on their faces. 'Don't worry. Once we're on the ground it will be a smoother ride.' She peered out of the window for a few moments. 'Hold on tight, we're landing now.'

The horses gave a loud whinny as the coach bumped to the ground. They could hear Malbeam calling to someone, the creak of metal gates being opened and then they were making their way along a shady pathway through a dense forest.

Vinnie leaned out of the window and shouted, 'Malbeam, let's head to the waterfall first.'

The coach swung off the pathway and they followed a sandy trail uphill. As they drew to a halt, Vinnie opened the door and jumped out, helping the others down.

'The best view is from the water.' She led them down a narrow slope to a lagoon. A boat was tied up to an ancient wooden pier. They scrambled in and Vinnie began to row the boat away from the pier. 'There,' she said. 'Have you ever seen such a sight?'

Sage and her friends were silent as they looked at the scene before them. Two giant steps of rock rose up steeply in front of them. On the top level, two large waterfalls spilt down onto the second level. This split into three separate waterfalls that cascaded down into the lagoon.

'Wow! It's so beautiful,' Sophie sighed as the others nodded silently.

Vinnie gave a mysterious smile as she edged the boat closer to the falls. 'Watch carefully.'

As they watched, shadowy figures emerged in front of the streams of water. Sophie gasped as the figures solidified. 'Is that you, Vinnie?' she asked as a young woman and a girl settled themselves down on the sand, talking and laughing animatedly.

Vinnie nodded. 'I'm with my mother, I'm about ten there.'

'Oh, these are memories, aren't they?' Sage said.

Vinnie nodded again. 'I have many happy memories of days spent with my mother when Father was away on business. I have no happy memories of *him*! He would have had me married off to a man old enough to be my grandfather when I was fourteen years old. It was only the intervention of my mother that stopped him. She managed to convince him that I needed more guidance to be a good wife before such a commitment.'

She sighed. 'I was seventeen when Mama died. It was a terrible time. The day after we buried her, Father told me my wedding would go ahead the following week. That's when I decided ending my life would be preferable. But it didn't work out the way I had planned. Delbert came to my rescue. Look.'

Delbert appeared, dressed in an elaborate Tudor costume. He was talking to Vinnie, who now appeared older, dressed in the fashion of a young woman of that time. She was nodding slowly and seemed to be asking him questions, listening carefully as he answered.

'He was more of a father to me than my own flesh and blood. After saving me from death, he took me on a grand tour. We travelled around Europe and to many other places around the world, seeing many of its wonders. That's what gave me my interest in art and history—although I experienced some of the events and creations in contemporary times.'

Sophie said, 'Look, is that the Eiffel Tower? Paris looks different there.'

'Yes. That was in the 1920s. And the next image is the following year when we were in Egypt. We visited the Pyramids and joined an archaeological dig that summer; it was such fun!'

The images faded and were replaced by the young Vinnie with her mother. She looked wistful. 'I wonder if Delbert hadn't changed me...would I be with her now?'

Sage's face clouded over. 'You have some beautiful memories. Perhaps you could help me to build some of my parents.'

Vinnie shook her head. 'I'm so sorry, Sage. I've been so insensitive. Of course, we can build you some beautiful memories here and in Earth world.'

At that moment, Malbeam appeared on the pier, waving to them.

'We must go back now.'

Soon they were in the coach heading back up the hillside.

'Just over there, where you can see a plume of smoke, is the shifters' village. And just to the north is Grey's house where we will be this evening.'

The coach turned onto a wider road where only a little light filtered through the treetops.

'We're heading into the darkest part of the Forest now,' Vinnie explained. 'This is the Basin, the main hunting area for both vampires and shifters.'

They peered through the windows into the dim light. Creatures scurried unseen through the dense undergrowth and harsh caws sounded through the air.

'It's pretty spooky out there,' Sophie commented.

'Though vampires do grow accustomed to sunlight over the centuries, most of us prefer to avoid the light.'

'I thought vampires had to sleep in the daytime,' Paris said.

'Some of the more traditional ones choose to. Delbert does not socialise much before sunset, but I don't think he actually sleeps. I think he uses the time to study his antique and art collection. And to decide what he'd like to acquire next. Still, it keeps me in work and gives me an excuse to visit Earth world.'

'Do you work for Mai, too?' Sage asked.

'Yes, I trace artefacts for her...' Vinnie began. She stopped speaking as the coach began to sway from side to side. Malbeam's voice was heard urging the horses to quicken their pace again. Her nose twitched as a low growl was heard nearby and one of the horses let out a shrill whinny.

Vinnie leant out of the window. Sage, Sophie, and Paris watched in horror as her eyes took on a strange red glow and her lips curled back to reveal two long sharp canines. With a leap, she sprang through the window and headed for the front of the coach.

Sophie caught Paris' hand as the coach swayed more violently. A guttural cry went up as the growls grew more ominous. Sage leaned out of the window. 'There are two big cats up there. I think Vinnie needs our help.'

She slipped out of the window and disappeared from their sight. Malbeam held out his hand and pulled her up onto the front of the coach. 'We must keep the horses calm while Vinnie deals with the cats. Hold on fast to the reins.'

Sage watched as he eased his way onto Midnight's back, crooning softly as he patted her neck and then the neck of the second horse. Taking a deep breath, she held on tightly to the reins, trying to quell her fear as she watched the transformed Vinnie walking slowly towards the two cats. The creatures were thin and obviously hungry and were not going to give up the chance of a meal without a fight. Freeing one hand, Sage reached out and pulled the rising plumes of red and green from above one of the cats. As she struggled to hold on to the reins, Sophie appeared beside her. 'Give me the reins. You and Paris do your thing!'

'Keep condensing, Sage,' Paris's voice came from nearby. 'I'll cast some whites.'

For the next few moments, the air was filled, cleared and refilled with streams of different colours. As the animals grew quieter, Vinnie leapt forward and drew sharp claws across the face of the nearest one. It pulled back with a painful screech. The scent of the cat's blood made Vinnie's eyes shine even more dangerously. Her tongue ran over her lips as she faced the cowering creature. With frightened yelps, the two cats turned tail and disappeared into the trees.

Vinnie walked away from the others and sat with her head in her hands.

Malbeam climbed down from the horse. He noticed Sage's concerned glance in Vinnie's direction. 'Just give her a few moments to herself.'

'Have you worked with vampires for long?' Paris asked him as he stroked the head of Midnight.

'Aye, going on for a hundred years now.'

Sophie frowned. 'A hundred years? But you're a goblin.'

Malbeam smiled. 'An old fae friend bequeathed her immortality to me when she realised that I was serious about my relationship with Ernesto. Ernesto is Delbert's bodyguard and right-hand man. He runs the house and takes care of everything for him. And you want to hear him sing. He has the voice of an angel.'

'Yes, I don't know what we'd do without Ernesto,' Vinnie said as she walked towards them. Her whole demeanour was cool and collected, with no trace of the wild vampire discernible. 'Well, if I had to get into a fight with a couple of mountain lions, I couldn't have chosen better company to be in. You three were absolutely amazing!'

Paris drew a hand over his brow. 'It was a bit scary, I must admit.'

'Let's get you over to Delbert's and you can clean yourselves up before supper time,' Malbeam said.

The door to the mansion was opened by a tall, well-built man a short while later.

'Ernesto, here are our Earth world visitors,' Vinnie said.

'He looks more like a rugby player than a singer,' Sophie whispered to Paris.

Delbert walked into the hallway and stopped as he was faced with the bedraggled group. 'My goodness! What have you been doing with the youngsters, Vinaconsuella?'

'We were enjoying a tour of the Dark Forest when we came across two hungry mountain lions in the Basin.'

His brow creased and he looked at Ernesto. 'That's a bit too close to shifter farmland, isn't it?'

Ernesto nodded. 'We must talk about it with Grey this evening. We'll need to deal with them before they get a taste for livestock—or young shifters.'

Vinnie turned to Sage and her friends. 'Nothing for you to worry about. I'll show you where you can clean up a bit before we go to Grey's.'

'I hope they don't think we're too scruffy,' Sage said, brushing down her trousers.

Delbert laughed. 'I wouldn't worry on that score. I'm just hoping they are in human form and wearing some kind of clothing.'

'Petra said everyone will be on their best behaviour for Lupe's fae partner and our Earth world guests. We'll have a wonderful evening,' Vinnie rebuked him.

***

Delbert picked an imaginary thread off his jacket as the coach drew up outside a sprawling stone building later that evening. A dark-skinned woman came out of the house holding a baby. The muscles in her arms flexed as she adjusted the child on her hip.

'Delbert, Vinnie! Welcome,' she said as they alighted. 'And you must be the visitors from Earth world. I'm Petra, Grey's daughter. This is my youngest, Cairn.'

Sage stepped forward and introduced herself and her friends as she led them into the house.

They entered a spacious, low ceilinged lounge. A group of men and women, enjoying an animated conversation, were seated on comfortable but worn sofas and armchairs on one side of the room. On the other side, two young children played a noisy game with wooden sticks.

Delbert rolled his eyes and whispered to Vinnie, 'I feel a headache coming on already.'

The conversation stopped as Petra led them to the adults. The oldest man stood up and gave a slight nod. 'Delbert, Vinnie. And these must be our Earth world visitors. You are most welcome. I hope you are enjoying your trip to our part of Aurum.'

Sophie nodded. 'It's been amazing.'

As they introduced themselves, one of the women turned to Sophie.

'Oh, you're the one who suggested doing away with the boundaries between the vampires and shifters. A great idea!'

'Hmm, maybe not such a great idea now that Mai wants to do away with all boundaries!' Grey scowled as Delbert nodded.

'Oh, come on! It's time we moved ahead...' a second young man began.

'As long as it's in the right direction,' another countered.

A heated discussion quickly followed.

Petra shook her head. 'I'm sure you've had enough of the noise already. Follow me.'

They went through a low doorway into a spacious kitchen where Saffron was seated chatting to a young woman.

'This is Chrysta, Rhodo's partner,' Petra told them. 'She's my sister-in-law. Here, Chrysta, you take Cairn while I check the oven.'

The young woman took the child onto her lap, smiling as a raucous laugh rang out from the neighbouring room. 'Come and join us in a more civilised conversation. Saffron's been telling me all about Earth world. It sounds so exciting with so many wonderful things to see. I'm going to persuade Rhodo to come with me on a trip there.'

'Earth world is not nearly as exciting as Aurum,' Sophie said. 'Here you have so much real magic, and all out in the open. I love being Gifted, but we have to keep it hidden in our everyday life.'

'I've heard about Gifted mortals; can you show me what you can do?' Chrysta asked them.

They spent the next half hour demonstrating their Gifts and regaling her with some funny anecdotes of events at Alora's house.

Suddenly, they were startled by loud growls and snarls outside the kitchen window.

'There are two wolves fighting in the yard!' Paris exclaimed as he looked out of the window.

Chrysta gave a sigh, shook her head and pushed open the window. 'Rhodo! Smoke! We have visitors remember. Get ready for supper—and that means shirts and shoes.'

Paris stood speechless as the two wolves transformed into two young men. They came into the kitchen, one still struggling to fasten a faded pair of jeans.

'Oh, not shoes, Chrysta?' The first man complained, grabbing a hunk of bread from a basket as he passed the table.

Chrysta shook her head again as the two men disappeared up the stairs. 'My partner, Rhodo, and his brother Smoke. Here Saffron, can you take the baby and give him his bottle while I go and round up the others for supper?'

Sophie sat down beside Saffron while Sage and Paris set out plates on the table.

'Hello, Cairn,' she said softly, stroking his tiny hand. A look of alarm crossed her face as soft fur appeared on the hand. 'What's happening? I thought shifters didn't…shift…until they were older.'

Petra looked up. 'Oh, that happens from time to time in the first few years. It's just his blood settling. Don't worry, he can't completely change. It'll wear off in a minute.'

The kitchen seemed to have more than the six male and three female shifters that Sage had counted sitting around the table. Several conversations were held simultaneously as plates were passed around.

Lupe patted Saffron's hand as she looked around her with a dazed expression. 'It's a bit different than Faeville, isn't it? Are you okay?' She gave him a smile and nodded. 'They are very welcoming, but very loud.'

'Vinnie was telling us how they met up with two mountain lions down by the Basin,' Grey said to Petra.

Petra looked shocked. 'Mountain lions? Near the Basin?'

Grey nodded. 'We'll have to organise a hunt as soon as we can. Possibly tomorrow. Delbert and Vinnie have gone to see how many vampires they can get to join us.'

At the word *hunt*, several of the young shifters began to talk excitedly. Grey raised his hand and they fell silent. 'None of you young ones has experience hunting lions. It's much different than going for boar or deer.'

'We used to hunt wild cat in Earth world,' Lupe told them. 'And sometimes panther. They can be difficult; we all had to work together.'

'We could use your advice, Lupe,' Grey said.

'It sounds very dangerous,' Saffron frowned.

'It's more dangerous to have a couple of mountain lions hanging around our farm animals and our children,' Petra pointed out.

Shortly after that, Delbert and Vinnie returned, joined by Mai.

'You have a serious problem on your hands,' Mai said as Petra handed her a mug of tea.

'There are ten vampires who are ready to join you in the hunt tomorrow,' Delbert announced.

'Together with the vampires, we can deal with it,' Grey said as the others nodded eagerly.

Sage felt a shiver run down her spine as she saw the cold predatory look in all their eyes.

Saffron seemed more concerned about Lupe's safety as they got ready to leave later that evening.

'Are you sure you won't be in danger?'

'We'll all look out for each other. It won't be much different to the hunts I took part in Earth world. In fact, it will be safer—we didn't have vampires to back us up then. Don't you worry, you go to the Fae Dance as you've already planned and I'll be here.'

Chrysta pouted. 'Oh, I wish we had occasions when we could dress up and enjoy music and dancing...'

'We have full moon nights.' Rhodo looked hurt.

'Don't get me wrong; I love racing through the forest, but I'd really like an evening where I could wear a beautiful dress and dance with you.'

Sophie looked worried. 'I haven't really got anything really dressy with me for tomorrow.'

'Me neither,' Sage added.

'I've got some dresses that you can borrow,' Saffron suggested.

'Why don't you come to the castle tomorrow afternoon, Saffron, and help the girls get ready for the evening?' Mai suggested.

'That's a great idea,' Lupe agreed. 'Then you won't be sitting around at home worrying about me.'

***

'So, how did you enjoy your trip to the Dark Forest?' Mai asked her three visitors when they returned to the castle.

'Very...interesting,' Paris answered slowly.

'Yes. They were all very nice, but a bit scary at times,' Sophie said.

'I felt quite nervous when they were discussing the hunt. Their eyes...' Sage shivered. 'No wonder vampires and shifters have such a terrifying reputation.'

Mai shrugged. 'They are hunters. That's the way they're made. But no vampire or shifter has ever harmed another Magical here in Aurum. That was one of the conditions of settling here. It doesn't stop them from posturing though. I suppose that's part of their nature, too.'

'They seem to have accepted Saffron, don't they?' Paris commented.

'Yes, and I'm so glad. I hope it will lead to more interaction between the different areas of Aurum.'

Chapter Twenty-Seven

'Here are Saffron and Peridot,' Mai said the following afternoon as a small dark green coach drew up outside the castle gate.

The women climbed out, both holding large bags.

'Paris!' Lichen leaned down from the driver's seat. 'Come and join us in the Glen. We've challenged our neighbours to a game of football and we need some experienced players.'

'Go on, Paris.' Mai smiled. 'I think this is going to be a girly afternoon.' As the coach drew away, she turned to the girls. 'How about you take your bags up to the bedroom? I'll bring up a tray of Meadowsip and Greenade.'

'Oh, Saffron, this material is gorgeous!' Sophie exclaimed a short while later, running her hands over a red gossamer gown.

Saffron looked at the gown Sophie was holding up against her. 'You would look stunning in that—but red is Flame's colour and she is sure to be wearing something in a very similar colour. You need a contrast...how about the cobalt blue one?'

Peridot picked up a peach-coloured gown from Sage's pile. 'Hmm, no. You're too pale to wear this. You need a more definite colour...that green would look better. And it will bring out the green in your eyes. You must have some goblin blood in your veins, with those eyes and your name.'

'Mum said she named me after my great-great-grandmother.'

'We'll have to do some research into your background.' Peridot smiled. 'Maybe we have family members in common.'

As the two girls tried on the selected dresses, Peridot unwound a velvet roll. Inside rubies, emeralds, sapphires, and diamonds shone. 'I've brought a few bits of jewellery that you could wear.'

'Oh, you both look so beautiful,' Mai said as she appeared with a silver tray. 'Refreshments, ladies, and let's put on some music to get into the mood.'

'What are you going to wear, Mai?' Saffron asked.

Mai shook out a long golden sheath dress with a slit at one side and slipped the silk garment over her head. Peridot pursed her lips. 'You need a classic Chinese hairstyle to compliment this dress. And I have the perfect thing to hold it in place.' She held up a long jade barrette shaped like a dragon.

The next few hours passed in a happy buzz of chatter.

'It's such a long time since I enjoyed a girly afternoon.' Mai sighed happily.

'Me, too!' Saffron said. 'Over sixty years, in fact. Sixty wasted years.'

'You're free of that horrible man now,' Sophie said. 'And you have Lupe, who's really lovely.'

A soft smile played around Saffron's lips. 'I'm so lucky.' Then her brow furrowed. 'I do hope he's okay.'

'He will be, he's not on his own,' Mai reassured her. 'The vampires and shifters are a formidable team.'

'That's true,' Sophie said. 'Just enjoy your evening.'

'What is a Fae Dance like?' Sage asked. 'I can't imagine.'

'It's hard to describe. It's just absolutely spectacular,' Peridot told her as she interwove strings of pearls into Mai's hair. 'Benigno works the dancers hard, but he does get the best from them. Each year they seem to get even better.'

'And after the performance, there's dancing for everyone,' Saffron added.

'We learnt some of the goblin dances. Are fae ones much different?' Sage asked.

'You have to be fae for some of them, but there'll be some goblin dances, too. Most of the goblins will be there,' Peridot told her. She looked at Mai. 'Your hair is perfect. In fact, though I say it myself, we all look pretty good.'

'Before we leave, there is one thing we must do,' Mai said. She left the room and returned a moment later carrying a tray.

'Mai, you've made some Chinese Fortune Cookies. Just like the old days!' Saffron clapped her hands together.

'It's a tradition before we start the Annual Festivities.' Mai turned to Sage and Sophie. 'What you have to do is choose a cookie and give it to another person. That person will select the next recipient, but it can't be the one who gave them the cookie. Now, who is going to go first?'

'Saffron,' Peridot suggested.

Saffron looked at the plate of cookies and picked up the one in the centre of the tray. 'This is for...Sage.'

Sage took the cookie and placed it on the plate in front of her. 'Okay. The next cookie goes to...Peridot.'

Soon each person had a cookie on the plate in front of them.

'Sage, you were given the first cookie, so you must open it first,' Peridot said. 'Let's see what your future love life holds.'

'Who is your mystery love?' Sophie laughed as her friend broke the cookie and watched as two orbs hovered over the table and then drew together.

'So, he's fae!' Saffron exclaimed.

'Well, that's a clear image of your future.' Mai smiled as the images disappeared. 'Who's next?'

Peridot broke open her cookie. The image that floated before her showed a pack of playing cards. The pack shuffled, then the cards turned over rapidly until the Knave of Hearts fell onto the table.

'I'm not sure what that means.' Peridot shook her head. 'You're next, Sophie.'

Sophie watched as the image floated from her cookie. It showed two doors next to each other. One of the doors opened and a young girl stepped out. The second door opened and a young man stepped out and took her hand.

'It's pretty obvious who you're going to end up with.' Saffron giggled as Sophie looked puzzled.

'Now you, Saffron.'

The fae carefully broke open her cookie and watched as a circle of orbs twirled around like bubbles; then each one burst and a litter of tiny pups fell onto the table.

'What we were all expecting!' Peridot laughed. 'Come on then, Mai. You must open your cookie now.

Mai shrugged. 'But you know that my cookie never contains a message.'

'There's always a first time.'

Mai sighed and broke open the cookie. Her face showed her astonishment as a pack of playing cards rose and shuffled themselves in front of her. Once again, the pack dealt all the cards face downwards on the table until the King of Hearts was laid upwards. She drew a deep breath and remained silent for a few minutes.

'They are a bit vague, aren't they?' Sophie said. 'Can anyone explain what mine means?'

'No, you have to work it out for yourself,' Saffron told her. 'That's part of the magic.'

Mai shook herself out of her reverie. 'Ready to go, girls? I think I heard the coach outside.'

Lichen let out a low whistle as the girls climbed into the coach. Paris looked at Sophie. 'You look lovely.' He gave a cough. 'I mean you *all* look lovely.'

***

There was a feeling of excitement in the air as they alighted in front of the fae theatre. Two young fae drove the coach away as they made their way inside. Sylvan was standing in the foyer. He raised his eyebrows in appreciation.

'Holly told me to meet you and escort you to your seats. Come this way.'

They nodded and greeted some of the people they had met on their visit as they made their way through the crowd. Holly waved them over.

'My, you girls are looking beautiful this evening. Come and sit down, the show is about to start.'

As they sat down, a tall fae wearing a white suit appeared and handed Mai an envelope. She gave him a smile as he left with a brief nod.

The lights dimmed and a hush fell over the auditorium.

The curtains parted to reveal a line of young fae. To the tinkling of bells and gentle pipes, they began to dance, weaving in and out of each other, and then made a circle. The next part of the dance was based on gymnastic moves that made Sophie gasp on several occasions. When they gave their final bow, Sophie was on her feet clapping.

'They're so good. And they're so young, too.'

'Benigno likes to train his dancers from an early age,' Saffron told her.

'If the little ones impressed you, wait until you see the older dancers,' Holly added.

The lights dimmed once again and the music began. The second group of dancers entered as if they were skating gracefully across the stage, then one by one they orbed and hovered in the air before returning to fae shape and continuing their dance with flashes of colour rising from them as they moved. It was hard to see each individual dancer at times as they moved so quickly, sometimes as fae and sometimes orbing. It ended with blinding flashes of colour as each orb rose higher, until, with the last notes of the music, they floated down and posed gracefully in human shape.

Once again, Sophie was on her feet, clapping and cheering as the dancers left the stage.

'I can see you are enjoying the show.' Mai smiled at Sophie.

'It's absolutely amazing!'

The final act was based on a circus theme, with trapeze artists, riders on white horses, led by a ringmaster who appeared and disappeared throughout the scene. For the finale, each fae orbed and became part of a colourful firework display, almost convincing the audience they were watching Catherine wheels and rockets exploding before their eyes.

Then the entire cast of performers came onto the stage to a loud applause, which increased in volume as Benigno strode out to take centre stage.

'He is a brilliant teacher,' Brunswick said as Benigno raised his arms and took a last elegant bow before walking off stage with his dancers.

'He's a genius.' Sophie sighed.

'Let's move to the foyer and find Mercy and the others,' Holly suggested. 'We can get a table while we wait for the dancing to start.'

Mai put her hand on Sage's arm as the three youngsters went to follow her. 'Follow me.'

She led them around the back of the stage and along a narrow corridor to a plain wooden door. After a light tap, the door was opened by the same fae who had appeared before the show. He greeted her with a smile.

'Good evening, Herman,' Mai said as they entered a luxuriously furnished room. In front of an ornate gilded mantelpiece was a chintz sofa and two armchairs. Around the room, a scattering of occasional tables and chests held glass domes filled with colourful moving images. Benigno was seated on a reclining armchair. He stood up and clasped her hands warmly. 'Mai, my dear girl, I'm so glad to see you here.'

'Benigno, you know I never miss the Fae Dance. I've brought our Earth world visitors to meet you, too.'

'Ah, Earth world; I haven't been there for about thirty years now. I'm delighted to meet you. What did you think of the show?'

'It was spectacular!' Paris said.

'It was wonderful!' Sage added as Sophie nodded her head vigorously in agreement. 'We have *nothing* like this in Earth world.'

Sage peered closely at a colourful dome. 'They're tiny dancers.'

'Yes.' Benigno nodded. 'Each dome is a working model of the previous shows we have put on.' He walked towards the largest dome. 'Nineteen forty. One of my favourites. What a troupe!'

'The new dancers are already showing a lot of promise,' Herman remarked as he poured tea into dainty china cups and passed them around.

'Yes, I'm looking forward to working with them in the new term,' Benigno agreed.

'But first we're having a holiday, with no talk of work!' Herman said resolutely.

'Into the White Mists?' Mai asked.

'As usual.' Benigno smiled.

'Hmm, let me see…Caribbean?'

'You know me so well!'

Mai looked at the puzzled faces of Sage and her friends. 'If you look into the distance along The Plains, you can see the start of the White Mists. For certain people, those with immortality and a lot of experience in magic, the White Mists can lead to another place, somewhere in your imagination, a place for your idyllic holiday.'

'And being a creature of habit, I usually conjure up a Caribbean island. Absolute paradise.' Benigno sighed. 'Why don't you join us for a few days, Mai? Put your feet up.'

'I'm tempted. But I still have a lot of work to do to sort out the new visitor passes for Gifted and Magically touched from Earth world.'

Benigno shuddered. 'I don't mean any offence to you youngsters, but I was rather appalled with how things were on my last visit to Earth world. I wasn't very impressed with what they call *progress*. I wouldn't like our beautiful Aurum to go the same way.'

'No, we're not going to let that happen, Benigno. Aurum will remain as it always has done. Earth world visitors will have to forego all modern devices while they are here. And each visit will be limited to a certain time. Once the visa expires, the person will find themselves back on the other side of the Portal.'

'I could live here quite happily.' Sophie sighed. 'If my family lived here, I would never want to leave.'

'We'll definitely be back for another visit,' Paris agreed.

They chatted for a while about the sights they had seen on their trip, with suggestions from Benigno on other places worth a visit, until Mai stood up. 'We'd better get back to the others. It was so nice to chat to you again, Benigno.'

Back in the auditorium, the scene had changed. The stage was lowered to floor height and one wall had been opened up on to a fragrant garden where fae couples, elves, witches, and satyrs swirled and danced past, leaving colourful trails as they swept by. An orb hovered nearby, then Saffron appeared beside them.

'Hi there. Have you been to see Benigno? Holly said that's where you'd be. We've a table over there, come and join us.'

Holly and Brunswick were sitting with Vera and a young girl.

'Cora has been so looking forward to meeting our visitors from Earth world,' Holly said.

Sage introduced herself and her two friends to a girl of about their age.

'We were very impressed to see you in the dragon races,' Paris told her.

Cora laughed. Sage noticed she was similar in build and colouring to her mother, with a pale complexion and rather pointed features, but she had a more relaxed air about her.

'I didn't really do too well, did I? Falling off in the first lap.'

'You were very brave to take part in the first place,' Sophie said.

'You live in Earth world, don't you? I'd love to go there. Vinnie has told me such exciting stories about it. She manages to stay safe, and you Gifted people do too, don't you?'

'Well, I have never felt in any danger, but we do have to keep our true natures hidden from normal humans,' Paris said.

'Yes, it can be difficult at times. Luckily, we have a strong community in The Valley and Alora, our Spell Master, teaches us all how to keep ourselves safe,' Sophie added.

Cora turned to her mother. 'See; it wouldn't be that dangerous to visit Earth world.'

The older woman raised an eyebrow. 'It may be safe for the Gifted ones used to living among normal humans, but for us witches, it's a different thing altogether. Our ancestors suffered terribly over there and were glad to find sanctuary here in Aurum. Remember the stories you father used to tell you?'

Mai patted Vera's hand. 'Life in Earth world isn't all bad, you know. Many Gifted wouldn't live anywhere else.'

Brunswick shook his head. 'I think Vera is right to be cautious about visiting Earth world, Mai…'

'Oh, Brunswick, I'd love to get the chance to visit some of the places that Vinnie has told us about. I had hoped…' Holly interjected.

As the conversation about the possibility of visits between the two worlds continued, Sylvan turned to Sage and held out his hand. 'Come on. Would you like to dance?'

She looked nervous. 'I don't know how…'

He smiled. 'You're fae, you'll feel it.'

She took his hand. Following Sylvan's lead, she quickly gained confidence as they circled the floor.

'Their feet don't always touch the ground, do they?' Paris said turning to watch the dancers. 'They glide and fly, too.'

'Wait until they play a goblin dance, then we can show them what we're made of,' Sophie joked. 'Can I have the first goblin dance with you?'

'You're on!'

The music drew to a close and they were soon joined by Flame, Flora, Peridot, and some other young fae and goblins. As Sylvan and Sage arrived a moment later, Holly gave her a round of applause. 'Danced like a true fae, Sage! Well done!'

'*Half* fae,' said Flame. 'And I see even Sophie is dressed up as fae tonight.'

Sophie spread out her dress. 'Isn't it beautiful? Saffron lent it to me.'

'It really suits you. You look stunning.' Paris nodded appreciatively.

The music began again and Brunswick stood up, taking his wife's hand. 'Goblin time! Come on, let's dance.'

Soon most of the group had paired up and headed to the dance floor and only Sophie, Paris, and Flame remained.

Sophie looked at Paris as Flame grabbed his hand and pulled him towards the dance floor. 'Come on, I'll show you how to dance.'

'Sorry, Flame, I've already booked this dance with Sophie.' He gave her an apologetic smile.

The fae stood with a dark expression on her face as she watched the two go on to the floor laughing as they made a stumbling start to the dance.

'Why would he choose her and not me? What's *she* got that I haven't got?'

'She's pretty, very funny and, I heard, also very brave,' a voice said behind her.

She swung around. 'Oh, it's only you, Kite.'

'Yes, *only* me.' The satyr smiled. 'Are we the only ones without dance partners? Would you care to partner me in a gambol?'

'I suppose so,' she replied ungraciously.

She stared over his shoulder while he chatted away as they made their way around the dance floor.

'Why are you so relentlessly good humoured, Kite?' she interrupted him rudely.

'Eternity is a bit too long to be in a bad mood.'

'Oh, so you have no plans to bequeath your immortality and settle down to family life then?'

'Well, not unless I meet a sweet-tempered young woman who I know will be the perfect companion for me and the perfect mother for our adorable children.'

Flame tossed back her head. 'Well, I hope you don't think that I...'

'My dear girl, I don't for one minute think that you could be a sweet-tempered young woman.'

Some of the dancers nearby exchanged glances as, with eyes blazing, Flame ground to a halt.

Suddenly, she threw back her head and laughed. 'I don't know whether to slap you or kiss you.'

'And I don't know which would be more terrifying for me,' Kite replied as he swung her back into the dance.

On the far side of the dance floor, Paris and Sophie stopped as the music drew to a close. The following tune was a much livelier one and as many of the dancers moved into two circles, Paris grabbed Sophie's hand and pulled her into the garden area. 'I don't think I can manage that dance, I'm afraid.'

'I'm ready to sit down for a while, anyway,' she replied, spotting a bench nearby.

'You really do look stunning tonight, Sophie. I mean, not just tonight. Well, I mean, you don't always look stunning, but you're always pretty, well, beautiful, really...of course, it's not just about looks, I know that you're an intelligent young woman, too...'

Sophie laughed and tucked her hand into his arm. 'I think you're complimenting me!'

'Would you like a walk around the garden?' Sylvan asked Sage as the music drew to a close.

'Oh, romance is in the air tonight,' she commented as they passed by Sophie and Paris, talking softly, with their heads close together.

Sylvan smiled. 'If we orb and head for the old oak tree on the hillside, there's a great view of the garden and the surrounding countryside.'

Sage looked nervous. 'I've never returned to normal shape anywhere except on solid ground.'

'Don't worry, I'll catch you and make sure you come to no harm.'

Moments later they were both hovering over the tree. Sylvan reappeared, settling on to a wide branch. He held out his arms. 'Come on.'

Sage was soon seated on his lap with her arms fastened around his neck.

'Sorry.' She gave an embarrassed laugh, her face blushing as she met his eyes.

He gave a cough. 'That's okay. Just get your breath back. There. Now you can appreciate the view.'

She let out a gasp as she gazed at the scene before her. Hundreds of coloured lights were flashing and drifting up from Faeville. In the distance, The Plains sloped down to the tiny green lights of Goblin Glen. On the horizon, the sun was sinking behind the hills and mountains of Dragon Land.

'It's so beautiful!'

'It certainly is, isn't it?' He squeezed her hand. 'There's one more place I'd like to take you. Ready to orb?'

The two orbs made their way to the outskirts of Faeville. Sage hesitated for a moment before following Sylvan into the Lilac Brae. As he landed on the ground and resumed fae shape, he put his fingers to his lips. For a few moments, they stood silently in the darkness. Sage felt a light squeeze of her hand and her eyes widened as a pale shape walked hesitantly towards them.

'A unicorn!'

The animal gave a soft snicker as it was joined by a group of twig-like creatures.

'Wood nymphs,' Sylvan whispered. He held out his hand as one of the creatures took a step forward and sniffed the air.

'Syl-van.' The voice that came from the rough bark lips was hoarse.

Sylvan nodded. 'Yes. I have brought my friend to meet you.'

'Hu-man?' A second creature scowled. 'No human!'

'Sage is half fae, the daughter of Daphne.'

Excited squeals went up. 'Daph-ne! Daugh-ter of Daph-ne!'

They ran forwards and grabbed her arms. Their skin felt rough and spiky as they pulled her towards the unicorn. In contrast, his silvery coat was smooth and warm. His eyes locked with hers and she heard her mother's name echo inside her head as an image of Daphne as a young girl with her arms wrapped around the neck of the magnificent beast filled her mind.

'He knew my mother,' Sage whispered to Sylvan as the image faded. They both stood silently as the wood nymphs led the unicorn away into the mists.

'Oh, Sylvan, that was amazing!' she said as they walked slowly back towards Faeville.

They stopped as they neared the dance floor.

'It's going to be so hard to leave Aurum.'

'But you will come back here again, won't you?'

'Oh, yes. I plan on bringing my grandparents with me. They'll love it.'

A sudden fluttering sound close by made her jump. Sylvan put an arm around her and drew her closer to him. 'It's only an owl.' He took one of her hands. 'I would like to visit you in Earth world sometimes, if that's okay with you.'

'I'd really like that, Sylvan.'

Chapter Twenty-Eight

Dawn was beginning to break as Sophie and Sage prepared for bed that night.

'What a summer holiday this has been.' Sage sighed as she slipped under the covers.

'Yes,' Sophie agreed dreamily. Suddenly she sat up. 'Sage, I must tell you something. I hope you're not upset. It won't affect our friendship in any way, but...'

'You mean about you and Paris? I'm not upset at all, not even surprised. I just wondered what was taking you both so long, especially after the fortune cookie predicting that you'd become involved with the boy next door.'

'So that's what it meant! And I have a pretty good idea who you'll be orbing with.'

Sage was glad she couldn't see her blush in the darkness. 'I wonder who Mai's king of hearts is?'

'And the knave of hearts must be in his party. Peridot looked quite puzzled,' Sophie continued. She lay back down. 'Thank goodness you're okay with me and Paris. I'd hate anything to spoil our friendship. I hope we'll be friends forever.'

'I'm sure we will,' Sage agreed as she drifted off to sleep.

***

The sun was high in the sky when the girls were woken up by a tap on the door.

'Hey, lazy bones! You're wasting our last day in Aurum,' Paris said as he put his head around the door. 'We've been invited for a farewell lunch today. See you down in the kitchen in five minutes.'

Saffron was sitting in the kitchen with Mai, a worried look on her face as the girls entered.

'I'm sure everything will be fine. You're all going to have to get on eventually and this is a great opportunity to make a start.' Mai patted her hand. 'Everyone will be on their best behaviour; I'll make sure of that.'

Saffron looked up as the girls came in. 'I invited Mercy, Flame, and Flora over to our new home for lunch today before I found out that Lupe has also invited several vampires and shifters over today. Sylvan has promised to be there, you'll all come, too, won't you?'

'This will be a lovely ending to your visit to Aurum, won't it?' Mai smiled at the girls.

'Yes.' Sage nodded. 'Everyone was so welcoming at Grey and Petra's home the other day.'

'I don't know what Mercy and the other fae will feel about this.' Saffron sighed. 'I'd better go and let them know. Maybe they'll change their minds about visiting us.'

Mai stood up. 'I'll go and see them. I think you could invite Kite and some of his satyr friends and Vera and Cora to make it more of a mix. We can get Mercy to bake some of her special fae cakes to keep everyone happy. You have a word with Peridot and see what goblin goodies she can rustle up. Flavia will love an excuse to bake up a few treats, too.' She turned to Sage. 'Can you three entertain yourselves for a few hours?'

'Oh, Mai.' Saffron gave a timid smile. 'I knew you'd make me feel better.'

'It'll be great fun!' Paris smiled as the two women left and then turned to the two girls. 'But I'm glad Mai will be there.'

Sophie nodded as she poured herself a cup of tea. 'Me, too.'

'What do you fancy doing on our last morning?' Sage asked as she buttered a slice of toast.

'Hmm, a walk around the castle grounds?' Paris suggested. 'We could go through the woods at the back as far as the lake. We haven't explored that bit yet.'

Soon the three friends were heading through the Great Hall.

'Can we have a peek at the bedroom one last time?' Sophie asked as she pushed open the door and peered inside. 'I'd love to have a four-poster bed like this one. And the view from the window is beautiful.'

'Look; this wasn't here before, was it?' Paris was standing in front of a large portrait on the wall. It was of a young man, blonde and of muscular build. He was wearing a pale silk shirt with a leather waistcoat. Soft grey breeches were tucked into knee high boots. His hands rested on the wide red sash around his waist. There was a look of kindness in his eyes and a touch of humour around his mouth.

'That must be the portrait Peridot painted for Mai,' Sage said. 'I wonder who he is?'

'Mai never mentioned it to us or offered to show us, so maybe she didn't want us to see it.' Paris looked uneasy.

'You may be right.' Sage nodded. 'Let's go.'

The sun was hot outside after the coolness of the castle. They were glad to reach the edge of the lake and sit down on its bank.

'It's a very big lake, isn't it?' Sage remarked. 'You can't see the other side, it's quite misty, even on a hot day like today.'

Sophie took off her shoes and dipped her feet in the water. 'I wish I had my swimsuit with me so I could go for a swim.'

'There's a rowing boat over there.' Paris pointed to an old wooden boat tied up at the side of the lake. 'We could take that out; it looks cooler out on the water.'

Sophie and Paris took an oar each and began to head out towards the middle of the lake.

'Look!' Sage cried. 'The mist is clearing and there's an island ahead. It must be the one Mai goes to.'

Sophie and Paris rested their oars and looked around. All three were silent for a moment as two shapes emerged, hovering over the water.

'Oh, my life! Are they memories?' Sophie's eyes widened.

Sage nodded. 'They must be.' The couple danced closer to the boat, smiling at each other as they swirled by. The woman was wearing a long white cotton dress, while the man wore a cream silk shirt and plain dark woollen breeches. 'That's Mai, isn't it?'

'And she's dancing with the man in the portrait!'

By now the boat was drifting closer to the island. As the couple danced away, the sky grew dark and there was a rumble of thunder. A flash of lightning lit up the sky.

'I think we had better head back,' Paris said, grabbing his oar. By now rain had started to fall and a strong wind was blowing.

'This isn't good,' Sophie whispered as Sage sat down beside her and grabbed the oar, too.

'Just keep pulling!' Paris urged.

As they struggled against the howling wind, several ghostly figures wearing chain mail and with their faces obscured by metal helmets appeared and began to push the boat back towards the lakeside away from the island. When they found themselves once again in the sunshine, the pale shapes evaporated.

'What were they?' Sage whispered.

'Mai's over there by the landing stage.' Sage waved to her.

'I wondered where you had got to, then Flavia suggested you might have come down here,' Mai said as they tied up the boat.

'Did you see the storm?' Sophie asked her. 'Everything here looks dry.'

'The weather here has been beautiful.' Mai frowned. She looked at them. 'Did you reach the island?'

'No, just before we got there, the storm blew up and we headed back,' Paris told her.

'Or tried to,' Sophie interjected. 'We were really struggling until those ghostly soldiers appeared and helped us out.'

Seeing the puzzled look on Mai's face, Sage explained. 'There were four of them. Once we were back in the sunlight, they just faded away.'

'And we saw a memory of you, Mai,' Sophie said excitedly. 'You were wearing a long white dress and dancing with the man in the portrait. You both looked so happy!'

She suddenly stopped talking as Mai's eyes grew moist and she quickly turned away.

'We're so sorry if we did anything wrong,' Sage said, hurrying after her. 'We didn't mean to upset you.'

Mai stopped and took a deep breath, shaking her head. 'No, you haven't done anything wrong; it's just...'

'Another story for another day?' Paris gently suggested.

She wiped a tear away and nodded.

Back in the kitchen, there was a tempting aroma as Flavia packed items into several bags. 'Ah, you found the youngsters. And just in good time, that sounds like a coach now.'

'It's Peridot,' Paris said, looking out of the doorway.

'Put these baskets in the back of the coach,' Flavia told him. 'Be careful of that big one, keep it upright.'

Soon, the coach was loaded and the youngsters climbed inside.

'Is Saffron still nervous?' Sage asked Peridot as they set off.

She nodded. 'Yes, even though Vinnie called over to assure her that all the vampires have promised to be on their very best behaviour. Ernesto will be there, too, to make sure they do.'

'I wouldn't like to get on the wrong side of Ernesto,' Paris ventured, as he pictured the giant of a man.

'Malbeam said he is a beautiful singer,' Sophie commented.

Peridot smiled. 'He has an incredible voice. We must ask him to sing today.'

***

There was a golden coach standing outside Saffron's house as they drew up. Mercy was handing Lupe a large basket, while Flame and Flora carried smaller ones into the house where Mai and Saffron were arranging the tables.

'We have enough food to feed an army here,' Sage quipped as they began to unload Flavia's offerings. 'Let's hope everyone is hungry.'

'Vampires don't eat anything, do they?' Sophie said.

'No, but the shifters will make up for that!' Peridot laughed.

They were all standing back to admire the spread as the sound of another coach was heard. Lupe stepped outside and greeted the new arrivals.

He was smiling as he led Delbert, Vinnie, Ernesto, and two other vampires into their home and introduced them to everyone.

'It's a beautiful house, Saffron,' Vinnie said, touching her hand briefly. 'And it's in such a pretty place.'

'Lovely, but rather bright,' a second woman said. 'Many of our kind prefer a little more shade.'

'If you'd like to come through to the lounge, we've drawn the blinds,' Saffron said, leading her through a doorway.

Vinnie sidled up to Mai. 'We shouldn't have any trouble. All the vampires were warned to feed well before coming here today.'

Loud shouts from outside heralded the arrival of the shifters. Lupe grinned as he went outside again. Grey was helping Petra from the coach followed by Chrysta and Rhodo.

'Hi there, Lupe,' Chrysta said, looking around her. 'You've a nice place here.'

'Yes, and you're close enough to the Dark Forest, too,' Petra added.

'Where can I leave the horses?' a young shifter called down from the driver's seat.

'There's a paddock over there.' Lupe pointed. 'I'll give you a hand while the rest of you follow Saffron inside.'

Soon, the vampire's horses were happily grazing with the dark green goblin ponies.

'More guests,' Lupe commented as two centaurs rode into view. On their backs were Vera and Cora. Behind them a group of satyrs were chattering and laughing as they made their way to the house.

The centaurs stopped to speak to the horses on the paddock as the others made their way inside where the shifters were eyeing up the laden table.

Sage helped Saffron hand out plates as she urged everyone to help themselves. Flame raised her eyebrows as she watched a young shifter pile his plate high. 'Someone has a good appetite!'

The lad blushed and put the spoon down. 'Oh, I'm sorry. I'm overdoing it, aren't I?'

'No, no.' Flame patted his arm. 'I like a man who can enjoy his food.'

He gave a short laugh and made his way to where Malbeam was seated with a filled plate.

'I can see why Saffron fell for a shifter,' Flame murmured to Flora. 'Are they hunky or what?' She smiled as Lupe approached them with a decanter of Meadowsip. 'Lupe, who is that young man over there?'

'That's Geo. No-one can handle a horse like he can. He's even impressed Malbeam and that tells you something.' Lupe headed for Mercy and Saffron with the Meadowsip.

'Hmm, horses…we already have something in common. I wonder if he'd be interested in coming for a ride with me. It would be a great way to forge links between our communities, wouldn't it?'

Flora shook her head as she watched Flame twirl a lock of her red hair around her finger as she sashayed towards the two coach drivers.

Paris nudged Sophie as they watched Flame flirting with the shy young man. 'I think the shifters have more reason to be afraid of fae than the other way round!'

Shaking his head at something Flame said, Geo quickly followed Malbeam back to the paddock and horses.

Saffron sat down with Sage and her friends. 'There are no problems with the shifters and us, but it's hard to get the fae and vampires to mix.'

'That's probably because we're eating and they're not,' Sophie said.

Sage nodded, putting down her empty plate. 'Once everyone has eaten, I'm sure we can encourage them all to mingle.' She stood up. 'I'll go into the lounge now. Will you come with me, Sylvan?'

With a nervous smile, Sylvan stood up. 'Of course.'

There was the hum of quiet conversation going on as they entered the lounge. Sage headed for Delbert with Sylvan closely behind her. 'Delbert, I never got the chance to say how much I enjoyed seeing you in Vinnie's memories. You must have seen so much in your life.'

Delbert sat up, looking pleased. 'I have indeed, young lady. Which memories did Vinnie show you?'

'She showed us memories of you in Egypt, on an archaeological dig there. Did you discover many treasures?'

Vinnie sat down beside Delbert and they talked together of the tiles and broken pottery they had helped unearth. As they talked, others gathered around them.

Flame stifled a yawn. 'It sounds dusty and hot! And all for a few broken plates.'

'And we saw memories of you both dressed very elegantly dancing in a magnificent ballroom,' Sophie continued, pretending not to hear Flame's comments.

'Ah, yes, the famous glass ballroom.' Delbert sighed. 'Paris was a great place to be in those days.'

'It still is the romantic capital of the world today.' Vinnie smiled. 'Though maybe not quite so glamorous these days.'

'Oh, I'd love to visit Paris,' Chrysta said wistfully. 'When we visit Earth world, Rhodo, that's one place that we just have to go to. I'll wear a long flowing gown and we'll dance in a beautiful ballroom!'

'Paris sounds like just the place for me,' Flame said. 'I could do with some romance in my life.'

'Oh, Flame.' Flora giggled.

A cross look passed over her friend's face and she took a step back, bumping into a young vampire.

'Sorry,' he said, taking her hand to steady her.

She moved away. 'Oh, you're so cold!'

He pulled his hand back quickly, apologising again. Flame reached out and took his hand in hers. 'Actually, that's just what I need as I was beginning to feel rather hot in here. Perhaps you could help me to get a bit of fresh air?' She linked her arm through his and they headed for the French windows. As she stepped outside into the garden, she took a deep breath. 'There, I'm feeling better already.'

The young man hung back as she touched a rose which was bathed in an orange glow from the setting sun. 'This is so beautiful, isn't it? So romantic, don't you think?'

Tossing her red hair back over her shoulder, she smiled to herself noticing the effect she was having on her escort. With his eyes fixed on her slender, white neck, he stepped towards her.

'It is indeed a beautiful sight.'

A frisson ran down her spine as he placed his hand lightly on her back and guided her further from the house.

'I think maybe we should be getting back...' Flame protested weakly, making no attempt to resist.

'Let's just enjoy this moment before the spell is broken,' he murmured, moving closer to her.

'Where is Flame?' Mercy asked Flora, looking around the dimly lit lounge.

'She was here a minute ago.'

'See if you can find her,' Mercy said. She tapped Vinnie's arm and gestured for her to follow her. 'Flame's missing.'

Vinnie scanned the darkening room. 'So is Samar. He was here a moment ago.'

Flora appeared next to them. 'She isn't anywhere in the house. Lupe has gone to check outside.'

Vinnie caught Ernesto's eye across the room and they both headed for the garden.

'Samar told me he had recently fed, so he shouldn't be any danger to the fae,' Vinnie told him. 'I just hope he was telling the truth.'

Ernesto stopped her and listened. 'Over there.' With a few quick strides, he crossed the lawn and grabbed Samar's arm, pulling him away from Flame.

Flame gave a cry of pain as she felt herself roughly manhandled into the centre of the lawn by Vinnie. 'What do you think you're doing?'

'Just go inside!' she hissed, shielding her from Samar. The young vampire's face was distorted with rage and desire as he struggled to free himself from Ernesto's grip. A moment later, the garden gate swung open and the two men disappeared.

A crowd had gathered by the doorway. Mercy ran forward and clasped Flame to her. 'Oh, my child, what happened?'

'Nothing! I was enjoying a quiet chat with Samar and Vinnie nearly broke my arm getting me away from him.' Pouting, she rubbed her arm. 'Why is everyone determined to ruin my love life?'

As she stormed inside, Delbert gave Vinnie a questioning look.

'It looks like Samar was lying when he said he had fed before coming here today. Ernesto has taken him home.'

Delbert's face grew grave as Mai told him of the events in the garden. 'I'm so sorry. Samar will be severely punished for his actions today. He has brought shame upon us all. Perhaps the vampires cannot be trusted to mix with the others.'

Mai shook her head and laid a hand on his arm. 'In all fairness to Samar, Flame can be a very forward young woman. Let's just be thankful that nothing happened today. With guidance and practise we can all live together; I know we can.'

There were murmurs as they walked back into the lounge. Flame gave Vinnie a dark look as she continued to nurse her arm.

'It's getting dark. Let's light a few candles, Saffron,' Lupe suggested. Sage and Sophie hurried to help him.

'Do you know what happened out there?' Sage asked Saffron.

She looked close to tears. 'It looks like one of the vampires had his sights set on Flame.'

'Or maybe *she* had her sights set on *him*,' Sophie suggested. 'She looks more annoyed than scared to me.'

'We mustn't let this spoil the day,' Lupe said to Peridot as he caught sight of Saffron's face.

She nodded and headed for a corner of the lounge. 'A good party needs music! Saffron, come and we'll play the song we practised earlier.' She picked up a flute as Saffron sat down and began to pluck at the strings of a harp, shakily at first, then becoming more confident as the people around her relaxed and began to enjoy the music.

No-one noticed Ernesto appear in the doorway until Flame hurried towards him.

'Where is Samar?'

'He had to leave.'

'But…'

'Ernesto! Just in time!' Delbert said. 'We have listened to a beautiful fae melody and now you must sing for us.'

Flame's lips narrowed as he gave a slight bow and walked away.

He stood at the front of the room and cleared his throat. The room grew silent as the giant of a man closed his eyes and began to sing in a rich tenor voice. Soon everyone was enthralled as he sang a song of longing and lost love. As the last notes faded away, there was silence followed by loud applause.

'That was wonderful,' Paris exclaimed.

'I told you, he has the voice of an angel.' Malbeam beamed with pride.

'Oh, Flame, wasn't that just so romantic?' Flora sighed.

'Absolutely. It's a tragedy when true love isn't allowed to follow its course.'

'Are you thinking of Saffron and Lupe?' Chrysta asked her.

'Well, actually...'

'Because I totally agree with you. They're a young couple obviously in love. No-one should be making problems for them. I'm so glad we're all on the same side!'

Chapter Twenty-Nine

'What a night!' Sophie said at breakfast the next morning.

'It certainly was,' Vinnie agreed. 'Luckily, not many people were aware of what was actually happening and thought that Flame had merely had a tiff with me.'

'What is going to happen with Flame and Samar?' Paris asked.

'Flame has been put to work unpicking Benigno's gossamer costumes ready to make next year's costumes which is a tedious job but nothing like what poor Samar has to do. He is to spend four months helping the ogres look after the trolls in the swamps which is not a very pleasant job. As you know, trolls generally act as toddlers and need a lot of cleaning up after them and they can cause quite a bit of damage if they wander into the wrong places or argue amongst themselves,' Mai told them. 'To be fair to Flame, she was very remorseful when Mercy explained how serious things were. When she realised that she had put her life at risk and that Samar could have been exiled from Aurum permanently, she was devastated.'

'And how did Samar react?' Sage asked.

'He's just thankful Flame wasn't hurt and he's not been exiled. He's learnt the hard way that vampires do not mix with fae or humans without feeding beforehand,' Vinnie said.

'Are Saffron and Lupe okay?' Sage continued.

'Yes.' Mai nodded. 'Most of their guests have said how much they enjoyed themselves and how much they admire Saffron and Lupe for being brave enough to host a party for fae, shifters, and vampires. I feel they're going to be a great help to build bridges between the different people that live here.'

Sophie looked up. 'Do we have time to go and say goodbye to Saffron and Lupe before we leave?'

Mai nodded. 'Be back here by noon.'

***

Saffron smiled as she opened the door to the three youngsters. 'I'm so glad you came! Oh, I can't believe this is your last day, I'm getting used to having you around. You were such a great help yesterday.'

As they sat down in the kitchen, there was a knock on the door and Peridot and Vinnie came in.

'Peridot said you would probably be here,' Vinnie said. 'We wanted to say a last goodbye.'

'Goodbye for *now*,' Peridot added. 'We'll see you here on your next visit.'

'We'll definitely be back,' Sophie agreed. 'It's been such a brilliant holiday—finishing up with such excitement here yesterday!'

'Yes, but Mai said that it all worked out well in the end,' Sage said.

'And that Flame got her comeuppance!' Sophie added.

Saffron shook her head slowly. 'You know I do feel a bit sorry for her. I called to see her this morning; she was surrounded by gossamer thread—it's one of the most tedious jobs. After Benigno's annual dance, all of the costumes have to be taken apart and the different coloured threads rewound to be used for the next set of costumes.'

'She got off lightly compared to Samar,' Vinnie pointed out.

'Yes, troll keeper isn't the most enviable of jobs!' Lupe said. 'The ogres will be glad to have some help. They'll certainly make him work hard.'

The conversation went on to the more enjoyable parts of the previous day.

'The food, the music, talking to all the different kinds of people—it was a great party,' Paris said as the others nodded in agreement.

'Next time you visit, we'll have another one.' Peridot smiled as they stood up ready to leave.

As they made their way back to the castle, Sophie stopped and looked around at Faeville spread out on one side with Goblin Glen on the other side. 'I'm so sorry to leave this place. Even the Dark Forest doesn't look so scary now.'

Sage frowned as she looked towards the trees bordering the Dark Forest. There was a tiny glow high up in one of the branches. Sophie and Paris were walking on ahead deep in conversation, so she quickly orbed and headed for the light. She found herself seated in a topmost branch beside Flame. Both looked at each other in surprise.

'What are you doing here, Flame?' Sage asked her. 'Aren't you supposed to be at Benigno's?'

'I…I just needed some air for a moment.'

'At the edge of the Dark Forest? After all that's happened?'

Flame's face crumpled. 'Oh, please don't tell anyone.' She held out a scrap of parchment. 'I know I'm banned from getting in touch with Samar, but I just had to let him know how sorry I am for all the trouble I've caused him. He could have been exiled from Aurum *forever*, all because of me! I know I can be a flirt and a tease, but I *never* for a moment wanted to cause so much trouble.'

Sage looked at the parchment. It held a single word "*Sorry*" followed by the letter *F*. 'If you send this and he tells anyone about it, you'll be in worse trouble than you are already, Flame.'

'I'll take that risk.' Flame balled the parchment in her hand and closed her eyes muttering a few words under her breath. She opened her hand and the parchment fluttered upwards and vanished into the trees.

'I better get back to Benigno's before they miss me,' Flame said. 'You won't...'

Sage shook her head, 'No, I won't say anything. I hope he doesn't either, for your sake.'

Flame gave her a brief hug before she orbed and disappeared from view. With a sigh, Sage returned to the pathway behind her two friends.

'There you are, Sage,' Sophie said. 'We were just wondering where you'd got to.'

'Just having a last look around.'

Mai was with Flavia in the castle kitchen when they arrived back.

'Sit down and have a cup of tea and a fae biscuit before you set off,' Flavia said to them. 'You won't taste anything as good as these back in Earth world.'

'That's true,' Mai said taking a bite from one of the biscuits herself. 'Alora is a great cook but hers just don't taste the same.'

'Of course, they don't! They need to be fae recipe, baked by a fae and made in Aurum,' Flavia snorted.

'It's a pity we can't take them with us,' Paris said as he helped himself to a second biscuit.

'They wouldn't taste the same in Earth world,' Flavia said.

Mai stood up. 'It's nearly time to leave. Can you bring your bags into the garden?'

The three youngsters gave Flavia a final hug.

'Perhaps we'll see you in Earth world at some time,' Paris suggested.

She shook her head. 'I'm too old for such adventures, but make sure you come and visit us again soon, won't you?'

'Oh, we'll certainly be back!' Sophie said emphatically.

There was the sound of a voice outside and Sage's face broke into a smile as Sylvan appeared in the doorway.

'I'm so glad I'm not too late,' he said, his eyes lingering on Sage. 'I just wanted to wish you all a safe journey home.'

'Thank you, Sylvan,' she replied. 'I hope it's not too long before we all meet up again.'

'I'm planning on a trip to Earth world myself pretty soon. I haven't been there in over forty years; perhaps you could show me around.'

'You can count on us, but Earth world's not half as exciting as Aurum,' said Sophie.

Mai stood in the middle of the garden. 'We'll land just outside the Portal, then we'll do a second jump to The Coterie, where your families will be waiting for you. Now, give me your hands...'

***

After a few dizzying moments, they found themselves outside the front door of The Coterie where Alora stood with a smile on her face.

'Welcome home! Come inside, everyone is dying to see you again.'

Mai picked up a cup of tea and sat down at the kitchen table beside Alora. In the next room they could hear the excited babble as the three youngsters regaled their family members with their adventures.

'They certainly had a good trip,' Alora commented.

'The first of many, I imagine,' Mai replied. 'And soon we'll have other Gifted visiting us in Aurum.'

Chapter Thirty

'It sounds as if you had a wonderful holiday,' Ellen said to Sophie as they sat in the kitchen a few days later. 'Sage had so much to tell us about your adventures—flying on dragons, goblin dances, parties with vampires and shifters!'

'Oh, it was absolutely amazing! I can't wait to go back there. Aunt Mary is really keen and we're both hoping to persuade Mum to come with us.'

'Sage has already convinced us that we would enjoy the trip,' Ellen continued.

'Yes, Grandad will have such a great time talking to the dragons. And you'll love Mercy, Nan. She knew Mum really well.'

'I told Mai we're putting our name down for a trip as soon as the visas are sorted,' Jim said as he came into the kitchen. 'I've been trying to persuade Adam and Elvis to come too, but they're not convinced.' He looked at the tiny creatures in his palm and chuckled. 'Adam says it's just another place run by human types.'

Sophie looked at her mobile. 'Paris asked if we could meet him by the park gates, Sage.'

'You two get going.' Ellen smiled. 'You might as well get out and enjoy yourselves before school opens up again next week.'

'Every time I see a plane in the sky, I think it's a dragon.' Sophie sighed as they made their way along the road.

'Yes, it does seem strange being back here; a bit flat somehow. It feels as if we were gone for more than a week.'

'There's Paris.' Sophie waved at him. 'And look who's with him.'

'Sylvan.' Sage smiled broadly as the two boys reached them. 'I never expected to see you so soon. What a lovely surprise.'

'It's a very short visit, I'm afraid. I have to be back in Dragon Land tomorrow at noon.'

'So, what would you like to do now you're in Earth world? Do you want to go to Alora's and meet some other Gifted people?' Sophie asked him.

'Oh no. I want a whole day without magic. I want to live like an Earth world person. There is one thing in particular I've always wanted to do—ride on one of those tall buses.'

'You mean a double decker?' Paris smiled. 'That's easy enough to arrange.'

'They look really good fun. Vinnie gave me some Earth world money, so today is my treat. Can you think of anything else we can do?'

Sage looked thoughtful. 'We could take a double decker to Queen's Pier—that takes about half an hour and goes through some beautiful countryside. The Queen's Pier funfair is pretty good.'

'That sounds like a good plan. The next bus for the pier leaves in ten minutes. We'll just make it if we hurry,' Paris said.

Fifteen minutes later, they were seated on the front seat on the top deck of the bus. Sylvan was absorbed in the view from the window. 'This is a great way to see the countryside, isn't it?'

'Have you been to a funfair before?' Sage asked him as they queued at the entrance gate.

'I went to one with Saffron and some other fae about eighty years ago. It didn't look anything like this.'

'This one has some of the best rides in the country. What shall we go on first?' Sophie asked.

'The rollercoaster, of course!' Paris' eyes lit up. 'They've added two new loops!'

'It'll probably just feel like flying to you, Sylvan,' Sage remarked.

She was surprised at his reaction to the ride. As they got off, his face was pale and beads of sweat lined his forehead.

'Are you okay? I thought it would be pretty tame for a fae.'

'It was nothing like flying! When I fly, I'm in control. On the rollercoaster, I was completely at the machine's mercy. Now let's find something we can control. Ah...' He stood beside the dodgem cars. 'This looks fun!'

Sylvan enjoyed it so much, they ended up having three more goes.

'How about some candy floss?' Sophie suggested when they finally left the ride.

Sylvan's eyes widened as he watched a woman pour sugar and other ingredients into a large metal cylinder, then wound up the sugary confection on a wooden stick.

'Is she using magic?' he whispered to Sage.

'I've seen people skating on ice,' he said as they stood beside a rollerblade rink. 'But these people are skating without ice.'

'They have little wheels on their skates instead of blades,' Paris explained.

'Little wheels on your shoes? What a great idea! We have to try this!'

Sylvan and Sage sped effortlessly and gracefully around the rink, while Paris struggled to keep upright. Sophie laughed as she helped him to his feet yet again. 'This just isn't your thing, is it?'

As the sun started to go down, the four friends made their way to the pier.

'I'm starving,' Sophie said. 'How about we have pizza and ice-cream at Pedro's?'

'I've eaten ice cream, but I've never tried pizza,' Sylvan admitted.

'You haven't lived if you haven't tried Pedro's pizza!'

He sniffed appreciatively as they settled into a booth in Pedro's. 'If it tastes as good as it smells...'

'It's even better,' Sophie promised.

It was dark when they finally climbed on board the bus to take them back home. Sylvan pulled Sage close to him. 'I've had the most wonderful day ever. With the best of company.'

Sophie turned from the seat in front of them. 'It's been such a great day. And I thought we'd be bored back in Earth world.'

Sage nodded. 'Earth world and Aurum—as long as you are in good company, they're both great places to be.'

'You're right. And we're lucky enough to be able to enjoy good company in both worlds. Being Gifted or Magical is the best thing ever,' Paris added.

Sage smiled. 'It definitely is. And we're going to make the most of both worlds!'

About Trish Moran

Trish Moran was born in Dublin, Ireland and moved to the Midlands, UK at a young age. Her first teaching job took her to London and she later taught in Greece. After several years, she travelled to Australia and worked as a bank teller in Melbourne.

After over a decade outside the UK, she moved back to the small Midlands town where she grew up.

Trish has always been an avid reader; one of her friends describes her as a readaholic, nervously lining up her next book as she comes to the end of the present one. She enjoys reading a wide variety of books which includes YA – especially fantasy and stories of more down to earth dysfunctional families; adult thrillers with complicated plots; and stories with quirky characters. She loves to discover a book with a new slant and think, 'Gosh, what a great idea! I wish I'd thought of that!'

In her thirties, Trish decided she would like to try writing, and completed several (unpublished) short stories and novellas before embarking on the Clone Trilogy - YA Sci Fi; Mirror Image, Altered Image and Perfect Image, published with Accent Press.

Shrinking Violet, published with Solstice Publishing was her first venture into YA Paranormal.

The idea for the Enchanted Series came to her on a trip to a medieval castle and overhearing a young child saying, 'Where do the dragons and wizards live now, mummy?' And it expanded from there.

As well as reading and writing; Trish enjoys going to the gym, walking and nature photography.

Social Media

Facebook: https://www.facebook.com/trishmoranauthor/

Twitter: https://twitter.com/trishmoran99

Blog: www.trishmoranblog.com

Other Books by Trish Moran

Shrinking Violet

https://www.amazon.co.uk/dp/B08H5Q9TLK/ref=sr_1_1?dchild
=1&keywords=Trish+Moran+Shrinking+Violet&qid=1598979465
&s=books&sr=1-1

As many teenagers know, life can be tough. Violet, Suranna and Charlie are well aware of this fact.

How can Violet learn how to overcome her shyness and speak up for herself?

Will Suranna ever be able to overcome the stigma of her dysfunctional family and achieve her academic goals?

Can Charlie follow his dream and stand up for himself at school and at home?

When three new students make their appearance at the school during the busy autumn term; things start to happen and their lives begin to change. They find themselves caught up in action and drama they never imagined would happen to them.

After an exciting term, the mysterious students disappear. But will the mark they made on these three students live on?

Made in the USA
Monee, IL
11 May 2021